THE DEPTFORD MURDER

An absolutely gripping crime mystery with a massive twist

JEZ PINFOLD

DCI Bec Pope Series Book 1

JOFFE BOOKS

Joffe Books, London
www.joffebooks.com

First published in Great Britain in 2022

Cover art by Nick Castle

ISBN: 978-1-80405-647-9

PROLOGUE

This was the start. And also the ending. A paradox. He liked paradoxes. The notion that something could be both true and false at the same time fascinated him. Every time was a thrill, but this time it felt different. Special.

It was autumn, and it felt colder today. He had been watching the house for three days now. It was early, a fine condensation beginning to appear on the inside of the windows. He guessed the central heating had just turned on. Soon there would be signs of life, curtains would be opened, and he would be able to see those inside. He could feel his heart beating. Yes, it had definitely quickened. He was patient, generally, and had no problem waiting. No problem at all, if it was worth it.

He'd been here before. The wait, the anticipation, the enjoyment. And there was the truth: he enjoyed what was about to happen. Enjoyed it more than anything else. He no longer felt the chill air. Now he felt the warmth of expectancy and the knowledge that today would be the day.

There was movement now in the house. It was like clockwork. The lights coming on, the curtains upstairs being pushed open, the morning routine. Breakfast, work, school. The same every day. The predictability allowed him to plan and consider.

The curtains in one upstairs room drawn open, then, fifteen seconds later, the curtains in the next room. One of the children's. It was almost a science. At eight fifteen the man would leave the house. At exactly eight forty the two children would be bundled out of the front door, would turn left out of the drive and go to school.

That left just one remaining.

He knew that the discipline he possessed was exemplary. Had he been an athlete in training, or a surgeon in the operating theatre, he would be pre-eminent in his field. He was the same as those people, but he existed on a plane that very few human beings could inhabit. The same, but different. Another paradox.

He would wait. Time for her to shower, get dressed, apply make-up. To get ready. Then he would go to work. Then, this would start, this ending. And today would be special.

It was time for him to begin.

CHAPTER 1

Things were not harmonious in Detective Chief Inspector Rebecca Pope's household as she arrived home at 7.30 p.m. Opening the front door, she heard raised voices and the unmistakable timbre of her eldest stepdaughter's voice in conflict with her father.

'You've got to be kidding me? I'm sixteen years old, I have a boyfriend and you're still trying to lay down the law about where I go and when I come back. It's like being in Stalin's Russia.'

Pope stayed where she was in the hallway, simultaneously impressed that Chloe could make the historical reference and irritated that she would talk to her father in that way. As always, she tried to work out the extent to which she should become involved in whatever crisis was unfolding between Alex and his daughters.

'Chloe, you are indeed sixteen. So, not eighteen, when you will be free to make all your own decisions. But while you are still at school, still living under my roof, still studying for exams next summer, I'm afraid you still have to abide by my rules.' Alex had put it pretty succinctly, but Pope doubted this was the end of the discussion.

'Give me one good reason why,' demanded Chloe.

'I've just given you three good reasons,' said Alex, 'so let's leave it there, shall we?'

Chloe was furious. Furious in the way that only teenage girls can be when they are denied what their heart desires. Small problems become catastrophic events.

'This is ridiculous,' shouted Chloe. She stormed out of the kitchen, sweeping past Pope, and thudded up the stairs. The door to her bedroom slammed shut emphatically.

From the doorway into the open-plan room beyond, Pope looked at Alex, unsure whether to smile. Irony needed to be judged carefully. He raised his eyebrows, which she took as a good sign. She walked over and kissed him.

'What's the problem?' she asked.

'Oh. The usual. Chloe wants to go to a party on Friday night and stay over. I told her she can go, but she'd need to come home and she couldn't stay over with Tyler. She thinks I'm being, as you heard, Stalinist in my approach to household rules,' replied Alex.

'At least she's learning something in history,' said Pope.

Alex shot her a look, which advised caution in the humour department. She poured herself a glass of Rioja, to match the glass in front of Alex.

'How was your day?' he asked.

'OK. I'm following up leads on a mugging in Covent Garden. The usual tourist stuff, but this time the victim ended up in hospital with a fractured skull.'

'It doesn't sound the kind of thing a Homicide DCI would be working on,' said Alex.

'Well, technically we're Robbery and Homicide. I usually have the pleasure of tackling the latter, but we're short-staffed at the moment. As the victim was attacked and suffered quite serious injuries, I've been given the case.'

Alex looked at his watch. 'You're late home.' He left the statement hanging, turning it into a question which required an answer.

'Sorry. The roads were chaotic. You know how it can be when you're out in the field — unpredictable at times.' She realized her mistake immediately.

'If you took the promotion, that wouldn't be an issue.'

Pope had been offered promotion two months ago. It was still on the table. It would mean more money, regular hours and less dangerous situations in which she found herself. It would also mean a desk job, which Pope thought sounded incredibly tedious. She had no desire to work any more closely with the higher ranks of the Metropolitan Police. Before she could change the subject, Hannah, Alex's youngest daughter, raced into the room. Pope was very grateful.

'Hi, Bec. Dad, some friends are going ice skating at Streatham rink on Saturday, can I go?' She was clearly excited. This was big news.

'What time, and who's going?' asked Alex.

'Not sure, probably after lunch. Just a bunch of girls in my class. Can I go? Please?'

'I guess so,' agreed Alex.

'Thanks, Dad.' Hannah rushed over, gave her father a big hug and ran out of the kitchen with a huge smile on her face. This was her first year at secondary school, and the business of forming and cementing friendships was the number one priority for Hannah.

'I spoke to my father today,' said Pope, attempting to ensure that the conversation did not return to the subject of her promotion. 'He's still not well. I can tell there's something wrong, but he won't tell me what's going on and insists that it's all routine. I know something's not right. I need to see him face to face and ask him outright.'

This was not easy for Bec Pope. Her father had walked out when she was twelve years old, leaving her and her mother to fend for themselves. It was a difficult time and she rarely saw her father in the years that followed. When her mother died a few years ago, her father barely registered his daughter's grief. Relations between them had always been tenuous at best, and she didn't know how to deal with this new situation. But she knew she would need to arrange to see her dad.

'Why don't you go out to dinner with him this week? You'll worry about it if you don't.'

'I'll give him a ring tomorrow,' said Pope, trying to convince herself.

Just then, she felt a vibration in her pocket, followed by the shrill sound of her ringtone. She made a mental note to change it. She retrieved the phone and saw that the call was from her Detective Inspector, James Brody. A slight twinge of anxiety hit her.

'Hi, Brody.'

Alex looked up at her, then quickly averted his eyes. She caught the glance.

She listened to the other end of the line, and her face became harder. Furrows formed above her eyes. She stiffened and looked instantly less at ease in her own skin.

'OK. I'll meet you there.' She replaced the phone in her pocket. 'Shit.'

Alex looked at her. Despite hitting forty last year, Bec looked younger. She was certainly an attractive woman, but suddenly it was as if all the cares of the world had landed on her shoulders in an instant.

'What is it?' he asked, rising from his chair.

'There's been a murder. A church in Deptford.'

Alex ran his hand through his hair. 'Oh, no,' he said. 'That's terrible. Why are they sending you? Isn't there any-one else on duty?'

'I'm the senior Homicide DCI available.'

Alex looked at Pope. She knew that he wanted to ask her if there was any chance they could send someone else. Someone else to work the murder. But he knew the answer, so he didn't bother.

Pope left the house, closing the front door behind her. She steeled herself. The beginning of a murder investigation was always tough. A mix of adrenaline, sadness and fear.

With a liberal dose of exhaustion thrown in for good measure. It would be a quick drive. She had twenty minutes to collect herself and prepare for a murder scene.

She had been home for less than twenty minutes.

CHAPTER 2

Pope drove quickly through the streets of South London. As she passed Peckham and hit New Cross the scenery became more rundown. A notorious area of London, although, as almost everywhere else in the city, it was currently undergoing regeneration in an attempt to make it more profitable for landlords and property owners. It had always seemed to Pope that gentrification largely meant inflated house prices that drove out locals, and artisan bakeries that charged exorbitant prices for sourdough bread. Even with these signs of gentrification, the area seemed to cling doggedly to its old rough reputation. As she drove further along the New Cross Road, she saw the familiar groups of young men who hadn't been pushed out by students. All bravado and insecurity masquerading as aggression. The Albanian and Turkish coffee shops seemed to increase in number every year, groups of middle-aged and older men spilling out on to the pavement, smoking and drinking small cups of very strong brews to remind them of home.

She crossed over towards Deptford, and when she arrived at the entrance to the churchyard, drove down the narrow road that afforded access to the church. She pulled up in front of the main entrance to St Paul's. Looking around, she noticed only two CCTV cameras, both trained on the construction site next door.

Pope saw the squad cars and the flashing blue lights before she killed the engine. She could see James Brody outside the main entrance. It was wide open, a parade of officers and forensic technicians going in and out. He was surrounded by men and women in white head-to-toe overalls that made them all look faintly ridiculous in the context of the architectural beauty of the church.

The last time Bec Pope had set foot in a church had been seven years ago. The funeral of Tina Waterson, aged thirteen. It was her first case as a Homicide detective. Four teenage girls had been abducted, presumed murdered by a serial killer in London. Three bodies had never been found but the fourth, Tina, was discovered on wasteland near Bermondsey. They had investigated the case for over a year, but to no avail. At the funeral, the girl's mother had attacked Pope, landing two hard blows before she could get out of the way and other family members could pull the mother back. She blamed Pope, her inexperience, and Pope agreed with her. She was still haunted by the failure to close the case. Technically, it was still open.

Her thoughts were interrupted as Brody walked towards her. 'Hi, Bec.'

'What have we got?'

Brody looked down at his feet, then straight at her. 'Difficult to explain. You'd better come in and have a look for yourself.'

She took a beat, took a breath, then walked into the church.

St Paul's managed to avoid the feeling that many churches seem to engender. Pope thought that to the non-believer the typical dark interiors felt oppressive, caused by a lack of natural light and the presence of light-altering stained glass found in the windows. The abundance of dark, wooden pews and other fittings only seemed to heighten this effect. St Paul's seemed different, however. It was bright and airy, and the white-and-gold interior, lit by large, opulent chandeliers, added to the sense of space. The large window at one end was oddly warped, as if being pulled in by a black hole.

As she entered, memories of childhood visits to church flooded her head. Primary school, a crocodile of five- and six-year-olds holding hands on the walk from classroom to pew every Wednesday morning. And the ill-judged sermons, on adultery, sloth and envy, delivered to those who had no idea what they meant, by those who had no idea how to talk to children. A lifelong guarantee of religious indifference.

Then she saw her.

To the left stood a large raised wooden pulpit, wrought-iron steps led up to it. Ornate railings by the sides. And on top of the pulpit, draped over the brass lectern, a body. Laid out like an offering to the gods. Pope stood still, took in the scene. Then, like a believer, she walked slowly towards it.

Before she ascended the stairs she turned to Brody.

'Are we sure it's murder?'

'We're sure. The marks around her neck, the bruising, the position of the body. It can't be suicide.'

Brody went first, walked carefully up the steps. Pope followed. You were never really prepared to see a dead body. She had been a police officer for nineteen years, and she had worked in the Homicide squad for seven. She had seen a fair number of murder victims when she had spent a year working in America on secondment to the NYPD, but it was rarer in London. Pope felt the tension in her chest as she climbed the stairs and followed Brody.

And there she was.

'There's no sign of a struggle. She seems. . . laid out. Carefully. Forensics think she was killed somewhere else,' said Brody.

Pope stood and looked at her for some time. Neither Pope nor Brody saying anything. Brody was right, the body appeared carefully positioned. This was not a hastily dumped dead body, but a carefully arranged corpse, prepared for an audience. She wore jeans and a light, V-neck jumper. She was barefoot.

Pope was silent. Her attention was drawn to an envelope arranged on the dead woman's chest. It was plain white. Printed on the front, she saw *DCI Rebecca Pope*. She started.

'Has anybody opened it?' asked Pope.

'No, not yet. Forensics wanted to wait for you.'

Pope moved closer and inspected the body. 'Tell me what you see,' she suggested to Brody.

'OK. The wound on her head looks like it might be from falling. Ligature marks around the neck. What looks like finger marks on the larynx, so she couldn't scream or call for help. By the look of the spread of bruising, he knew where to find the internal carotid artery, where he applied pressure, resulting in a loss of blood to the brain. My guess is that the coroner will find that's the cause of death. The purple bruising to the windpipe also suggests that the murderer applied pressure there, which ensured death was fairly quick. He knew what he was doing.'

'You go on too many forensic courses,' said Pope.

She reached into her pocket and pulled out a pair of latex gloves, which she put on. Brody did the same. Several Forensics officers were now beside them, squashed together awkwardly on the circular iron staircase.

'Have you taken all the photos you need? Fingerprints?' Pope asked the lead forensic technician.

'Yeah. You can open it.'

She bent down and carefully lifted the envelope. She could feel by the weight that there was something inside, maybe a card of some sort. It felt too heavy to be a sheet of paper. Blank on the front, except for the printed name. Her name. She turned it over. Nothing.

She carefully lifted the flap, doing her best to protect any forensic evidence that might be present. It opened easily. She took out the piece of white card inside. She looked at it. It was a pre-printed card with *Invitation* written in silver lettering on one side. She turned it over and on the other side she saw the same typeface as on the front of the envelope. *Dear Rebecca. You're invited.* That was all.

After showing the contents to Brody, Pope handed the card and the envelope to one of the Forensics officers, who carefully placed both parts in a plastic evidence bag and sealed the contents, before walking back down the steps.

'"You're invited",' said Brody. 'What the hell is that? Invited to what?'

'Good question. Maybe Forensics will be able to get something from it.'

At that moment Pope's sergeant, Adam Miller, came rushing into the church.

'We have a possible ID on the victim,' he said, slightly out of breath. 'A man phoned in a missing person report, matches our victim's description. Susan Harper. Address in Camberwell.'

'OK. You stay here, Miller. Text me the address and keep me informed. Brody, let's go.'

Pope took one more look at the dead body and walked down the iron steps. As she walked towards the door she noticed a black iron candleholder at the back of the church. It had six rows of small, circular spaces, about ten to twelve of which were occupied by burning white candles. She wondered if anyone would be lighting a candle for Susan Harper.

* * *

They crossed back through Peckham and into Camberwell. From there the GPS earned its keep by navigating through the warren of minor roads to their destination.

Brody had been on the phone gathering information. He summarized what he'd found out as they drove.

'Victim is Susan Harper, thirty-eight. Stay-at-home mum to Zoe, fourteen, and Jamie, twelve. Married to Mike Harper, an English teacher at St John's Academy in Vauxhall.' Pope knew the school — it had a tough reputation.

'Everything normal this morning, husband left for work as usual, kids left for school. Mike had a meeting after work, and the son was at football practice. Zoe, the daughter, went to a friend's house after school, then came home around 5.30 p.m. She found the downstairs in disarray. Mum wasn't there and wasn't answering her phone. She called her dad, who came home and dialled 999. At 7.04 p.m. police answered a call from the distressed vicar at St Paul's, where they found the body of Susan Harper. ID's now been confirmed, they've got a photo from the husband.'

Brody closed his notebook. 'The liaison officer says the family are still inside. They're in a hell of a state, as you can imagine.'

Pope ran through the timeline in her mind, picturing the family leaving in the morning and the daughter returning in the late afternoon.

When they arrived at the Harper house, Pope followed Brody up the short path through the front garden. It looked well tended, with a range of attractive-looking flowers and plants in the border around the small lawn. As they approached, a junior officer Pope didn't know was standing in the porch and nodded to them. They walked in through the front door, which was a light wood with stained-glass panels. It looked to have been recently replaced or renovated in an attempt at period authenticity.

'Let's see what we're dealing with, then,' said Pope.

She took out her notebook and found the next clean page. She jotted the case details, name of victim and address. The hallway looked like any suburban hall: a small high table containing a telephone, keys and a mobile phone, placed next to a family photograph and an ornamental bowl. Either the victim's or her husband's, she assumed. A number of pegs were attached to the wall, groaning under the weight of a range of summer and winter coats and jackets for four people. Underneath was a shoe rack, equally burdened down. When Pope was a kid she had two pairs of shoes. One for school, and one for everything else, a pair of trainers. The rug on the floor usually covered a large section of the polished wooden floorboards beneath, but was now creased up and unruly. A vase, presumably from the small table, had been knocked to the ground and had shattered. There were flowers and a large wet patch on the floor, spread out over about a third of the area. It was clear that there had been a struggle here.

Pope summarized. 'So, someone comes to the door. Susan Harper opens the door and is attacked, either immediately or at some point afterwards. The attack happened in the hallway.'

'It starts in the hall, yes,' corrected Brody, 'and then continues in the living room.'

She followed him into the room that led off the hallway. Three Forensics officers were busy working. There were further signs of struggle. Cushions from the sofa were spread out on the floor and one of the armchairs, with a stick-back wooden frame, had been knocked over. There was a small yellow plastic marker next to the chair, with the number one written on it. Several photo frames were also on the floor, the glass at the front of them smashed. They had another yellow marker next to them, number two. Pope looked at the pictures. One of the Harper family on holiday somewhere hot and sunny. Another of the two children, Zoe and Jamie. A third with an older couple, presumably the kids' grandparents. Typical snaps found in any family home. Pope bent down by the sofa. There was a small patch of blood on the carpet. Another numbered marker indicated the evidence.

'Anything?' Pope asked the forensic technician standing closest to her.

'Not yet. We've only just started in here. The hall is next. We assume the blood belongs to the victim,' he said, indicating the dark patch on the floor.

Pope wrote down a couple of comments in her notebook. They spent a few more minutes looking around the living room and taking note of the environment. When she was satisfied that there wasn't anything else that appeared immediately helpful, Pope said, 'Let's go upstairs.'

They climbed the stairs. The Harpers' bedroom was the first door on the left. They walked in. The room looked like a typical suburban, middle-class bedroom. Nothing appeared to have been disturbed.

Pope asked, 'Has anything been taken from the house?'

'Nothing. The husband doesn't think anything is missing.' There was a pause.

'This doesn't look like a straightforward burglary or an opportunist attack. I think he knew when she would be alone and he waited for that time,' said Pope. 'He also did this at a point where he would have enough time to kill her, move her and leave without being seen. That either suggests that he was lucky, or that he planned this very carefully. Maybe watched the house beforehand.' Pope sighed. 'The moving of the body is the thing that I don't get. Why take her all the way to a church in Deptford? It doesn't make sense. It's too dangerous. Too many opportunities to be seen.'

She thought for a moment.

'I'm going to go and talk to the husband. Have a closer look around up here. Check the kids' bedrooms.'

Pope walked downstairs, towards the kitchen, paused and prepared herself for the interview with Mike Harper. Like all police officers, she hated this part of the job. As she entered the kitchen, she saw him. The two children were sitting at the table, hugging, tears in their eyes. Mike Harper was standing by the sink, looking out at the garden. He turned when Pope spoke.

'Mr Harper,' she said, holding out her hand. 'DCI Pope, I'll be leading the investigation.' He held out his hand and awkwardly shook hers. 'I'm sorry we have to meet under these circumstances. I'm very sorry for your loss.'

Mike Harper nodded. His eyes were ringed with red, raw from crying, his face strained with the effort of trying to hold it together for his kids.

'I need to ask you a few questions. Shall we go next door?'

He understood, looked at the two children who nodded their agreement, and they moved out of the kitchen and into the dining room. It was small and looked to be seldom used.

'How are you doing, Mr Harper?'

He didn't answer, but sat down in one of the chairs and bowed his head.

Pope gave him a minute to compose himself. He had obviously needed time away from the children.

Mike Harper looked up and wiped his eyes with the back of his sleeve. 'Sorry, DCI Pope.'

'I just need to ask you a few questions at this stage, I know you need to be with your children. We can talk in more detail later.'

He nodded. Prepared himself.

'Can you think of anything unusual in the last few days? Around the house? Any visitors, phone calls, emails either of you received?'

He seemed to be trying to recollect. He shook his head. 'Nothing I can think of.'

'Is there anyone your wife has recently argued with? Anyone who might hold a grudge against her? Anyone who had cause to do this?'

He looked surprised. 'No, no. Everyone loved Susie.' His voice caught. Quieter. 'Everyone loved her.'

'Had Susie gone anywhere different? Or any routine visits in the last week? Somewhere she regularly goes at the same time each week?'

'No, I don't think so. She was supposed to be meeting her friend Jo today. They were going to. . .' He trailed off, unable to finish the sentence, looked down.

'Yes, officers are talking to your wife's friend at the moment.'

Now the difficult part. Pope paused, then: 'Is there any chance that she was seeing someone else? Romantically?'

Mike Harper started. 'Seeing someone else? What do you mean. . .?'

'I know this is difficult. I know it's not what you want to think about. But I wouldn't ask if it wasn't important.'

He raised his voice now, grief turning to anger. 'No, DCI Pope. My wife was not having an affair.' He shook his head. 'I can't believe you asked that. Jesus. I need to be with my kids.' Mike Harper got up and left the room.

Pope realized it was pointless pursuing this tonight. She sighed. What a job.

She got up and walked out to the hallway. Other than the bruises around Susan Harper's neck, and a gash on her head that had presumably caused the bloodstain on the carpet, it was difficult to extrapolate any further. Hopefully the medical examiner would be able to find something of use. What worried Pope was that if the murderer was careful enough to scope out the house, organized enough to remove and transport the body, and capable of arranging the body so perfectly, then he could very well be meticulous enough to ensure that he left no forensic evidence. Once again, Pope had a real sense of foreboding.

She stood looking at the scene. *What happened here, Susie Harper? Why did you open the door? Why did this happen to you?* It was then that something in the corner of the hall, on the small table by the front door, caught her eye. Partially hidden between a photograph frame and a bowl containing keys. She walked over, peered closely and examined the object.

'You are kidding me,' she said quietly to herself. She reached out. There were two possibilities. And she very much hoped that one was more likely than the other.

* * *

The images on the screen moved as he watched them, the pixels dancing in front of his eyes. He watched a man on the screen look around, scrutinizing every corner of the hall. Fair hair, about five feet eleven inches. He watched him move around the room with the delicious knowledge that he had absolutely no idea he was being watched. This made it even more exciting, more rewarding. The man on the screen had in his hand a small notebook and seemed to be making notes. He felt his pulse and noted the slight quickening. His hands were moist, barely perceptible, but a definite change. The added bonus of a rerun, he thought.

He inhaled sharply when a second figure appeared in the tableau. A woman. Dark brown hair, blue eyes, about five feet eight inches. She wore a black suit, tailored, and a white shirt underneath. He thought they looked good together, the man and the brown-haired woman. As they talked, he watched their body language. He listened to their conversation. The woman spoke more and had the authority. She knew what she was talking about and had understood the scene quickly and perceptively.

They left the room. After some time, the woman returned, stood silently and seemed to be thinking. She began to move around. Then they were looking right at each other.

He moved up to the screen so he could be closer to her. They both moved closer. The woman seemed to be saying something to herself. Suddenly she reached out and the screen went fuzzy, and there was nothing more to see.

He smiled, stood up and stretched. He had been sitting watching this screen for a long time. The daughter coming home and discovering his work had been something of a highlight. Worth the wait. But watching Detective Chief Inspector Bec Pope at work, watching her find the camera. That made it all worthwhile.

CHAPTER 3

After finishing at the crime scene, Pope sent Brody home while the technicians and forensic team completed their work. He was reluctant to leave, loyal to the last, but she insisted. Pope waited until they had gone, so she could be the last person to speak to the family. She explained what would happen next, then left and drove home.

It was 2.30 a.m. by the time she arrived back and quietly let herself into the house. She took off her coat, poured herself a scotch and sat in an armchair in the living room. She wanted jazz, maybe some Miles Davis, to relax, but it was way too late. So she sat in silence with the whisky and let insomnia do its worst.

She thought about the card and what it meant, who it could have come from. A long list began to form in her mind, the years as a police officer providing many possible suspects. Then she played the individual elements of the crime scene through her head. The image of Susan Harper stayed, refusing to leave. Sleep, as ever, took a long time to arrive.

When she woke at six fifteen, she realized that she had never made it upstairs. She texted her team to tell them to be at the station for an 8 a.m. briefing, then headed for a shower.

She left the house quietly before 7 a.m., before anyone else was even awake.

* * *

The Robbery and Homicide briefing room at Charing Cross Police Station had seen better days. It was a good size, able to hold upwards of thirty officers at a time for meetings. But in most respects, it illustrated the underfunding of the police force in Britain in the twenty-first century. The chairs and desks were adequate, but worn. If you looked very hard, you might be able to find a chair that was not covered in years of coffee and tea stains, a desk that didn't have varnish peeling at the corners. It was years since it had been given a slap of paint, and it showed. The tall, narrow windows let in curtains of light, in which the dust particles played in the early morning, giving an eerie, almost Gothic feel to the room. In the corner there was a coffee machine, and a kettle stood on a small table for preparing tea for the officers. A carton of milk, some tea and coffee, and a bag of sugar sat rather forlornly beside them. At the front of the room was a flipchart with a large white pad attached, and some thick marker pens on the thin tray underneath. Next to it, an electronic screen was attached to the wall, in turn connected to a rather ancient-looking desktop computer. It was functional, but it wasn't the Ritz.

Pope was not the first to arrive. Brody was already there, organizing the chairs, ensuring a clean page on the flipchart and checking they had milk for the coffee. He made a cup for himself and one for Pope.

'Good morning,' said Brody, as he put milk in their coffee.

'Morning,' replied Pope.

He handed her the coffee and took a sip from his. 'Did you get much sleep last night?'

She assumed that her appearance gave away the previous night's insomnia. 'Yeah,' she lied.

Brody raised his eyebrows, his scepticism obvious.

Pope changed the subject. 'It's going to be a difficult briefing this morning. I need to show the team the crime scene photos and brief them on the camera.'

'What do you want me to do?' asked Brody.

'If you can pass out the information to everybody, I think I'll be fine with the rest. You can be my glamorous assistant if I need anything.'

'Great. That's what I joined up for. Look forward to it.'

At about 7.55 a.m. the others started to arrive. They acknowledged Pope and Brody as they came in and sat down. Sergeant Adam Miller sat in the front row. At twenty-four he was still relatively inexperienced, but what he lacked in years on the job he made up for in enthusiasm, intelligence and hard work. Miller was the third permanent member of Pope's regular squad. Next to him sat the two constables Pope used, Mike Hawley and Ana McEwan. They were both reliable and conscientious. Next to them sat Stephen Thompson, from the Tech Support Department. Pope had asked him to come to the meeting today to brief them on one particular aspect of the case. Behind them sat a number of other officers. Pope did not regularly work with them, but knew them all to varying degrees. Only her boss was not present. She decided to start anyway.

She took a deep breath. 'Good morning, everyone, thanks for making it here so early.' As she was speaking to the assembled group, Brody handed out a photocopied pack of information to each officer.

'Detective Inspector Brody is handing out the details of the case, and assignments for today, which you can read when we've finished. This is a bad one, and it will have already caught the attention of the media, so don't leave these lying around and be careful who you talk to.

'Last night, local officers got a call to a missing person in Camberwell. While they were on the scene, we were called to St Paul's church in Deptford, where the vicar had discovered a body. This turned out to be our missing person. Susan

Harper, white, female, aged thirty-eight, wife and mother. She had been strangled, we think at her home in Camberwell, then taken to the church at some point yesterday afternoon. Husband and family seem to be eliminated from the enquiry at this stage, but obviously this will need following up. It looks initially as if this was done by someone from outside the immediate family.' This was the easy part.

'Unfortunately, there are some aspects of the case that suggest that this is not going to be a straightforward investigation.' She stopped. A man quietly entered through the door at the back of the room. Everyone turned to see who it was. If Pope didn't know better, she would have sworn that this late entrance was designed specifically to ensure that they did. Detective Superintendent Richard Fletcher walked to the back of the room, found the centre, directly in front of Pope, and leaned against the wall. His movements were fluid and precise, and this served to create an unsettling effect. It all seemed too careful, too calculated.

'Sorry I'm late. Do continue, DCI Pope.'

Pope took up where she had left off. 'As I was saying, there are some troubling aspects to this case already. Firstly, there is every indication this wasn't some opportunistic killing. I'd say the murderer was meticulous in his planning.'

A female officer in the second to last row put her hand up.

'Yes, Verdy?' Pope was irritated by another interruption.

'Do we know it was a male killer, or are you just assuming that?'

Verdy seemed pleased with the question, as if she had introduced a key point in a debate. Pope paused. Verdy was always the first to remind everyone that women were just as capable as men of committing horrific crimes.

'No, we don't know for sure that a man committed this murder. However, as you'll be aware, men commit approximately ninety per cent of homicides, and as you'll see in a minute, our killer possessed considerable strength, so I am fairly certain that this is the case. However, as you imply, we will keep an open mind in our investigation.'

Verdy nodded, satisfied that she had made Pope concede a point.

'As I was saying, the level of planning and care in this murder was considerable. We think the killer may have scoped out the house and the family beforehand and waited until he knew the victim would be alone. The details are in your pack, but at this stage we think he strangled the victim downstairs at the property in Camberwell, before transporting the body to the church and laying her out on the pulpit.' Pope could see the shock and concern on the faces of the officers in the room and paused a moment. The only one who did not visibly react to the information was Richard Fletcher, at the back of the room. He continued to stare at Pope with an unflinching gaze. Again, Pope felt vaguely unsettled.

She flicked a switch and the monitor attached to the wall began to glow blue. There was a beep, and the screen came to life. Brody switched the lights off and Pope had everyone's attention. On the screen Susan Harper lay supine across the pulpit at St Paul's. Her arms, legs and head draped over the edges.

'This is how the victim was found. You can see the placing of the body is very deliberate, very controlled.'

Pope scrolled though a series of photos, each showing a different perspective of the placement of Susan Harper's body on the pulpit. The officers sat silently, some taking notes. Pope had asked Miller not to include images that showed the card laid on the victim's body.

She clicked to the next image, a closer angle, showing the marks around Susan Harper's neck and throat. The body looked serene from a distance, but close up the brutality was more obvious.

Finally, Pope showed the assembled officers pictures of the crime scene at the Harpers' house. 'As you can see, the killer appears to have attacked Susan Harper at the door. And the struggle continued in the living room.'

When the pictures had cycled through to the end, Brody switched on the lights. The room had an air of anticipation.

'You have copies of the key photographs in your packs,' said Pope.

'There's one more thing you need to know before we get started, and it is not in your pack. This is not to leave the room.' She cast a look at the less experienced members of the team to make sure they understood. 'A miniature video camera was left in the hallway, apparently by the killer when he left the victim. This seems to have been transmitting while DI Brody and I were examining the crime scene, and possibly since the murder was committed. We know that this type of motion-sensor camera is sometimes used for security and monitoring. However, Mr Harper denies having any knowledge of it. So, we are working on the assumption that the camera was left by the murderer. I've asked Stephen Thompson of Tech Support to be at the meeting today, so he can explain this in a little more detail. Stephen?'

Thompson stood and moved to the front of the room. Pope could see that he was not used to public speaking and was clearly out of his comfort zone. He had a tablet in his hand, which he put down on the desk. He did not refer to the notes he had made on it during his brief presentation.

'Good morning, everyone.' He paused, and the assembled officers looked at him in anticipation. He cleared his throat.

'DCI Pope found a small device at the crime scene that, on closer examination, turned out to be a covert spy camera.'

Verdy put up her hand again. 'Is this one of those nanny cams?'

'That's right. It's very small and unobtrusive, and can be placed anywhere.' Thompson looked relieved to have a question he could answer. 'It records both video and audio via an omni-directional antenna, meaning that it picks up anything that is happening in the room with a wide-angled field of vision. This is then wirelessly transmitted to a remote receiver, which can then, theoretically, be monitored anywhere with a Wi-Fi signal.'

A murmur of interest spread through the room.

'We are currently analyzing the device in the lab, but these are widely available both online and in shops and it is almost impossible to trace the signal, in terms of where it is being monitored. If, indeed, it is. We may be able to extract the footage and, of course, we are checking for forensic details, fingerprints, that sort of thing.'

Thompson collected up his tablet, moved around the table and quickly returned to his seat.

'Thanks very much, Sergeant Thompson,' said Pope, resuming her place at the front. 'Clearly this case presents us with a number of key avenues to explore. First, the victim. Why choose this family, this woman? Is there a connection with the killer? Most murders are, of course, committed by someone known to the victim, so that needs to be our first line of enquiry. Second, did anyone see the perpetrator, possibly without knowing what they were seeing? He could well have been scoping out the house for days, if not weeks, so someone might have seen something. We need to canvass the entire area. Thirdly, why would he move the body and stage it in the church? Why choose St Paul's? I think this is going to be key. It is highly unusual and suggests that this was not an opportunist murder or a burglary. This was personal. Finally, the video recorder. I'm not sure what that says about our perpetrator, but we need to find out quickly.'

Verdy's hand went up again. Pope nodded to her.

'Do you have any theories about the use of the video recorder?'

Pope paused for a moment. It was a good question and one she wasn't quite sure how to answer.

'There is the possibility that he likes to watch the scene. That he enjoys the spectacle of what he's done. But clearly we're at an early stage with this.'

Verdy nodded, digesting this. The room was quiet.

'Your assignments for today are in your packs. We meet here again this time tomorrow morning. I'll be meeting with DI Brody and DS Miller this evening for an interim review, so please make sure you let me know your progress by end of shift today. OK, thanks very much, everyone.'

The officers present leafed through their papers, checked their work for the day, and who they were teamed with. They paired up with other officers, talking quietly as they left the room. The gravity of the situation was not lost on any of them.

Stephen Thompson picked up his tablet and passed Pope on his way out.

'Thanks for that, Stephen.'

'No problem.'

'I need you to keep me updated on anything you get. Straightaway,' said Pope.

'Will do. As soon as we know anything, you'll know,' he assured her. He joined the others leaving the briefing room.

Within a couple of minutes the only ones left in the room were Pope, Brody, Miller and Superintendent Fletcher, who indicated to Pope that he wanted to have a word with her alone. Pope said she would meet Brody and Miller in their office in a few minutes. They left the room, leaving Pope and Fletcher in the large space.

'Good briefing, Bec. Clear and concise. Explaining the situation without sensationalizing the details.'

Pope waited, wondering where he was going with this. She could never quite read her boss.

'But why didn't you brief them on the card?'

She hesitated. 'I wasn't sure that it was the right time to do that.'

'Why not?'

'I need everyone focused on the task. I don't know how relevant this is going to be. And it's quite personal.'

She could see Fletcher weighing up her decision.

'They'll need to know about this soon. It's obviously important.'

'Yes,' agreed Pope, 'but until we understand what's going on, it will only be a distraction. Give me time to work out what we're dealing with first.'

He seemed to accept her explanation.

'We need a press conference today, Bec. The media have already got hold of this and they're starting to make their own stories out of rumour and half-facts. I think a public appeal is a good idea, see if anyone can help out in sightings of this guy.'

'Something tells me that we're unlikely to get anything of value from the public,' she replied.

'Perhaps,' he conceded. 'It does work best in opportunistic crimes. . .'

'This guy strikes me as someone who doesn't take chances. I've put a request for a rush on the autopsy of Susan Harper, and I'll go down to the coroner straight after this to see what we've got. But I have a feeling we're not going to find anything useful. Someone who is this careful in the details is unlikely to have made mistakes.'

'But it is possible.'

'Yes, it's possible, which is why we're investigating with this in mind. However, we need to be prepared to look at other angles in this case. If he's as meticulous as he seems, we may not find anything useful in terms of forensics,' said Pope.

'This is going to be a big story, Bec,' said Fletcher seriously. 'The victim is a housewife, not a gang member, and this is going to be all over the media. We need a quick result on this, or the department is going to look shoddy. I hope you understand that.'

Of course she understood. How the department looked publicly reflected on Fletcher. He was eyeing the next step up the career ladder in the Metropolitan Police, and a quick result in this case would give him a helping hand in promotion to Chief Superintendent.

'Yes, but I think any murder is a big story, whoever the victim is,' said Pope evenly.

Fletcher made to interrupt, to protest, but Pope continued.

'So, of course we'll do our best to get a quick identification and arrest here. But something doesn't feel right about this guy.' Pope wondered if she would regret revealing what she was about to say. 'What I'm really worried about is that this may not be his only victim. He seems very well organized, and very capable, and often single murders do not present like this. The first thing I'm going to do is cross-check the details with other similar cases in London and the UK, to see if there's any comparable MO elsewhere on other crimes. This just doesn't feel like a first murder. I hope I'm wrong.'

She looked at Fletcher, who was clearly not happy with what he'd heard, but unable to argue with anything Pope had laid out for him.

'Just get this guy and do it quickly. Press conference this afternoon. I'll let you know the details. And, Pope, I want to know any information as soon as you do. Top brass will be on me like a rash, and I'll need to have something to tell them. Preferably, something positive,' said Fletcher.

'I'll do my best not to make your phone calls with your superiors uncomfortable, sir. This will, of course, be uppermost in my mind at all times.'

Fletcher looked at her and seemed to be weighing up the sarcasm. His tone changed. 'Bec, this is connected to you. Personally. Be careful.'

He left the briefing room, without looking back. Pope headed towards her office.

When she got there, the open-plan office was busy, but quiet.

Brody and Miller were both hard at work. They both looked up and stopped what they were doing.

'Don't tell me. We need to catch this guy quickly, no napping on the job,' said Brody.

'So young, so cynical,' replied Pope. 'And pretty much word for word.'

Fletcher was predictable. He wanted to solve the crimes, but he was rather too focused on his own career, and sometimes it seemed as if that took priority.

'I've put out a request to ACRO for each force to cross-reference with what we know so far,' said Miller. 'We can add details after we've had the coroner's report, but I thought it was important to get this out as soon as possible. I've also started to look through your past cases, any recent prison releases, anyone who might hold a grudge. Any personal connections.'

'Good,' said Pope. 'And expedite forensics on the card left at the scene. Chase them. I want that back ASAP.'

'Will do,' said Miller.

There was a silence. Brody broke it. 'Bec, this guy. . . does this seem like a one-off to you? I mean. . .'

'I know what you mean,' said Pope. 'And it's a possibility. That's why I asked Adam to cross-reference with other forces. But for now, our focus needs to be the murder of Susan Harper. If information comes back that leads us to think otherwise, we'll re-evaluate.'

Brody and Miller nodded in agreement.

'Adam,' said Pope. 'I also want you to liaise with Tech Support to see what they've come up with re the camera. Brody and I will head to the coroner to see what we can get there.'

Miller turned back to his computer screen and began typing again.

'I'll meet you downstairs in a couple of minutes,' she said to Brody. He nodded and left the room.

Pope headed to the bathroom. While washing her hands, she looked at herself in the large mirror that covered most of the wall above the washbasins. She didn't know too many murder detectives who had the time or inclination to worry too much about their appearance, but the mirror was there anyway. Her reflection looked back at her. There were hints of a few grey hairs, lines on her forehead that she didn't remember seeing before. She was forty-one. She felt older. Alcohol, insomnia and the job were a vicious trifecta.

As she looked at herself, she wondered whether she had the energy for another murder case. It was a rhetorical question. Susan Harper, like every other victim, deserved the best that she could give her. Fatigue, whether physical or emotional, was simply not an option.

And an "invitation", with her name printed on it, guaranteed that she had no choice.

Pope dried her hands and prepared herself for a visit to the Metropolitan Police medical examiner.

CHAPTER 4

Pope and Brody made their way to the underground garage beneath Charing Cross Police Station. The station was an impressive building from the outside. Originally built in the 1830s as a hospital, it was later converted into a police station by a sympathetic and talented architect. They headed down to Pope's current squad car. She threw the keys over to Brody.

'I guess I'll drive.' He grinned as they both got in.

They always referred to the forensic pathologist as the medical examiner, or, more usually, the ME. Pope hated to admit it, but it was almost certainly picked up from watching American crime dramas on TV. Rachel Okafor had been one of the chief forensic pathologists used by the Met for over ten years, and she knew what she was doing. She was also succinct in her reporting, professional and, crucially, quick.

Brody pulled on to Agar Street, headed down the Strand and crossed the Thames over Waterloo Bridge. Blue skies with just a few thin white clouds high above provided a perfect backdrop for the majestic view in each direction. To the left St Paul's Cathedral and the City of London. To the right, the London Eye and the Houses of Parliament. Pope doubted that there was a better view in London. Traffic was not particularly heavy and they cruised past the National Theatre and the South Bank, sprawling on each side of the bridge with a 1950s Brutalism that you either loved or hated. Pope loved it. She had seen a lot of jazz at the Royal Festival Hall, and the building held a special place in her heart.

'The sky today. So clear,' said Brody, hunching down in the driver's seat a little so he could look up. 'Reminds me of the sky in New York on 9/11.'

Pope looked at him. 'How on earth—' She stopped herself. Too late. Brody's predilection for conspiracy theories was well known in the station, particularly 9/11. For an intelligent man, Brody had some odd ideas about, well, any potential conspiracy you could think of. His intellectual Achilles' heel.

'I'm reading an interesting book that details the latest theories behind the twin towers collapse. Lots of photographs, including the planes actually hitting. The sky today has that same quality.'

Pope didn't want to engage. She kept quiet.

'Did you know that there were Israeli agents filming just after the planes crashed? Right there, downtown?'

Pope looked resolutely out of the window.

Brody seemed to take that as a sign to continue. 'The financial aspects are fascinating. In the few days leading up there were really unusual transactions on the shares of United and American Airlines. The two airlines involved. Lots of buying of put options. Very odd.'

Despite herself, Pope was interested. 'What's a "put option"?'

'It's a kind of financial option designed to pay out if a stock drops below a certain level. Like an insurance, really. Suggests that there must have been insider knowledge in advance of 9/11.'

'But all these theories have been debunked, haven't they? Most people don't believe all these claims anymore.'

'They've been discredited by government sources, but they would be, wouldn't they? If they're involved. And it's

31

difficult for people to come out and question the official line because they get widely criticized and ridiculed. That's the problem. That's why JFK's still so troubling.'

'OK, OK. Enough. I'm not going down the JFK road again. Not after last time.'

'But you have to admit. . .'

'I'm not doing this now.' Pope looked out of the window to her left. 'Other things to think about.'

She preferred it when Brody was reading about forensics, his other interest. Far more useful.

They were both quiet as Brody steered them through Elephant and Castle and on to King's College Hospital, an enormous sprawl of buildings. He pulled into the car park and found a parking spot. They headed to the Pathology offices and arrived at reception.

'Hi, Detective Chief Inspector Pope and Detective Inspector Brody, here to see Dr Okafor,' explained Pope to the receptionist.

'Yes, you're expected, DCI Pope. If you'd like to take these visitors' badges, then go through, second door on the left.' Pope knew the way. She clipped the temporary badge on to her jacket, feeling like a delegate at a sales conference.

They found the door and Brody knocked.

'Come in,' said a voice from behind the door.

'Do take a seat,' said Okafor after they had shaken hands, gesturing to two upright chairs on the other side of the large desk that she sat behind.

'You're here about Susan Harper,' she said, half to herself as she looked at the file on her desk. She had obviously been checking the details when they arrived. 'Right, here we are. Susan Harper, aged thirty-eight. White female, five feet six inches tall, nine stone and six pounds in weight. Relatively fit and healthy, no sign of any pre-existing conditions that I detected.'

Pope and Brody waited through the necessary preamble, trying not to show their impatience. Rachel Okafor noticed anyway.

'So, what you want to know is cause of death.' She continued looking through her notes. 'Mrs Harper's body shows signs of great pressure to the neck and throat. Her hyoid bone is fractured. There are ligature marks around her neck, as well as bruising. The forensic evidence suggests that she was strangled by a rope, or more precisely, a medium-width waxed nylon cord, very tough, as well as being manually strangled.'

'You mean by his hands?' clarified Pope.

'Yes, that's correct.'

'Her larynx and trachea both show signs of trauma and considerable bruising, as does her neck and either side of her windpipe. Cause of death, technically, is loss of blood to the brain and asphyxiation by compression of the internal carotid artery.'

Pope looked at Brody. He had said almost exactly the same thing at the crime scene the previous day.

Okafor continued. 'It appears that your killer strangled the victim first with a strong rope, and then finished the job with his hands. There is no evidence of any sexual activity. I would say two things in addition. Firstly, this man, and I am assuming it is a man, is strong. It is not easy to strangle another human being who, as the survival instinct kicks in, fights for their life. Secondly, he knew exactly what he was doing. He knew to attack the larynx, trachea and windpipe to ensure that she couldn't scream and draw attention to what was going on. He also knew where to find the carotid artery and, even more impressive, or worrying, depending on your point of view, he knew where the internal carotid artery lies in the human body, rather than the external carotid artery, which serves a different purpose in supplying blood to the face and neck, rather than the brain.' She closed the file, steepled her hands together on the desk, and looked at the detectives in front of her, waiting for any questions.

Pope thought for a minute. 'You say he knew what he was doing. Is there a chance that this was luck, or a scattergun approach of hitting everything in that anatomical area?'

'No, I am fairly certain that that is not what happened here. The sites of bruising are too precise and, it's difficult to explain, but when stranglers know what they're doing, it is just different. Again, more precise. Most strangulations are either accidental or amateur, impulsive. This is different,' replied Okafor.

'One more question,' said Pope. 'I know it's not really your area, but from what you have seen, and what you have just suggested, do you think that this is his first victim? I mean—'

'Yes, I know what you mean,' interrupted Okafor. She paused, thinking how best to phrase the answer. 'This is purely informed supposition, but no. If I had to guess I would say that your killer seems efficient and knowledgeable in human anatomy and the techniques of strangulation. But don't quote me.'

Pope and Brody looked at each other, but it was very hard to work out what their expressions meant. Maybe they didn't know themselves.

They thanked Okafor and she saw them out of her office.

'No offence,' she said as they were leaving, 'but I hope not to see you again for a while.'

Pope looked back and smiled, then turned around and left with her partner.

* * *

When Pope and Brody arrived back at the station the desk sergeant handed Pope a memo.

'It's from Superintendent Fletcher.'

Pope read the note and showed it to Brody. *Press conference at 12.15 p.m.* was all it said. She looked at her watch: eleven fifteen. Brody headed to the office to see how Miller had got on and write up his notes from their visit to the coroner. Pope went the other way.

She waited outside Fletcher's office, until she was called in. There she found Fletcher wearing his full police superintendent uniform. Although he wasn't yet wearing his peaked cap, he looked as if he was going to a passing-out parade for new recruits. It had clearly been cleaned and pressed and looked brand new. She wondered silently if Fletcher had a whole wardrobe full of them that he whipped out whenever the need arose. She didn't ask him. Pope understood the function of such uniforms: to other police officers it denoted authority and respect, tradition and importance. For members of the public, it reassured them that all was in safe, professional hands. The same theory as airline pilots. The small chain that hung across the fastening to the jacket looked odd, a throwback to a bygone age. All part of the image, to differentiate Fletcher from the other police officers around him. Tradition and expectation dictated that Fletcher had to dress for the occasion, but he also seemed to enjoy wearing the outfit. Pope couldn't think of anything worse. She looked down at her own, rather crumpled suit. The comparison did her no favours.

Pope spoke first. 'Very smart, sir.'

'Thank you, Bec. Are you here about the press conference?'

'Yes. How would you like to play it?'

'I'd like you to lead. Is there anything you'd like to keep back?'

'I don't think we should mention the camera,' replied Pope. 'Tech is on it, but we don't know anything useful yet. It won't serve any purpose other than to unsettle the public. It also gives us something we can use to weed out crank callers. Same with the card on the body. We'll need a bit more time on that.'

Fletcher nodded. 'OK. Keep it brief, only a few questions. I don't want this sensationalized. The media will be all over it as it is.'

'OK. I'll see you in there at twelve fifteen.'

'Bec.' Fletcher called after her as she was opening the door. 'Wear something smart.'

'I'll do my best, sir.' Pope left the superintendent's office. She'd be wearing what she was currently wearing.

* * *

35

By 12.10 p.m. the press and TV journalists were already assembled and there was an expectant buzz in the room. It was packed. Microphones with huge fuzzy covers were clustered at the front of the room, in front of a lectern. Cameras and crews, and even more journalists with voice recorders, all waited, ready to spring into electronic action. Others had notepads and pencils at the ready, the old-school crime reporters who had not embraced modern technology.

Pope and Fletcher stood at the front of the room. Although Fletcher had asked Pope to lead, he couldn't resist the limelight. Fletcher welcomed everyone and outlined the context, then handed over to Pope. She cleared her throat, and explained the talking points they had agreed. As ever, it was a fine line between offering useful information that might lead to calls from members of the public, all while respecting the family of the victim by not giving the grisly details of how their loved one was murdered. She also had to avoid anything that the assembled bloodhounds could turn into a salacious story. When she had finished, she judged that she had walked that tightrope reasonably well.

'Are there any questions?' she asked.

Almost all the hands in the room shot up. She picked a journalist from *The Times*, who she had dealt with before and whom she knew to be professional.

'DCI Pope, do you have any leads yet?' he asked.

'This is our first day of investigating a crime that was committed yesterday, so we hope to be able to share some information soon. We are following a number of leads at this time.' Standard response number one.

'What leads are you following?' persisted the journalist.

'I can't comment on that. The investigation is ongoing.' Standard response number two.

She pointed to a woman who she recognized as a crime reporter for the *Daily Mirror*.

'Can you confirm that Susan Harper was strangled, DCI Pope?'

She hid her anger. She knew that reporters often paid police officers for information on cases but was not happy that the leak had happened so soon.

'I can't confirm that at present. Again, investigations are ongoing. I'm afraid I don't have time for any more questions.' She stepped down from the podium.

As she left the conference room through a side door with Fletcher, the barrage of shouting, questions and flash bulbs continued behind them.

'Another bloody leak!' Fletcher exclaimed. 'I want you to find the source and send them to me as soon as possible.'

Pope nodded, but deep down she knew she'd never find the person responsible.

* * *

He turned the sound up on the TV. A gathering of journalists and reporters. A man and a woman at the front of the room in the bright lights brought by the TV crews. One in a police uniform. The other, DCI Bec Pope.

He stared down at the screen. He stepped backwards, waiting. Then he leaned in close to the screen. The resolution was so good these days that you could see every hair on the head, every pore on the face.

The police officer in uniform addressed the camera. The man seemed to be looking straight at him, straight through the camera. A wave of anger rose up in him. He spat on the screen, hitting the man square on his nice, clean uniform. He wiped the back of his hand across his mouth and then, catching himself, used his sleeve to wipe the screen. He hated to lose control.

The woman was now speaking to the audience, but she seemed to be talking to those in the room, rather than speaking to, and for, the cameras. She then asked for questions. Of course there would be questions. The first one came.

'We are following a number of leads at this time,' she answered someone he couldn't see.

Is that right? *he wondered. 'A number of leads. . .' He had left a few "leads", as she called them.*

When the question about strangulation came, he looked closely at the screen. DCI Pope had not said anything about the cause of death. He examined the police officer's expression. He breathed in, seeing the barely perceptible twitch in her face. He could smell the anger coming from the woman on the screen as she refused to confirm the cause of death. Pope and the other officer left the room.

He imagined the conversation they were having: the recriminations, the anger, the frustration. Not that any of this mattered, of course. Soon their attention would be pulled in another direction, and they wouldn't be able to have the luxury of spending time searching for leaks.

Soon he would give them something else on which to focus.

Then, they would begin to grasp the nature of what they were dealing with.

Then, they would realize that this was very different to anything they had had to deal with before.

Unique.

Terrifying.

He rewound the image until he reached the expression on Pope's face when she was asked to confirm the cause of death to be strangulation. He froze the video.

He reached to the stereo and pressed play. The opening bars of "I've Got the World on a String" by Frank Sinatra. He turned the volume up until he could feel the music through the floor. A sudden burst of brass for an introduction, until Sinatra's vocals came in, and then, soon afterwards, the full band. He stood up again and faced the TV screen. He looked at Bec Pope. He felt the music inside him. It made him feel omnipotent.

He lifted his head to the ceiling and the sky beyond and screamed. At the image, at the music, fuelled by the adrenaline coursing through him as he thought about what he was about to do. He could not hear himself, but he could feel it, feel the roar in his lungs and in his chest.

It was nearly time.

CHAPTER 5

Pope walked out on to Agar Street and crossed Charing Cross Road in front of the National Portrait Gallery. She needed to think, and she needed some fresh air. She turned into Leicester Square, extremely busy but suitably anonymous. She bought a cup of coffee from a café and found an empty bench facing the north side of the square. The coffee was average at best, but it served as a prop to occupy her hands and help her focus.

She watched as office workers rushed to get somewhere important, to make use of the little time they were allowed for lunch, grabbing a bite to eat and carrying out errands. Tourists wandered at a much more leisurely pace — couples and families, mostly, with the occasional backpacker, stopping to watch the street entertainers who sprayed themselves silver and breakdanced to seventies hip-hop. A thin gauze of fatigue was beginning to work on her. The sky became a bleached-out backdrop. She could fall asleep right there, sleep for days. She longed to catch up on the hours she had failed to sleep last night, and the night before, and the night before that. Insomnia had come calling around a year after she joined Homicide. About the time she was moved off the Tina Waterson case. And it had stayed.

She was jolted awake by a vibration in her pocket and realized her phone was ringing. She pulled it out and checked the screen: *Dad*. Pope didn't want to talk to him at the moment, so let the phone ring out. He left no message. She put the phone away, but then immediately felt guilty. There was something wrong with her dad, and it was only a matter of time before he told her what it was. Maybe that's why he was calling, or maybe something had happened to him.

She knew that this would bug her until she knew, so dialled him back. He picked up on the third ring.

'Bec, I just tried to call you.'

'Sorry, I didn't get to the phone in time. How are you?'

'I'm OK, thanks. What are you doing?' he asked.

'I'm just grabbing a coffee,' said Bec, truthfully, 'then I need to get back to work.'

'Yes, I saw your case on the news. Terrible.' Did she detect criticism in his voice? His tone was hard to read. It was always hard to read.

Pope looked at her watch. 'I've really got to get back to the office. Was there anything specific you wanted?' Pope knew she shouldn't be so brusque, but her dad tended not to take subtle hints and she had discovered over the years that the direct approach was often more successful.

'What are you doing tonight?' her father asked. 'Fancy getting something to eat?'

Pope was surprised. Her father rarely initiated meetings, usually having more important things to do than catch up with his daughter.

'I'm kind of at the start of this case, and I'm going to be really busy—'

Her father cut in. 'Come on, Bec. Even murder detectives have to eat. I haven't seen you for ages. I can come to you.'

Pope wondered if he wanted to speak to her about his health. She thought for a moment.

'OK, how about Vesuvio on Wellington Street, just off the Strand? We went there once years ago. Do you remember?'

'I'll find it,' said her father. He obviously didn't remember. 'Shall we say 9 p.m.?'

'9 p.m. should be fine. I'll book a table.'

'Great, see you then.' Her father hung up.

Pope wasn't quite sure why she had agreed to the dinner, but she knew she had to see him sometime, and he was right, she did have to eat. She finished her coffee and threw the paper cup into a rubbish bin next to the seat. She took a deep breath, lifted herself off the bench and headed back to the squad room.

When she arrived back at the station, it was a hive of activity. Police officers seemed to be walking in all different directions, carrying memos and reports and going to meetings. Several tourists were waiting in the reception area, presumably to report a theft or pickpocketing. She headed upstairs to her office.

'Hi. Have we heard back from Tech?' she asked as she walked in.

'We have, but I'm afraid it isn't good news,' replied Miller.

Pope sat down behind her desk. 'Go on.'

'They've taken it apart, and they inspected the crime scene this morning. There're no identifying features that will allow them to work out where it's from or where or how the signal was being picked up. They couldn't find anything at the Harpers' house to see where it was transmitting to. You can buy these types of cameras in lots of places. They're actually quite common, particularly in business and diplomatic circles, apparently.'

'So they're mainly used for businesses and diplomats to spy on each other?' asked Pope.

'More to record meetings and interviews to provide evidence where nothing is put in writing,' said Miller. 'And, I suppose, in some cases for blackmail or industrial espionage, yes,' he conceded.

'And are we even sure our killer is the one who put it there?' asked Brody who had joined them at Pope's desk.

41

'No, we're not. At the moment, there doesn't seem to be any other explanation, but as we can't work out where it came from or where the signal was transmitting to, no, we're not sure.'

'Have you had anything back about the card?' Pope asked Miller.

'No. Forensics can't get anything. No prints. It's totally clean.'

Brody updated Pope on other aspects of the investigation. PCs Hawley and McEwan were canvassing the neighbours and other residents of the Harpers' street. Other officers were at Mike Harper's school. Yet others were sitting behind computers trying to cross-reference, input information and make links. In total there were fifteen officers and detectives working on the Susan Harper murder case.

'Any news from ACRO yet?' Pope asked as she skimmed her emails. The Criminal Records Office coordinated police records across the country. But it relied on information from individual forces.

Miller rolled his eyes. 'Three guesses. They've either got too much to do, not enough to do or there isn't anyone there to do it. I'll let you know when I hear anything.'

Pope and Brody decided to return to the crime scene, and then interview Susan Harper's husband. That took them most of the afternoon. Brody had suggested that looking again at the Harper's house might reveal something. But despite a lengthy examination of the whole house and garden, nothing appeared to help them make any further progress. Likewise, interviewing Mike Harper did not offer anything new. He was devastated and his grief appeared genuine. Both Pope and Brody were certain that he was not involved. He had a watertight alibi, as he had been teaching a full day at school. Thirty witnesses at any point in the day. Likewise, both children had attended school all day. Pope didn't really suspect that the children would be involved in the murder of their mother.

Brody drove them back to the station. There were still friends and family members to interview, but Pope had a feeling that they were unlikely to provide them with any clues to Susan Harper's murder.

'I don't think he knew her,' said Pope after they had been driving in silence for a few minutes.

'What makes you think that?' asked Brody.

'The way he knew exactly what he was doing, the likely recce of the house and family in advance, the moving of the body. To me that suggests a psychopath. He didn't get in there, kill her and get out quick. He took his time, set up a scene for us to find, or at least to gratify his own needs. I agree with Dr Okafor. I think he's killed before,' said Pope.

'Do you think he'll kill again?'

'I don't know,' said Pope.

* * *

They arrived back at the station at 5.30 p.m. Miller caught them up with what other officers had reported from canvassing, interviews and computer work. Nothing of any real interest so far. Brody and Pope divided up the information they had gathered during the day and set to writing it up in their daily reports. At about 7 p.m. Miller went home, leaving just the two of them in the office. Pope called Alex to explain that she was still at work, and that she was meeting her father for dinner so she would be back late. In turn, Alex told her the latest developments in the Chloe saga. After a short while Pope finished the call, sighed, looked up to the ceiling, then returned to the laborious job of writing police reports.

At 8 p.m., she and Brody were finishing up the last of the work.

'I have to meet my father in an hour,' she said. 'I need a drink to fortify myself. Care to join me?'

'Sounds good,' he said, packing his notes away as the printer produced paper copies of their reports.

They left the station and headed to the Coal Hole, a pub on the Strand just a few minutes' walk away. It was close to the restaurant where Pope was meeting her father. She ordered a house red wine, Brody a pint of bitter. She paid, and they found a seat in the far corner of the pub. Pope looked around. A few tourists, a lot of young office workers out after work, before inconveniences such as career, marriage and children. A couple of office romances. A few middle-aged men on their own, finding companionship with alcohol before they headed home.

She and Brody discussed the case for a bit until, simultaneously, they both seemed to decide that they had talked enough about work, and the topic of conversation changed.

'How's your father?' he asked.

'I'm not really sure,' replied Pope. 'I think he's got something to tell me about his health. I know he's had some doctor and hospital visits, but we don't talk or see each other that much. Despite the fact that he's only a few miles across the river from me. I wonder if he is going to talk to me about it tonight. Hence the fortification.' She smiled, lifting her wine and taking a sip.

'Everything all right at home?' he continued. 'I couldn't help overhearing a bit earlier when you were on the phone to Alex.'

'He's having trouble with Chloe. She wants to stay over with her boyfriend after a party on Friday night. Alex wants me to back him up, no doubt he wants me to tell Chloe some scary stories about the consequences of being an errant teenager in a big city.' They both smiled, picturing the scene. 'And Alex isn't too happy that this case will mean I'll be away from home a lot, for who knows how long.'

Brody looked at her. 'She's sixteen, Bec. Tell her she has to be home, she'll hate you for a week, and then it'll be back to normal. It's more important that she's safe.'

She saw that he realized this was obvious advice, and not really his place to give it.

'Yeah, I know. But she and Alex butt heads so much these days, it's difficult to navigate the minefield. It's like being a UN peacekeeper, but no one really respects your authority to make decisions and lay down the law.'

'Ah, the joys of being a stepparent,' replied Brody.

Pope looked at her watch and saw that she was supposed to be at the restaurant ten minutes ago. She also realized that she had forgotten to book, and hoped that there would be a table for them. She finished the remains of her wine.

'I've got to go,' she said. 'Why don't you join us? It's only over the road, and I'm sure my father would be happy to meet you.'

Brody smiled. 'No, I should get going. Thanks anyway. Have a good time with your dad.'

She smiled. 'Yes, that's a possibility, I suppose. Don't spend too much time reading about 9/11.'

'You're kidding? I'm just getting to the chapter on the bin Laden interviews. Fascinating. . .'

She rolled her eyes, and he stopped.

Pope wanted to stay. She hadn't had enough of his company and she wanted to spend more time in the corner of this pub with him. But she had to go and she already was late.

Pope headed east and turned up Wellington Street, which carried on to Covent Garden. Vesuvio, an Italian restaurant popular with locals, actors and theatregoers, was on the left. She headed down the stairs and checked to see if her father had arrived. He was sitting at a table with a bottle of wine in front of him. Pope pointed him out to the waiter and walked over to the table.

Her father stood up as she arrived. 'Bec, good to see you,' he said, giving her a hug. Pope sat down opposite.

John Pope was sixty-one, but looked about ten years younger. His hair was still full and very dark with only a hint of greying at the temples. Pope assumed this was without the aid of dye. He was tall and athletic, and kept himself in excellent shape. A habit picked up as a young man in the army and never lost, he exercised regularly, ate healthily and rarely drank. Tonight was obviously an exception. Pope reached over and picked up the bottle of red wine on the table, pouring herself a glass.

'So, how are things?' Pope asked as she took a sip of the wine.

Her father had chosen well, although anything would be better than the uninspiring wine she had downed in the pub beforehand.

'Fine, thanks. You?' replied her father.

'OK. This case has taken over everything really, and will continue to do so until we catch the guy. I've got a big team to work on it, which is great, but it means I've also got to manage them all while doing what I have to do.'

Her father nodded his understanding. He had been a senior manager with the same multinational financial services company for over thirty years. It had been the bane of her mother's life: the constant business trips abroad, the late nights entertaining clients and the constant ringing of the phone when he was at home. He had left when Pope was twelve. It had been very hard, but at least it stopped the arguments.

They were momentarily interrupted when the waiter arrived to take their orders. Pope ordered pasta and, after a moment's hesitation, a green salad to go with it. Her father ordered seafood. The waiter repeated their choices and left quickly, a model of quiet efficiency. Pope looked around. The restaurant was about half full. The pre-theatre crowd had long since left, and it would be a while until the post-crowd arrived. Soon after that would be the actors from the nearby theatres, entertaining family and friends who had attended their shows.

'How are Alex and the kids?' asked her father. He never used the girls' names, and rarely visited. Stepfamilies were not worth the effort for him. Nothing to be gained.

'They're fine. Alex's work is going well, very busy. Hannah and Chloe—' she deliberately used their names — 'are well. Hannah's working hard to make friends and settle into her first year in secondary school. Chloe is, well, let's just say that she's excelling in the role of "stereotypical teenage

46

girl". Parties, boyfriends, arguments with her parents, that kind of thing.' She waited for John Pope to show an interest. She'd be waiting a very long time, she thought.

Pope talked a little more about her home life, in the vague hope that her father might show an interest. Once their meals arrived, Pope noticed that she seemed to be eating quickly, unused to sitting down for a leisurely meal. At home she would usually end up snacking on leftovers after everyone else had gone to bed. Her father, on the other hand, seemed to be eating slowly, deliberately, as if he was thinking about something. Pope wondered if it was because of a medical condition, but wasn't sure how to broach the subject.

They talked and drank as they ate, largely about Susan Harper's murder. He wanted to know all the details, how they were investigating the crime and whether they had any suspects. Pope eventually said, 'I can't really talk any more about the case. The investigation has only just started and is essentially confidential.' She changed the subject. 'How's your health these days?'

John Pope looked directly at his daughter. 'I'm fine. The doctors are just running some tests, as they tend to do when you reach my age. They're over-cautious at work, and need us to get checked out regularly.' Her father continued to hold eye contact with her.

Pope could tell he was lying. She was torn between respecting her father's clear wish not to discuss the state of his health, and a natural desire to know what was going on in her family, such as it was.

'So it's nothing particular you're being tested for?' she persisted.

'No. Just routine.' Brief. Closing the conversation down.

'OK, well, that's good to hear, I guess,' replied Pope. In her work she was used to pressing people to tell the truth, especially when she knew she wasn't getting it. But here, now, with her father, she couldn't do that. She got the feeling that however hard she pushed, her father wasn't going to tell her anything.

They talked for a while longer, about nothing of consequence, until her father asked the waiter for the bill.

Outside it was just starting to rain, and the streets were emptier than usual. What water had collected on the ground reflected the streetlights and car headlights and brake lights, creating a warm, watercolour glow bouncing off the tarmac. They said their goodbyes, made hollow promises to catch up very soon and went their separate ways. Pope glanced back, watched her father walking towards Covent Garden. He was imposing as he moved, and the few people who passed him got out of his way on the pavement, rather than the other way around. She wondered if this subconscious show of dominance was merely covering the vulnerability he was currently feeling after the medical tests to which he had been subjected. She shook her head. She'd have to leave the cod psychology to others.

She was sure of one thing, however. Her father had lied to her this evening, and this was the last thing she needed to be worrying about.

CHAPTER 6

He stood silently in the shadows, unmoving. Watched. Across the street and twenty yards away. Everyone in the houses in this street were either asleep, in bed or on the way there. He had been watching for an hour. She had come home fifteen minutes ago, found her keys in her handbag and let herself in. All the while oblivious to his presence. The lights turning on in the house tracked her progress: hall, living room, kitchen. She wouldn't be long. But he was in no hurry.

He knew she lived alone and often worked late, or went out for a drink or a meal with friends after work. She always took the underground, never the bus, and walked back from the station at the same quick pace. She always came home alone. She spent no more than an hour downstairs, before going upstairs to get ready to go to sleep.

He would never get over the predictability of human beings. The invented routines around which they organized their lives, as if they were immutable boundaries. This predictability, of course, was useful. His planning was made easy by routine.

He took a deep breath, savouring the moment. The euphoria he knew he was about to experience. The anticipation.

He waited, and then the lights in each room went off in quick succession. He walked silently across the street, pulling on a pair of thin gloves as he went. The harsh white of the streetlight was now on him, cutting a slice through the darkness and picking him out as its subject for illumination.

He needed to be quick.

He knocked on the front door: three sharp raps. He could sense the confusion inside, and heard footsteps coming down the stairs. Tiredness, disorientation, a mild anxiety he could almost taste through the door.

A brief pause. 'Who's there?'

'It's Mark from number fourteen. They delivered a parcel for you this morning to my place. I've got it here.'

'It's pretty late.'

'Yes, sorry. I came round earlier but you weren't in. I just noticed your lights on. I guess I can come back tomorrow if you don't want it now.'

'No, no, it's fine. Thanks. Hold on.' She unbolted the door and pulled it open. 'Sorry, I'm just—'

She didn't complete the sentence. He punched her hard in the face. She grunted with the blow, stumbled backwards and fell to the floor, unconscious. He walked in and quietly closed the door behind him.

He stood looking over her. She had fallen awkwardly and her neck was twisted unnaturally away from her body. He would have to fix that. He reached into his pocket and his fingers found a length of medium–thick waxed rope.

He leaned down and lifted her head from the floor. The rope slipped easily and quickly around her neck. He pulled it tighter, then looped it round his hands at either end. His shoulders lifted as he pulled on the two ends of the rope with enormous force.

He could hear her attempting to gasp, felt the natural survival instinct as she began to kick her legs and try to dislodge his grip with her hands. But she was semi-conscious, and he was much, much stronger. Suddenly the lack of air caused her to struggle much more violently. She seemed to find some inner strength, tearing at his arms and hands. And then she slumped.

He removed the rope and wound it into a tight, small coil and placed it into his left pocket. He watched her for several minutes. The lifeless body was fascinating. Quiet peace after the furious struggle only seconds before.

He reached down and lifted the body. She was easy to carry. He lifted her up the stairs carefully, ensuring that nothing was disturbed on the way. Inside the bedroom, he placed her carefully on the bed. He took off his shoes and climbed on to the bed. He straddled the body and looked down, placed his hands carefully around her throat and pressed. Gently at first, but then gaining in power until the tissue began tearing beneath his hands. He looked up to the ceiling, relishing the moment of ecstasy and, as the hyoid bone in her neck cracked with a barely audible sound, let out a short exhalation. He released his grip slowly until his hands were free. Marks around her neck started to appear.

He stepped carefully off the bed, before repositioning her body. She would look peaceful, sleeping. At rest. He looked around the room for the first time. The objects he saw didn't interest him. The trinkets of a life were entirely meaningless. He opened the curtains, knowing that they would not be closed by anyone examining this room. He removed a small electronic device from his pocket, reached up and placed it unsteadily on the corner of the curtain rail. It immediately fell on to the windowsill. He went downstairs and searched through drawers and cupboards until he found a roll of tape. He returned upstairs and used several small pieces of tape to secure it in place. This was difficult in his thin gloves, but he wanted to know it would stay in place. He reached up and turned on the camera. A small red light came on in the top right corner and then blinked away.

He paused a moment, gazing down at the woman laying peacefully in her bed. Then he reached into his pocket and produced a crisp white envelope, printed black text on the front, and placed it carefully on the dead woman's chest. He smiled, then went downstairs, carefully replaced the roll of tape in its drawer. He checked the hallway to ensure that everything was as it should be, and quietly left, closing the door behind him.

He walked from the house in almost total darkness. He knew that soon there would be another visitor to the house: Bec Pope.

* * *

Pope had drunk too much red wine to drive herself home and so she hailed a black cab on the Strand. The taxi driver talked about his day, the people he had picked up and where he had taken them, and then moved on to politics. Pope was too tired and distracted to engage in conversation, and eventually the driver gave up and they rode the rest of the journey in silence.

As she looked out of the window the rain-soaked streets began to blur as the water drops on the window of the cab formed a haze between her and the rest of the world. Black taxis and men and women in suits merged in a bright fluorescent blur, streetlights and brake lights creating an ominous glow in the sheets of water that were now coming down. London looked clean in the rain, but she was too exhausted to appreciate it. She thought of her father and the unsatisfactory meeting they had just had. Her whole adult life had been punctuated with unsatisfactory meetings with her father. They had never really discussed him leaving her and her mother. She had been too young, and then there never seemed to be the right time. She knew it would come one day. But it would have to wait. She had the murder of Susan Harper to deal with and she wouldn't allow herself to be distracted.

Pope's taxi pulled up outside her front door. She paid the driver and got out. As the taxi drove off, she found her keys and let herself in.

Alex was in the living room, watching a movie on TV, a large glass of red wine on the coffee table beside him. She took off her coat, went over and gave him a kiss. He held on to her, then picked up the remote control and muted the TV.

'Don't turn it off on my account,' said Pope, as she went into the kitchen and poured a glass of wine from the open bottle on the counter.

'It's OK, it was pretty dull. Just a time-passer,' said Alex.

'Where are the girls?'

'Hannah's in bed and Chloe is upstairs getting ready for bed. I hope. It is eleven thirty,' he said evenly.

She looked at her watch, sat down next to him and took a long drink from the glass.

Alex looked at the glass, then looked at her. 'Good meal with your father?' he said with a smile.

'It was OK,' she replied. 'We went to Vesuvio. The food was good.'

'Did he talk to you about his tests?' asked Alex.

'No, not really. I asked him, but he said they were "just routine", a regular check-up ordered by his company.'

'Maybe that's what it is.'

'I could tell he was lying to me. There's definitely something wrong. But he changed the subject very quickly,' said Pope.

'Are you worried?'

'For now I've got to focus on the case. I'll deal with it once that's over. We talk, but we never really talk, if you know what I mean. We never discuss the important things, just skate around the surface.' Pope looked at the TV absently for a while, as Alex looked at her. Just then they heard footsteps going up the stairs and a bedroom door closing.

'Damn,' said Alex. 'That will be Hannah. She must have heard us talking about your father.'

'They're not really close,' said Pope.

'No, but after losing her mother, whenever illness touches her family or friends, she tends to overreact. And she's probably thinking about you and how you'll be feeling. She's sensitive, and she's very fond of you. You know that,' said Alex.

'Sorry. Shall I go up and talk to her?'

'No, leave it for a while. You need to unwind. I'll go up in a few minutes.'

Just then they heard footsteps coming down the stairs. Different footsteps, so they knew it was Chloe. She walked into the room and said hello to Pope. No hug. In some ways, even after two years, she was still an outsider with Chloe. She wondered whether this would ever change.

Chloe walked into the kitchen and seemed to be doing something, but Pope couldn't work out what. She sensed it was a tactic to enable her to come down and the real reason for her presence would soon make itself known.

Chloe walked casually back into the living room and stood facing her father.

'Dad, I really have to go to this party on Friday night.' She looked at Alex, then at Pope. They both returned her look, but didn't say anything. Chloe's second attempt at getting permission.

'It's in North London, and it'll be late, so I'm thinking I'll stay at a friend's house so I don't have to get all the way home. OK?' She said it as casually as she could, but there was an underlying nervousness, as if she knew she was asking for something that they would think was unacceptable.

'Tyler's going to be there, right?' asked Alex. Tyler Watts was Chloe's boyfriend. Six months and she was head over heels in love. Pope knew that Alex didn't like Tyler. Not only was he Alex's precious daughter's boyfriend, but he was a skater, a slacker and a smoker. In trouble at school, presumably doing no work, and a terrible influence on "his" Chloe. Chloe had some idea of her father's feelings, but Alex did his best to appear outwardly supportive of their relationship. He tried to keep his opinions to himself.

'Yes, I think so.' Chloe said it with a pretence of not really being sure, as if it was incidental to the issue at hand.

'Well, he can bring you back, then,' said Alex. 'The party's fine, but you can't stay over, I'm afraid. Back by twelve thirty, as usual at weekends. Anyway, we've already discussed this.'

Chloe looked at him, fury in her eyes. 'You're joking, right? All my friends are allowed out later than me, and Tyler won't be happy about leaving so ridiculously early, so I'll probably have to come home on my own.'

'If he's any sort of a boyfriend, he'll bring you home,' replied Alex.

'All my friends are staying over. I'll be the only one. Please.' She looked at her father.

'No, sorry, Chloe. You'll need to be back by twelve thirty, as I said.' Alex looked at Pope, and so did Chloe. They both wanted her input, but both wanted her to say something completely different.

Pope opened her mouth, about to speak.

'It's got nothing to do with you anyway!' Chloe shouted as she turned and stormed out of the room. She stopped at the door. 'You're not my mother.' She ran out of the room and up the stairs.

'Chloe!' Alex shouted after her.

'Don't worry, it's fine,' said Pope.

'It's not fine,' said Alex. 'I'm not having her talk to you like that.' He went to go after his daughter.

Pope caught him by the arm. 'I said it's fine. She'll get over it.'

She pulled him close and wrapped him in her arms.

Suddenly she heard her phone ringing in her pocket. Alex felt the vibration and he looked at her, his expression changing. She knew this was not the time to answer the telephone, not the time for anything except the moment of shared intimacy that Alex needed. But she was also the DCI on an open murder investigation and, sometimes, that needed to come first.

She removed her arms from Alex and he looked at her with a mixture of hurt and anger. She picked up the phone and pressed the green answer button.

'Pope,' she said, not having looked at the caller ID. 'Hi, Brody.' Alex's look was easy to read. She looked away.

'Christ,' she said. 'Where?' Pause. 'Why are we getting the call?' Another pause. Lengthier. Pope looked up at the ceiling.

She was aware of Alex close behind her, knew exactly what he was feeling.

'Are they sure?' continued Pope. 'OK, send a car to pick me up. I shouldn't drive.' A car was already on the way. She ended the call and looked at Alex.

'There's been another murder. I'm sorry.'

CHAPTER 7

A cordon had already been set up across the quiet Shoreditch street by the time Pope arrived. The door to house number twenty-six was open and the lights on inside. Pope recognized the two PCs Hawley and McEwan standing on duty just in front.

'Hawley, McEwan. Are Brody and Miller inside?'

'Yes, ma'am,' replied Hawley.

She walked up the short path and went inside. It was crime-scene busy. A number of officers were examining the downstairs rooms, and two forensic technicians marked potential evidence while a photographer took pictures of anything tagged. She could see signs of what had happened in the hallway. There was blood on the carpet at the bottom of the stairs and a small table had been knocked to the floor.

Pope found Brody and Miller in the kitchen, sitting at the table, deep in discussion. She stood by the door. There were only two chairs at the table.

'What do we have?'

Adam Miller spoke first. 'Female victim, Linda Wilson. Photo ID and driving licence in her purse confirms identity. Thirty years old, resident at this address. Works at a financial services firm in Westminster. She lives alone, but the body

56

was discovered by her partner, Meena Shah. She's a para-medic and often comes over late, after her shift.'

'What else do we know about Shah?'

'She's at the station now. She's been on shift all day, plenty of witnesses,' Miller added, checking his notes. 'Quite a new relationship, apparently.'

'OK, so what happened?' asked Pope. She really wanted to ask only one question.

Miller continued. 'It looks like she was attacked in the hallway and appears to have been knocked down at the bottom of the stairs. There's blood on the carpet and signs of a struggle, so this is our best guess at this stage. You saw the techs examining the area.'

Pope nodded for him to continue.

'It seems that the victim was then taken upstairs and placed on her bed. . .' Miller paused. He knew that this was the point of no return. 'She looks to have been strangled. And carefully positioned. The ME is upstairs now confirming cause of death.' He closed his notebook and set it on the table.

'So, a similar MO as Susan Harper? But the body left in her house?' Pope asked. It wasn't really a question.

'Yes,' said Brody.

She looked past him and out into the darkness of the street beyond. He waited until she looked at him. 'It's him,' he said.

Pope had known this as soon as she'd got the call from Brody, but now she had the confirmation, it hit her in the stomach like a hard right hook.

'OK, let's go upstairs and see what the ME has to say.' She left the kitchen, excused herself past the technicians at the bottom of the stairs and climbed the staircase to the upper floor. Brody and Miller followed her.

As she entered the bedroom, she saw Rachel Okafor on her knees by the bed, taking samples from underneath the fingernails of the victim, Linda Wilson. Next to her was her assistant, Sam Brooks, a relatively new recruit to the coroner's service. He didn't seem particularly comfortable.

They made their introductions, and stood quietly for a moment, out of respect for the victim and the situation.

'I see you got the late shift,' said Pope. Okafor nodded curtly, still bagging samples.

She waited a moment. 'What do we have here, Rachel?'

Okafor paused, and then stopped what she was doing and stood up. 'You'll have to wait until we've carried out a full autopsy back at the morgue before I can give you anything definitive.'

'I realize that,' said Pope. 'But it would be really helpful if you could give us your impressions so far.'

Okafor thought for a moment. 'Off the record?' she asked.

'Off the record. Absolutely.'

She sighed. 'OK. My best guess at this stage is that Linda Wilson was struck an indeterminate number of times downstairs in the hall. She was then brought upstairs and placed on the bed. She was strangled, either downstairs or up here. Cause of death, on preliminary investigation—' she emphasized the word *preliminary* — 'is strangulation.'

She looked at Pope, waiting for the inevitable next question.

'Is it the same guy?' asked Pope. And then added unnecessarily, 'As Susan Harper?'

'It certainly looks that way,' replied Okafor.

Pope had been expecting her to hedge her bets. She waited for an explanation.

Okafor handed Pope a pair of blue latex gloves, then leaned down and produced a clear plastic evidence bag from beside her as Pope pulled them on. Inside, a white envelope. 'This was on the body. Lying on the chest.' She passed it to Pope.

Pope took a deep breath and removed the envelope from the bag. Everyone in the room had stopped what they were doing and were watching her. It was the same as the one they had found at the previous crime scene and had the same lettering on the front: *DCI Pope*. She carefully opened it. Inside she saw it was a photograph and slowly removed it, holding it at the corner. Once out of the envelope she saw that it was an image of her at the Harpers' house in Camberwell. Taken in the hallway, it showed her standing at the foot of the stairs, holding a pen and notebook, deep in thought. She showed it to Brody and Miller.

'Looks low res. It must be a still from the digital recorder we found at the previous crime scene,' said Brody. 'Christ.'

Pope turned the photograph over. On the back, printed from a computer, the words *Interesting times, Bec.* She saw her first name. Addressed by the murderer. Close. Personal.

Pope placed the photograph back in the envelope and put it in the evidence bag, which she resealed. She handed it back to Okafor.

'I'll get it to the lab,' said Okafor, adding it to the other bags beside her.

'Anything else?' asked Pope.

'I can't confirm anything for sure yet. But, looking at the bruise marks, and the likely ligature, and the damage that seems apparent underneath the skin, I would say that the strangulation was carried out in almost exactly the same way as on Susan Harper. I'll be able to confirm that when I've carried out the full autopsy,' repeated Okafor.

'Thanks, Rachel. I appreciate it. Mind if we take a look around?' asked Pope.

'Sure. Just don't get in my way.'

'We'll do our best.'

Pope, Brody and Miller walked around the bedroom, trying to get a sense of who Linda Wilson was. The room was sparsely furnished, which befitted the location. The furniture, what there was of it, looked expensive. Bleached wood and wrought iron, original floorboards. There was a unit made from bare wood and reclaimed pipes, no doubt from one of the converted warehouses in the area, in place of a wardrobe. It was hung with pressed garments straight from the dry cleaners. There was a small dressing table and mirror, with a substantial amount of cosmetics, neatly packed in small baskets to avoid clutter. There were no photographs. Nothing seemed out of place. She got the impression of a woman for whom work formed a large part of her life. Organized and fastidious. All that time spent organizing her life now rendered meaningless.

Her thoughts were interrupted by Brody. 'I think we're right that he knocked her out downstairs,' he said. 'There are no signs of a struggle in here. Unless he put it all back in place, she was probably unconscious when he brought her up.'

'Or he strangled her downstairs,' said Pope. 'She may have already been dead when he brought her up here.'

They reflected on that. A killer who kills in one place, and then moves the body elsewhere and positions them in a particular way. They all knew the implications of this were something they didn't really want to have to consider.

'It seems very quick,' said Pope after a moment. 'He killed Linda Wilson the day after he killed Susan Harper. A killer with multiple victims over time is very rare. But there is usually some time in between victims. In fact, it's almost textbook. But this. . .' She paused, trying to formulate a thought. 'This guy seems to have hit the ground running. Two in two days is highly unusual.'

They worked in silence for several minutes, taking in the room.

'Camera,' said Pope, suddenly, looking at Brody. In all the horror of what they were dealing with, they had completely forgotten about the camera in the previous crime scene.

It didn't take long to find what they were looking for. Pope saw it first. She took a chair from the dressing table and pulled it over to the edge of the curtains. She climbed up on to the chair and stared at the corner of the rail for some time. Sam Brooks took a number of photographs from underneath. Then Pope reached up and carefully removed the small black video camera that had been crudely fastened on to the rail with adhesive tape. She held it in her hand as she got off the chair. They all gathered round. It looked identical to the one found at Susan Harper's house.

'Jesus Christ!' Adam Miller was the first to speak. 'What the hell is going on here?'

* * *

Only a few hundred yards away, in a late-night hipster bar in a neighbouring street, the clientele were oblivious to the scene unfolding just around the corner. Groups of young professionals and students, and couples who didn't care about an early start the next morning, laughed and talked and drank.

The walls were clad in aluminium, beaten and uneven, and with a number of contrasty black-and-white photographs of iconic American cities: New York, San Francisco and Chicago. Not the obvious landmarks, but enough to be able to identify the city if you were in the know. The floors were untreated, giving the place a utilitarian feel. The tables were created out of disused railway sleepers and thick slabs of distressed oak. The seats were old church pews. The keyword was authentic. *Craft beers, organic wines and food sourced from local farmers' markets added to the ambience. The music was low key and contemporary, played at the perfect volume: not too loud to prohibit conversation, but loud enough so that no one could overhear. From the look of the customers, it was the perfect venue for a date. The bar staff were young, good-looking and fashionably dressed in black. The bar was full a few hours ago, but as the night grew later, it had emptied out and was now about half full.*

He sat at one of the oak tables in the corner of the large room, his back to the wall. In front of him was a glass of beer, which had been placed on a square napkin, American style. Next to the glass he held a telephone, a headphone in one ear. On the screen he watched someone lying in bed, eyes closed, propped up on several pillows, seemingly asleep. Next to her were two people, one woman and one man, both wearing white coveralls, with their shoes covered. The woman seemed to be talking into a small recorder, while the man was taking photographs, putting things given to him by the woman into bags, making notes in a small notebook.

He took a sip of beer. He glanced around the bar, but no one was paying any attention to him. They were all absorbed in their own little worlds. His attention returned to the small screen in front of him. Now there were three more participants in this scene. Two men and a woman had joined the original two, talking to the first woman, who had stopped what she was doing and was now standing facing them. He recognized DCI Bec Pope. He watched as the conversation continued. As he listened, he smiled to himself. The discussion over, the original two went back to what they had been doing, and the other three began searching the room in more detail. He saw them look carefully around and then, fascinated, watched as Bec Pope brought up a chair, stood on it and, for the second time in as many days, looked directly at him.

As he watched the small screen, he saw the perspective shift and realized that DCI Pope had found the camera and was staring into the lens. It had the effect that the two of them were face to face. He enjoyed the sensation and, as he looked the woman in the eyes, considered that it would soon be time for Bec Pope to become much more personally involved in the case she was currently investigating.

He closed the window on his screen, flicked the phone off and drained his glass. He felt satisfied. But then, he had only just begun. He stood up and walked to the counter. The bar had almost emptied now, and the staff were preparing to close up for the night. He signalled to the young woman behind the counter and handed her a £20 note.

Around twenty-two or twenty-three, she was dressed entirely in black: a polo neck jumper and tight, figure-hugging jeans. She had straight blonde hair tied in a ponytail. She was slim. She clearly looked after herself.

His eyes lingered on her body as she calculated and retrieved his change from the cash register. She handed him the change with a half-smile and he felt a short burst of electricity as their hands touched. He thanked her, looked in her eyes for a moment longer than necessary, and left.

CHAPTER 8

Pope had met Tobias Darke almost twenty years ago, while she was in training at Hendon Police College. Darke had given a lecture on the role of the forensic psychiatrist. Afterwards, while other recruits left to grab some lunch, Pope stayed behind to grill her lecturer on aspects of his work and implications for the work of the police. Darke, in turn, had been impressed with Pope's interest and enthusiasm, not to mention the intelligent questions she had asked, and had invited her to attend some of his lectures at University College London, where he was working in the medicine department at the time. Pope had attended as many as her training schedule would allow. For some years afterwards, until her workload became too heavy with increasing responsibility, she went to see Darke speak whenever she could.

As Pope drove, she thought about that initial lecture. It had completely changed the way she thought about psychiatry and the extent to which it could support the police and the criminal justice system. Darke had gone into detail about his work with inmates, not just evaluating violent criminals, but supporting them in their rehabilitation, as well as how he assisted the Metropolitan Police. These days, Darke lectured regularly at universities across the UK, and annually visited the Universities of Pennsylvania and California, Irvine, both of which offered thriving and highly oversubscribed criminology courses, to deliver guest lectures. His main work, however, was based at Broadmoor, a high-security psychiatric hospital around thirty miles west of London. Darke was a senior consultant with responsibility for the oversight of the work with the most serious offenders. These were usually violent offenders who were considered too dangerous for the general prison population and who needed much more individual and specialized care than most psychiatric hospitals were equipped to offer.

And so when Pope realized that in all likelihood they were dealing with a serial offender, she had called Darke. The two had consulted on a number of cases over the years. He had also helped Pope at a particularly difficult time in her early career when she had shot and killed a man after a tip-off about a robbery in Hatton Garden, London's jewellery quarter. When she found the camera at the second scene, Pope knew that they needed to seek an expert opinion from Darke.

Tobias Darke lived near Richmond Park in southwest London, primarily so that he could walk his dogs there each morning. It was also an easy commute to the hospital on the days he needed to be there, as well as offering easy access to Central London, the motorway network for his university visits, and Heathrow Airport for his international commitments.

Pope and Brody drew into the pebbled, horseshoe drive and got out of the car. Darke lived in an imposing Victorian house. It was early morning, and the dew was still evident on the well-maintained flowerbeds in the front garden. Pope rang the bell and they waited. They heard barking, then someone telling the dogs to be quiet, followed by footsteps. The front door opened.

'Bec, James!' Tobias Darke exclaimed. He embraced Pope and then Brody, as two golden retrievers weaved around their feet with tails wagging enthusiastically.

'Holmes, Watson! Back inside, go on,' he said, shooing the dogs back into the house. Pope smiled. The names still amused her, even after all these years. The dogs dutifully returned inside the house.

'Come in, come in,' said Darke, leading them into the grand hallway and closing the door behind them.

Darke was of average height, slightly overweight, with sandy hair beginning to grey a little. He had a full, bushy beard but it always appeared neatly trimmed and well cared for. He wore a tweed suit which looked expensive, a matching waistcoat, and a bright yellow tie. He looked every inch the cultured and erudite professor.

'Sit down,' he said, as he directed them into the living room. 'I'll put the kettle on and make us some tea.' Whatever time of day it was, Darke always drank, and offered, tea.

Pope and Brady sat on an overstuffed sofa in Darke's elegant, book-lined living room. Contemporary art hung on the walls, by artists Pope had never heard of. The bookshelves overflowed with scientific and medical reference books and hardback editions by Shakespeare and Dickens. Darke had once told her that if you really wanted to understand the human mind, you'd be better off reading Shakespeare than any psychology textbook. Not that it stopped him writing them. Several volumes, his name prominent on the spine, were present on the shelves, including two collections of adapted lectures that were standard issue for undergraduates at the universities at which he lectured.

Their host returned bearing a tray cluttered with his usual fine bone china tea service and an extra pot of hot water. They exchanged pleasantries until the tea had brewed to his satisfaction, then he poured them each a cup and sat back in his chair, saucer in hand. Brody accepted his and then placed it on the table between them. He was a coffee drinker. He hated tea.

'So,' Darke said, gazing piercingly between the pair of them, 'you have a problem.'

Pope looked at him. 'Yes, Tobias. We have a problem.'

'I spoke to Rachel Okafor at King's this morning, after your phone call. She filled me in on the forensic side of things. Can you give me the rest?' said Darke.

Pope took a beat, and then explained what they had found and the commonalities between the two murders. When she had finished, Darke was silent for some time, looking into his cup of tea. Pope and Brody waited patiently, letting him digest the details.

'It seems that there are a number of key points that are important at this stage, and on which you might initially focus in order to understand these crimes.'

Brody opened his notebook and took a pencil from his pocket.

'First, if, as you suspect, these murders were premeditated, it tells us something about the killer. Some multiple murderers are spontaneous, impulsive, and some are what we call "strategic". They plan carefully. There was a study a few years ago. . .' He paused. 'Out of a university in Illinois. It looked at exactly this difference and found that strategic killers tended to be highly intelligent, but also it is very common for them to have psychiatric disorders. This is bad news for you as an intelligent killer is less likely to make mistakes, less likely to leave easy clues,' said Darke.

'Maybe we look at patients with psychiatric disorders as a starting point?' said Pope.

Darke nodded, and continued. 'The second consideration is the method of the murder itself, which suggests some form of expertise or, at least, experience. The precise nature of the injuries you describe is not something that most members of the public would know about. Your killer may have some level of medical training or background.'

'If we look at cross-referencing current psychiatric patients who also had some form of medical training, we might find something there,' said Brody, as he wrote in his notebook.

'Yes,' agreed Darke. 'And don't forget armed forces medical personnel. The intersection of what you're looking for with post-traumatic stress disorder will be considerable.'

Brody noted this down.

'The third point is the staging of the victims,' said Darke. 'The FBI categorize these kinds of killers as "organized" murderers. They don't lose control, and generally stage or pose the victims for one of two reasons. The first is to mislead the investigation, a red herring of sorts. The second reason is to satisfy the emotional and fantasy needs of the perpetrator. This might include sending a message to the public or the person, or people, investigating the crime. The artefacts he left for you, Bec, suggest that this is indeed the case here.'

Pope and Brody looked at each other, and then at Darke, who nodded grimly. He seemed to know what they were thinking.

'And that leads me to the last, and most obvious, point: the placing of a video camera and a card at the scene. In the first murder, he wanted to watch you investigate the scene of the murder. In the second, he progressed to watching the body itself being discovered. I can't offer anything based on direct experience. I can tell you, however, that you're dealing with an intelligent, resourceful and disturbed perpetrator. He's playing with you. Finding out the reason for that will be the key here, I think,' said Darke. 'He obviously wants the connection to you personally, Bec, to be clear. Where are you with the card and the photograph? Any ideas?'

'Not yet,' replied Pope. 'They're still with Forensics. We're looking into anyone recently released who may have a connection to me.'

'Is there anyone who springs to mind?' asked Darke.

There was.

She hesitated. 'Not at the moment.' She looked at the floor, certain Darke would see right through her.

There was a slightly awkward silence. Brody broke it.

'He's killed two victims in two days. That's unusual, isn't it?'

'That frequency does seem unusual, yes. But you have to remember, there's really no "usual" when it comes to serial killers. And, most people define a "serial killer" as having three or more victims, so you're not there yet.'

'Rachel Okafor thinks he's killed before,' said Pope. 'Do you have an opinion on that? And on whether he might kill again?'

Darke thought for a moment. 'Well, it's very difficult to say for sure. But experience suggests that if the murderer was that proficient, he has almost certainly killed before. Most first murders are messy. These ones were not. In addition, there is often a gap after a first murder by a serial killer, while they come to terms with what they've done. The lack of one here suggests that he is very comfortable with murder.'

'And the second question?' prompted Pope.

'Whether he'll kill again? I doubt very much that he's finished,' said Darke. 'He's having too much fun with you. In my opinion, he'll only finish when you catch him.'

* * *

'Do you want to stop and get something to eat?' Pope asked Brody, as he drove them through Wandsworth, following the line of the Thames as it meandered beside them.

'Good idea.' He drove until he saw a café, then quickly pulled over into a parking space in front of it.

The place was done out like a traditional American diner, red booths and a soda fountain on the front counter. Huge pictures on the walls depicted New York City landmarks — the Chrysler Building, the Empire State Building, the Flatiron, the Brooklyn Bridge — and famous New Yorkers. There was a New York State number plate attached to the wall, and a Broadway street sign in green. Pope felt a sudden wave of nostalgia for the year she had spent in New York in her twenties.

The café was fairly busy. They chose a booth near the back and sat down.

When the waitress came over to take their order, Brody ordered a cream cheese bagel and a black coffee.

'When in Rome,' he said to Pope.

Pope ordered the "Number Six" breakfast. Eggs, toast and coffee.

'How would you like your eggs?' asked the waitress. She looked at her. 'Over easy?' she prompted. Pope was tempted to point out that this was London, not New York, but she chose not to, and instead said, 'Scrambled, please.'

'And your toast? White, wholemeal, rye, sourdough?' the waitress asked.

'Rye,' she replied. She looked at Brody. 'When in Rome.'

The waitress left with their order.

'Do you think he's right?' asked Brody quietly. 'About him wanting to watch us, targeting us for attention? Do you agree that he'll carry on killing?' There was tension in his voice, as well as professional enquiry.

'I don't know,' replied Pope. 'But I've worked with Darke for twenty years. He's always been an invaluable source of information and guidance in cases of violent crime. There aren't many people this side of the Atlantic who know as much about this stuff as he does. I've never known him to be wrong in the past. He knows what he's talking about.'

Brody nodded, but was quiet.

She looked at her watch. 'I'll text Miller and ask him to have everybody ready in an hour. We can meet when we get back.'

The waitress brought the food and the coffee. Pope was aware that they were both eating quickly, sensing the urgency of the work ahead of them. She made no attempt to slow down.

She couldn't get Tobias Darke's final comment out of her head: *he'll only finish when you catch him.*

CHAPTER 9

Adam Miller, Stephen Thompson and PCs Mike Hawley and Ana McEwan were waiting in the briefing room when Pope and Brody returned to the station. Brody made coffee for him and Pope and the six of them arranged themselves around the substantial rectangular desk that took up a large part of the room.

Pope started. 'OK. Let's see where we are and whether we've got anything useful. I want to keep it small, as we appear to have a leak in the department, and there's some things we need to discuss that I don't want made public knowledge.' They all nodded, simultaneously concerned about a possible leak of information from one of their own, and pleased to be considered trustworthy by their boss.

'Miller, anything from interviewing Linda Wilson's neighbours this morning?' asked Pope.

'Well, we started early with the immediate neighbours to get them before they went to work. Most of them were in, although a flat three doors down had no answer. It's a typical London street full of young professionals, so half of them didn't even recognize her from her photo. Those that knew her describe her as keeping to herself, friendly but quite reserved. She was discovered by her partner, Meena

70

Shah, a paramedic, when she came off late shift. None of the neighbours saw anything unusual last night, no one heard anything. He may have come on foot, in which case it's not surprising that he went unnoticed. It's not really the kind of neighbourhood where they look out for one another.'

Pope looked at Mike Hawley.

'We got pretty much the same impression,' said Hawley. He looked over at McEwan, who nodded in agreement. 'Most of the people we spoke to had seen her around but didn't know her name and hadn't spoken to her beyond an occasional "hello" in the street. No one saw anything last night.'

'OK. I want you to go back there this afternoon and widen the interviews. Talk to everyone on the street. I can't believe that no one in a whole road saw or heard anything. Take some extra uniforms with you,' said Pope.

Miller nodded, and wrote something down in his notebook.

'Thompson,' said Pope. 'Any luck with the camera?'

Stephen Thompson looked startled, as if he wasn't expecting to be asked anything. He picked up the iPad in front of him and unlocked it, looking at his notes.

'Yes, er, well. . .' he started, clearly uncomfortable with being in the spotlight. 'The camera was the same make and model as the one you found at Susan Harper's house, so there's a strong likelihood that they were left there by the same person.' He paused, waiting for a reaction, but everyone present knew this already. 'The good news is that if we can find where these were purchased, the fact that he bought two, or maybe more, means that the transaction might be easier to trace. That's what we're focusing on at the moment.'

'Is there anything new you can tell us based on the second camera?'

'Unfortunately not,' said Thompson. 'Beyond make and model, there's no fingerprints or anything else, just like the first one. It remote transmits, so there's no hard drive to look at, and beyond that, the only thing we can do is find where the transmission was picked up. That's like finding a needle in a haystack, though.'

'In what way?' asked Pope.

'It has a fairly small transmission radius, but the buildings are so densely packed that it is virtually impossible to locate exactly where the signal went. You'd have to actually catch him watching it to know where it was picked up. There's no other record,' said Thompson.

Pope thought about that for a minute. 'So, he must have been somewhere fairly close to watch the feed from the camera?' she asked Thompson.

'It's a strong possibility.'

'It's unlikely he was in a nearby house both times. Check out any public building within a distance where the camera could have transmitted a signal. Pubs, bars, restaurants, cafés, etc.,' said Pope. 'It may be that he went somewhere close by to enjoy the fruits of his labour.'

'Will do,' said Miller.

'Bear in mind, though,' said Thompson, 'that he could have used a signal boost and relay somewhere close by. That might enable him to pick up the signal from further away.'

'We'll check it out anyway. The camera's a key lead.'

Miller and Thompson both nodded.

Pope looked at Miller, hesitated for a moment. 'There's another thing I'd like you to do. Check on a name for me.'

Miller looked up.

'Mick Waterson. Michael.' She added. 'Last known address was number thirty-seven Wickham House. Check if he's still there and what he's up to these days. He used to have a car body repair business under the arches in Peckham.'

Miller scribbled down the details. 'No problem. Who is he?'

'An old problem. I just need a check on him. Might be nothing.'

Miller nodded and returned to his computer.

Brody looked at Pope, eyebrows raised. She shook her head minutely.

'Brody, can you fill them in on our meeting with Tobias Darke?' asked Pope.

Brody nodded slowly, then recounted their conversation with Darke.

'Darke thinks that he is using the camera to watch us when we arrive at the scene, although he was not certain about this. It may be that he just gets off on watching the victim for some time after he has left the scene, or maybe he likes to watch the crime scene and the discovery of the body. There is obviously a connection to Bec. A past case, maybe.'

'Thanks,' said Pope, feeling that she needed to take over. 'We need to focus on a number of key priorities now. Miller, as we said, you, Hawley, McEwan and the other uniforms available need to canvass the rest of Linda Wilson's street, and the local area. I want this done today, while memories are fresh. Thompson, you said that your guys were working on where the cameras may have been bought.'

'Yes, they're on that now,' he replied.

'Good. Also try to get a more specific idea of the radius of the camera's signal. This will assist our officers in coordinating their interviews in the area surrounding Linda Wilson's house.'

'OK,' said Thompson, jotting something down on his iPad.

'Brody, can you write up the notes of the meeting we had with Tobias Darke? I'll call Rachel Okafor at the morgue to see what we've got from the autopsy, and then,' Pope added, 'we need to start looking at cross-referencing our old cases to see if anything obvious jumps out — those we've arrested who have been recently released and who might fit some of the criteria Darke outlined.'

Pope was thinking about the cards and the photograph. These were going to be the key. She had to work out the connection. The killer wanted her to understand something, but what? She looked at her team.

'OK, thanks, everyone, let's get to work.'

They got up and left the room, leaving only Pope and Brody. He was about to say something, when the door opened and Richard Fletcher strode into the office. He closed the door behind him. Pope suspected he had been waiting for the room to clear and wondered why he hadn't just come to the meeting in the first place, rather than make her go through everything twice.

'Bring me up to speed. Where are we?' he said.

Pope filled her boss in as succinctly as she could. She knew why Fletcher was really here. He wanted the killer caught, of course he did. But he was also concerned with what nowadays were termed "the optics". Pope hated the expression and everything it implied.

'So, what you're telling me, is that at this point in time, we don't have any concrete leads.'

'We're only two days into this,' said Pope.

'And two dead bodies in, as well,' said Fletcher.

Pope fought the urge to punch her boss in the face. She took a beat. Again.

'I'm well aware of the victims. But there is little physical evidence at the scenes and none of it tells us anything conclusive,' reiterated Pope, 'we're working on it as we speak.'

'I need this guy caught, Bec,' said Fletcher. 'The news media is already running with the second victim. I don't need a multiple murderer at large in the city. You need to get ahead of this, and fast. I want updates every two hours, and I want a name.'

'Give me more officers, then,' said Pope.

'I can't give you any more than I have already, Bec, you know that,' replied Fletcher. 'I'll authorize as much overtime as you need, but that's as far as I can go. I'll expect to hear from you in two hours.' Fletcher let the door swing behind him on his way out.

Pope looked at Brody. 'He says "I" a lot, doesn't he?' she said.

Brody smiled, glad that Pope hadn't lost her cool.

'I need to call Rachel Okafor.' Pope returned to her desk and picked up the phone. She dialled the number and waited for her to pick up. She didn't have to wait long.

'Hi, Bec,' Okafor answered. 'Let me guess. Linda Wilson? Have I had a chance to look at her yet? What have I got on the cause of death?'

'In one.'

Brody watched her, listening carefully as Pope spoke. She picked up a pen and began to write in her pocketbook.

After several minutes, Pope said, 'Thanks, Rachel, I appreciate it. Let me know when you have the written report ready.'

She ended the call, added a few more notes and put her pen down on the desk.

'Anything new?' asked Brody.

'No, not really. Confirmed what she told us at the scene. The cause of death was strangulation. The injuries, the bruising and the other marks, match almost exactly those found on Susan Harper. The ligature marks are the same, and the pattern of breaks also matches exactly: the hyoid bone was fractured in the same place. She is going on record as saying that it was the same killer. This will be confirmed in the written report.'

'How much do we release to the media?' he asked.

'We'll let Fletcher decide that. But we'll need to keep something back, to be able to determine any genuine information we may get. I'll talk to him.' Pope sighed. She didn't really want to have another conversation with Fletcher at this stage, but she knew she had to.

They were both silent for a while.

Brody broke the silence. 'The way he killed them both in exactly the same way. The staging. The camera, the card. Who the hell are we dealing with here, Bec?'

* * *

He ate breakfast late. It had been a late night. He'd become impatient to stay up to watch the scene. Yes, it was a scene. Like a movie, and he was the director. He had set the scene and directed when the other actors would arrive, what they would do, what they would say, how they would act. Knew the expressions on their faces before they even got there, before they even saw what he had set up for them. Lights, camera, action.

He thought about the blonde girl behind the bar. There was a tension there, a connection. And he knew he had wanted her. He was very tempted to wait for her outside and consummate his desire. But he stopped himself. Too near where his other scene was being played out. One thing at a time. He admired his discipline. She had been very. . . He stopped himself.

'Discipline' he said.

He showered and got dressed. He enjoyed the luxury of a shower every day, whether he needed it or not. Growing up, he had been allowed to bathe only once each week. There was no reason not to have had more regular ablutions, except the exercise of power and control in preventing him from doing so.

When he was eight years old, his mother died in a car crash. His father was driving and had pulled out at a junction. A car sped through the light and smashed straight into the passenger door. His mother died instantly. His father was kept in hospital overnight. He had returned home the next day, a small plaster on his temple. He never spoke of the accident and never discussed the boy's mother. The responsibility for the accident was never established, and no prosecutions were ever brought.

Father and son lived as virtual strangers, until six months later when the father took a Smith & Wesson 9 mm handgun, stuck it in his mouth and blew his brains all over the bathroom wall. The boy came home from school and found his father, minus much of his head.

After that he was taken into care and passed through a series of children's homes. There he was treated as, by turns, a nuisance, a project, an invisible number on a bank balance. The other kids treated him like shit. They treated everyone like shit. He soon learned that this was the currency. You took it or you doled it out. He got beaten up a lot at first. Sometimes badly, sometimes very badly. On one occasion ending up in a hospital on the Kent coast with concussion and a fractured wrist. The boy who beat him was two years older. The day after he got out of hospital, the older boy was discovered in the garden, curled up under a sorry-looking apple tree, screaming. A pair of scissors sticking out of his thigh. There was blood everywhere. The older boy had refused to say who had done it, but everyone knew. He didn't get beaten up again.

Eventually it was decided that a communal setting was not conducive to his emotional or spiritual well-being. An earnest social worker called Valerie Jenkins had come to see him. A foster home key worker was assigned. A foster family in South London had been found and he was to move there immediately. Wasn't that wonderful? But he didn't feel anything. It was neither good nor bad. Just different.

By this time he was twelve. His new foster parents, Steven and Maddie White, were both teachers in London secondary schools. They had no children of their own but were regular foster carers. They felt they were doing a selfless, altruistic act by fostering children, and they genuinely liked young people. Most of them.

He lasted six months with the Whites.

Shortly after he arrived, the Whites' cat disappeared. It was found some days later by a neighbour in their back garden. Its tail had been severed, and it had been gutted from jaw to tail. The couple were distraught. But even in the midst of their grief, they couldn't help but notice a vague ambivalence in their young charge. He seemed upset but, they thought, it appeared that he was behaving as he felt he ought to behave. He seemed unusually interested in the details, in the violence of the act itself. They initially dismissed it. But the Whites expressed their disquiet to Valerie Jenkins, and she thought it would be better if he had a fresh start, so she removed him from the White home. The Whites regretted giving up on the boy. They were, however, also secretly relieved, something that they only admitted to each other long after he had left. It was difficult to articulate exactly why, but they had both felt that something was wrong with him. Maddie White, in particular, had been unsettled by the boy.

The well-meaning Ms Jenkins moved him back to a different children's home in another part of London. And then another, and another. Until eventually he ended up in one that was bigger, had male staff, and more older children, who she thought would be role models for him. She was right, but not, perhaps, in the way she had hoped.

When she dropped him off, she had made very clear that this was his final chance. Any more incidents and he would likely be facing a life of incarceration. After she had left, he sat in his room and thought. He wasn't scared by the thought of prison like most people were. He was tough and institutionalized. He would cope. But he wouldn't thrive.

Wouldn't be able to do the things he enjoyed doing, wouldn't be able to behave with relative impunity. He enjoyed violence and he enjoyed the power and respect his strength afforded him. But he wanted to travel. He wanted experiences. These things he could not do in prison.

So he decided to reinvent himself. He began to work hard at school and to study at home. He isolated himself from the others in the home and he worked for his exams. The foster carers, the headteacher and Valerie Jenkins all congratulated him when he passed his exams with flying colours. He knew they were really congratulating themselves. They had saved another victim. Reclaimed another life. A vindication of their beliefs, their values, their altruism. Charitable and giving.

He knew different, however. He was the same as he ever was, he only appeared different. And like so many people he encountered, they were too stupid to understand. People didn't change.

A long time had passed since then. He looked at himself in the mirror as he combed his hair. He had accomplished a great deal since he had walked out of the children's home on his seventeenth birthday. He was almost there. Almost finished. The grand finale, the final act. He hoped his actors were ready for what he had planned for them.

CHAPTER 10

The afternoon was spent poring over past cases in an attempt to find a link with the killer. Nothing. There were plenty of people who would have a motive for attacking Pope, and indeed Brody, but none were a match with the current killings.

Pope was frustrated. They were getting nowhere.

Tech were still working on the camera and where it might be transmitting, where it might have been purchased.

The forensic report on the second card and the photograph found nothing. No fingerprints, no residue, nothing.

Just as she was making herself and Brody another coffee, Miller returned from canvassing the area around Linda Wilson's house.

'How did it go? Anything?' asked Pope.

Miller sat down at his desk. 'Nothing useful yet. The others are still at it. I wanted to update you on that name you asked me to check.'

Pope looked at him expectantly.

'Mick Waterson. It was your first case on Homicide, right? Tina Waterson.'

Brody looked at her.

'Yeah. What did you get?'

'He's still in the same place, number thirty-seven Wickham House. Still working for himself according to the information I've got. Railway arches in Peckham, as you said.'

'Anything interesting?'

'Well, yes and no. He was arrested four years ago for drunk driving, lost his licence for eighteen months. And also arrested for GBH last year. CPS didn't pursue the case, though.'

'Why not?' asked Pope.

'Insufficient evidence. Apparently, a witness retracted his statement.'

Pope nodded. She could picture exactly what had happened.

'Do you think he could be involved?' asked Brody.

'I don't know. He certainly hates my guts, so he fulfils that part of the criteria. Whether he's capable of murder? I don't know. I think we'll go and pay him a visit in the morning. See what he has to say.'

'Something to look forward to,' Brody said.

She looked at her watch. 'Jesus, I should have been home hours ago.'

A ping on her phone told her that she had a text. She retrieved it from her pocket. Alex.

When are you getting home? I need to talk to you.

She tapped out a reply.

On my way. Everything OK?

'I need to get going,' she said to Brody.

'Me too,' said Brody.

They made half-hearted attempts to tidy their respective desks and left the office, turning off the sharp strip lights behind them.

They walked down the stairs and into the large reception area, discussing where they would start tomorrow as they went.

As they were talking, Pope was aware of a noise at the front door of the station. A tall, well-dressed man in his late fifties had stormed into the main reception area. It took Pope a second to realize that the man was shouting her name.

'DCI Pope! I need to talk to DCI Pope. Where is she? I need to talk to her now!' he shouted. His voice was filled with rage and desperation.

Pope stepped forward. 'I'm DCI Pope, sir. What can I do for you?'

The man stalked towards Pope, who stood her ground.

Brody instinctively moved towards Pope. He bent his arms slightly, a subconscious readiness to spring into action if required. The sergeant on duty had come out from behind his desk area.

'You're Pope?' he asked.

'Yes, I'm DCI Bec P—'

The man balled a fist and lunged at Pope. It was clumsy, clearly not something he was used to doing. Pope dodged the blow and sidestepped, deftly moving her attacker past her. She quickly took hold of his arm and pulled it up behind his back, effectively paralyzing him. A well-practised move. Brody and the other officers moved towards them, but Pope signalled for them to hold back.

'Let me go,' shouted the man, clearly in considerable pain. 'Let me go now.'

'I'll let you go if you talk to me and don't try to hit me again,' said Pope calmly.

'Let me go. You're hurting me,' he shouted.

'Your choice is to calm down and talk to me, or I'll have you arrested right here and you'll spend the night in the cells. Then we'll talk in the morning. You decide.' Pope gave his arm a tweak, to cause a little more pain and send a clearer message.

'OK, OK,' he said. Pope let go of him.

The visitor smoothed down his jacket and coat, and held his right arm. 'I'm sorry,' he said, looking at Pope.

'What can I do for you?' asked Pope again.

'My name is David Wilson. I'm Linda Wilson's father.'

Suddenly it made sense. Pope's stance softened. She moved towards Wilson. 'Why don't you come and sit down and we can talk?' she said, indicating a seating area against the left-hand side of the reception.

Wilson didn't move. There was still anger there. Less than before, perhaps, but still present.

'There was a victim before Linda.' His voice rose, and Pope could sense the potential for this to escalate again. 'You *knew* there was a serial killer. You knew and you didn't warn us. If you had, Linda would still be alive. This is your fault.'

Pope understood now.

He blamed her. It didn't matter that she hadn't put her hands around his daughter's throat. It didn't matter that it hadn't been Pope who ended her life. As far as David Wilson was concerned, she may as well have done. She had withheld information from the public. She had downplayed the risk. She had made a judgement call and she had got it wrong.

She looked around and saw that there were no other members of the public present.

'Mr Wilson, come sit down with me, so that we can talk about this.' She again indicated the chairs. Someone sitting down was almost always less aggressive than someone who was standing. It was also harder to hit someone when you were sitting down.

Wilson allowed himself to be guided over to the seating area. They both sat down, and Brody came and sat down directly across from Wilson.

'This is DI Brody, who is working your daughter's case with me. I'm very sorry for your loss, Mr Wilson,' said Pope. She let that hang in the air for a few seconds, while Wilson looked at the floor.

He looked up. 'Why didn't you warn us? The public? Why didn't you tell us what was going on?'

'We did inform the media. We held a press conference the day after we discovered the first victim. We outlined the circumstances of her death, and this was widely reported in the local and national press, as well as local TV news. But at the time we didn't know that there would be a second victim. We're doing all we can to find the perpetrator.'

Wilson sighed, then hung his head again and started to cry. The sobs shook his body, the anger giving way to grief. The loss of a child was something Pope could not even begin to imagine.

Pope offered to get Wilson a tea or coffee, but he declined. He stood up, and looked at Pope, his eyes red and filled with tears. He wiped them away with the edge of his coat sleeve. She realized he now just wanted to get out of there as quickly as possible.

'Please keep me informed, Pope. I'd rather hear it from you than from the newspaper or the TV,' said Wilson.

'Of course,' replied Pope. 'I'll be in touch as soon as we know anything concrete.'

He thanked Pope and moved towards the door. She watched him until he left the station without looking back.

'Are you OK?' Brody asked.

'Yes, I'm fine. Poor guy. He's angry and he doesn't know what to do with it. It's easier to blame someone, to focus what you're feeling somewhere. But eventually you just have to deal with it. I think that's what he just realized.'

'There's nothing we could have done differently. We couldn't have kept his daughter alive,' said Brody.

'I know,' said Pope.

Brody looked at her, unsure whether she really believed that or not. He knew her. She would be playing that question around in her mind all night.

* * *

When she arrived home, the first thing Bec Pope did was grab a beer from the fridge. She opened the cap and drank the whole bottle in several big draws. She tossed it into the rubbish bin, took out another, and only then sat down next to Alex on the sofa in the living room.

'That kind of day, eh?' he asked. He put his hand on the back of her neck and began to gently massage it. She leaned back. It felt good. She told him about her day, surrendering to the feeling of his hand on her skin.

'What was it that you wanted to talk to me about?' she asked.

He looked at her, seemed to be trying to gauge whether this was the right time to bring the subject up. He reached over to the coffee table, picked up a typed letter on headed paper and handed it to Pope. She took it and scanned the contents.

'Oh, God,' she said finally. It was a letter from the head-teacher of Chloe's school. Chloe had truanted from school the day before. She had also been in trouble for disruption in class and rudeness to members of staff. The letter asked them to make an appointment to see the head to discuss her behaviour. Pope leaned her head back against the sofa.

'She's never truanted before, has she?' asked Pope.

'Not as far as I know,' replied Alex. 'I'm furious with her.'

'Have you spoken to her about it yet?'

'Not yet. I thought you could be there for backup.'

Pope knew she needed to support him with this, but after the day she'd had, family drama was the last thing she needed.

'OK.'

Alex called up the stairs and asked Chloe to come down. After a suitable wait, she appeared in the living room. Alex was standing up, while Pope remained sitting down.

'How was school yesterday?' Alex asked her.

'OK. Boring, the usual,' said Chloe, with just a hint of uncertainty.

'We've had a letter from the school,' said Alex evenly. Fear momentarily flashed across Chloe's eyes. 'It says you truanted school yesterday.'

He paused and looked at his daughter. She didn't say anything, so Alex went on. 'It also says that you've been disrupting lessons and that you've been rude to teachers. This says we have to go into school to meet Mr Harding.'

Chloe said nothing. She was formulating her response. Pope had a good idea what it would be.

'What's going on, Chloe?' Alex asked her.

'Nothing.' Her look of defiance didn't bode well for how this would go.

'No, not nothing. Where were you yesterday?'

'I went shopping,' replied Chloe.

'Shopping? When you should have been at school? With who?' asked Alex.

'It doesn't matter,' said Chloe.

'Yes, it absolutely does matter,' said Alex, his voice steadily rising. 'Were you with Tyler?'

'Why do you always assume Tyler is involved?' she said defensively. 'You don't know what you're talking about. What have you got against him, anyway?'

Clearly Chloe had been with Tyler.

'Right. You're grounded. For a month,' said Alex.

'A month! You're insane! Why?' said Chloe. Now her voice was also rising.

'We'll talk about this later when you've calmed down and I've had a chance to think about this some more,' said Alex.

'No, we won't! School's crap! It's boring and full of idiots and all they care about is exams. It makes no difference whether I'm there or not. I'm not grounded and if I want to go out, I'll go out. I'm sixteen and you can't stop me.'

'Chloe—' Pope began.

Chloe turned on her. 'It's got nothing to do with you. Stay out of it,' she screamed. Before anything else could be said, she ran out of the room, slamming the door behind her. Heavy footsteps pounded up the stairs, the familiar soundtrack to teenage rebellion.

Pope and Alex looked at each other.

'Give me a hard-nut villain any day of the week. Teenagers are impossible,' she said.

He fell into the sofa. 'Can you pour me a glass of wine? I need medicating.'

She finished the remainder of her beer, opened a bottle of Rioja, and poured them each a large glass. She handed one to him and took a gulp of the wine in her glass. They sat in silence for a minute.

'I think we need diversion,' she said, picking up the remote control and turning on the TV. The London news headlines were playing, and she turned the volume up. Suddenly she sat forward. It was a picture of Linda Wilson in the background, behind the newsreader. First story.

The Metropolitan Police have today denied that they held back evidence of a serial killer currently roaming the streets of London. So far two victims have been strangled, and sources tell us that the murders were strikingly similar. Police sources say it is the same killer. The case is being led by DCI Rebecca Pope, but there are questions about how much information the public are being told. David Wilson, the father of the second victim Linda Wilson, says that if all the information had been released as soon as it was known, his daughter would still be alive.

'Did you know about this?' Alex asked her.

'Not the report. David Wilson came to see me just before I left the station. I knew nothing about this.'

The report cut to a doorstep interview with Wilson. It was still light out, so clearly the TV crew had found him earlier in the day, given him a skewed version of the truth and let him do the rest.

'DCI Pope has a lot to answer for,' David Wilson insisted as the interview ended.

'The serial killer, dubbed "the Cameraman", apparently leaves video cameras at the crime scenes to record what happens after he has left,' the presenter continued. 'Police say they have no leads at present. We will of course update you on this story as soon as we have any further information.'

Pope was speechless. Furious. "The Cameraman" for Christ's sake. Where had that come from? She was so angry she couldn't think clearly. She turned off the TV and sat back. She took a very large gulp of wine.

Seconds later, her mobile phone began to ring.

CHAPTER 11

Again, sleep eluded her. Her head was too full of the case. Everything about it troubled her. She considered the second card and what significance she should attach to it, and the camera and the implications of it being left at the scene. She thought about the leak in her team. Then she thought of Tina Waterson. She wasn't looking forward to visiting Tina's father.

Pope eventually managed to get to sleep at some point past 3 a.m., only to wake at six fifteen when her phone began ringing again. She didn't answer it, but let it run to voice-mail. It was Fletcher. Predictable.

She drove to the station, arriving exactly one hour after she had been woken by her boss's message. Alex had barely been awake, and after a tired goodbye he had turned over and gone back to sleep.

She felt alone on her drive into Charing Cross. She felt isolated at home. This was a common feeling during a murder investigation. The weight of her work made anything going on at home seem insignificant. Which, of course, it was in relation to a murder. But Alex and the girls felt the pressures of family life acutely, and although they were aware of the pressures she was under, they didn't truly understand them.

This only increased her sense of isolation. Nobody wanted to inhabit the life of a Homicide detective. Nobody wanted their lives to intersect with hers, because intersecting with her life meant being one of two things: victim or suspect.

These were the thoughts of Bec Pope as she arrived at work, parked her car and entered the building. She knew her first task would be to meet with Richard Fletcher to discuss the leak within the department. She walked up the stairs, trying not to think about the little sleep she had managed last night.

'Bec. My office now.' She hadn't even been able to take her coat off or make a cup of coffee.

She changed course and walked into the office at the far end of the hallway to her own. Fletcher had already disappeared inside.

'You saw the news last night, I take it?' said her boss, leaning forward in his chair, hands clasped together and elbows resting on his expansive desk.

'Yes, I saw it. I don't know—'

'The Cameraman! Where the hell did that come from?' Fletcher interrupted. 'I can't believe the media have that detail. Where did it come from?' he repeated.

A silly question. 'As I was saying,' replied Pope, 'I don't know where it came from.'

Fletcher ignored her tone. 'I've told you already, I want whoever is responsible found and sent directly to me. I'm not having this in my station. It's totally unacceptable.'

'I agree, sir. But that is going to have to wait. At the moment, I've got my hands full with a multiple murder investigation, so hunting for moles is taking a back seat. We've already had this conversation.'

'Have you any idea how this makes us look? The Cameraman! It's pathetic. There can't be many people who knew about the cameras. I want a list,' barked Fletcher.

'Listen.' Now Pope was angry. 'I know this makes our job more difficult, and that it will worry the public. As soon as the media gives a killer a stupid nickname, people start to think of famous serial killers and their imaginations go into overdrive. But all the more reason to spend all available resources catching this bastard. I can't waste time on anything else at present.'

Pope looked at Fletcher, who was clearly considering how to respond. She knew that years as a manager had taught him to be a diplomat.

'This kind of insubordination is not helpful, Pope—' Pope opened her mouth to tell Fletcher exactly what she thought of that — 'however, I understand that you're under a great deal of pressure with this case, and, of course, our number one priority is to catch this killer. Focus on the case, I'll follow up the leak. Keep me informed and up to date, I've got the media and Head Office on the phone constantly.'

'Right,' said Pope, as she left the office. She couldn't do Fletcher's job. She couldn't constantly worry about how it all reflected on the public perception of the force, and she'd never be able to keep her cool when her time was wasted by press and superiors. It was one of the reasons why she hadn't accepted the promotion that Alex was so keen for her to take.

She closed Fletcher's door behind her, burying all the things she really wanted to say to her boss, and walked to her own office.

Brody was already there.

'Morning. Are you having breakfast meetings with the boss these days? Going for promotion?'

'Too early for jokes,' she replied. 'Get your coat, we're going to see Mick Waterson.'

* * *

The Tina Waterson case had been a brutal introduction to the Homicide squad. Pope's boss at the time, Bruce Phillips, Homicide legend and old-school copper, had been convinced that Mick Waterson had killed his own daughter. This had informed how he had pursued the case. Pope wasn't so sure, but as a novice on the squad she was reluctant to challenge her boss and the rest of the team who followed his lead with a zeal bordering on hero worship.

Her first case as a Homicide detective. Less than a week into the job and the body was found, battered and dumped in wasteland. Tina Waterson was thirteen years old. Just a girl. Three other teenage girls had gone missing around the same time, similar circumstances, their bodies never found. The case had been splashed all over the front page for weeks. A leak had linked the three missing girls and the journalists had gone wild. Pictures of Pope and Bruce Phillips in the tabloids. Pope had struggled to hold it together. Then Phillips warned her that this was the job and if she couldn't hack it, now was the time to say. That did the trick. If you told Bec Pope she might not be able to handle something, she handled it.

Mick Waterson had no alibi for the time Tina Waterson went missing. He said he was in the pub, said he'd been drinking alone on the way home from work. But no one could corroborate it. Phillips had seized on this. The statistics proved the number of murderers who were already known to their victims. He decided that the father was guilty early on in the case and as a consequence Pope felt that other leads were not followed up as rigorously as they should have been, if at all. She had wrestled with how to deal with this, but Phillips was not the kind of man you went to with doubts. When he was sure, he was sure.

As a result, a case couldn't be made. No evidence, no motive, no prosecution. The case was active for a year, but no new leads or evidence were ever found. Phillips retired soon afterwards, reputation still more or less intact. Pope developed insomnia, and the ghosts of Tina Waterson and the other three girls stayed with her.

Pope gave Brody the edited version on the way to Peckham. Explained that Tina Waterson's parents had always blamed Phillips's focus on Mick, and Pope's inexperience in Homicide, for the lack of resolution to the case.

'He certainly held a grudge, and probably still does,' she said, by way of explanation for their visit. 'Don't expect a warm welcome.'

They pulled up by the railway arches in Peckham. She remembered the place. Little had changed except that the empty units now outnumbered those occupied.

She saw Waterson's auto body repair arch almost immediately, and a knot formed in her chest. A lot of memories and feelings coming back, all of them awful. She and Brody climbed out of the car and walked slowly towards the arch.

She could see him now, blue overalls, bending down behind a battered red Ford Escort. She'd forgotten how big Mick Waterson was. Intimidating. She cleared her throat, although he had undoubtedly heard the car pull up.

Mick Waterson lifted his head, saw Pope and registered. He froze for a moment, then stood up and spat viciously on the floor, maintaining eye contact with her.

'Mr Waterson,' said Pope. 'Mind if we have a word?'

'Is it about Tina?'

'No. It's about something else.'

'Then fuck you,' was his considered reply.

'We need to talk to you about something.'

'Fuck you,' he said again.

'I heard you the first time,' said Pope. 'It won't take long.'

He stared at her, then took in Brody, looked him up and down.

'Who's the monkey?'

'Hello, Mr Waterson. DI Brody.' He held up his warrant card.

'What are you working with this bitch for?'

Brody made to walk forward, Pope put a hand on his arm, shot him a look.

Waterson looked at him and laughed dismissively, spat again.

'Look, Mick. None of us wants to be here. But I can call for a van to take you down to the station if you'd prefer. You'll have just about enough time to lock up the arch if you're quick.'

'You could try.'

91

'Your choice. Here or the station. This is the last time I'm going to ask politely.' Now her voice had an edge. Pope needed to assert her control over the situation.

Waterson sighed. Seemed to be weighing up how much trouble he could cause them against how much trouble they could cause him. Pope held his gaze.

He picked up an oily blue cloth and wiped his hands, probably putting more oil on his hands than he was wiping off.

'Is that prick Phillips dead yet?'

'Not yet.'

'Shame. What do you want? Make it quick, I'm busy.'

'Just a couple of questions, then we'll be on our way,' said Pope.

He stared at her, waiting.

'Do you know a woman called Susan Harper?'

'No.' Quick.

She and Brody watched him carefully.

'What about Linda Wilson.'

'No,' Waterson replied.

'Think carefully, Mick. You don't know either name?'

'Never heard of either of them. Like I said.'

'Where were you on Tuesday morning, between 8 a.m. and 12 p.m.?' This was the window Okafor had given them for when Susan Harper had been murdered.

Waterson thought for a moment, then looked at her. 'Around.'

'Around?' repeated Pope.

'That's what I said.'

'Any chance you could be a little more specific?' asked Pope.

'Here. Working.'

'Can anyone corroborate that? Anyone else here?'

'Nope. I work alone.' He looked at her defiantly.

'That's not really going to cut it, Mick.'

'That's your problem.'

'It's yours, actually,' said Brody.

Mick Waterson looked at Brody and laughed. He looked back to Pope. 'Where do you find 'em?'

'And what about Wednesday evening, between 8 p.m. and midnight?' Linda Wilson.

'At home.'

'With Trish?'

He looked at her with distaste, as if she had no right to even utter his wife's name.

'No.'

'You were home alone?'

'Yup.'

'Where was Trish?'

'Out.'

'Not very helpful, Mick.'

'Not my job to be helpful to you.'

'It seems not. Where was Trish on Wednesday evening?' asked Pope.

'Out with her mates. Don't know where.'

Pope stared at him. 'We'll need to talk to her.'

'Good luck with that. She hates your guts.' He half smiled.

Pope needed to think, needed a different approach.

'OK, Mick. We'll be back in touch. Let Trish know we'll need to talk to her as soon as possible.'

'You can do that yourself.'

'Sorry to have troubled you.'

'I bet you fucking are.'

She and Brody turned to leave.

'Give Trish my best,' said Pope.

'I'm sure it'll make her fucking day.'

As Pope was opening the car door, Mick Waterson called after her. 'DCI Pope?'

She turned.

'Have you found Tina's killer yet?'

'No, Mick. I'm afraid I haven't.'

* * *

'He doesn't like you very much, does he?' said Brody, as they passed Elephant and Castle towards Waterloo. The air was heavy with the smell of traffic.

'I think that's fair to say.'

'What do you think?'

Pope considered the question. 'Difficult to say. He blames me and Bruce Phillips for not catching Tina's killer, so he has every reason to have it in for me. He could've written the cards. He's certainly been violent in the past and he seems not to have let it go. There's not a lot of point talking to Trish yet, as he's not using her as an alibi. I'll get Miller to do some more digging, see if there's any CCTV around the garage and his house we can check to verify his alibi. Then we'll get him in and talk to him on our territory.'

Brody went to say something, hesitated.

'What?' asked Pope.

'He doesn't seem to have much of a motive,' said Brody apologetically. 'I mean, disliking you seems a pretty weak reason to kill two complete strangers. And he hasn't bothered to construct an alibi, which I would expect him to do if he was trying to cover his tracks.'

'Let's see what Miller can find.' She was reluctant to accept Brody's hesitation. 'We do need to talk to him again, though,' she reiterated.

Brody looked out of the window. They were silent for the remainder of the drive.

CHAPTER 12

It was 8.30 p.m. and Brody was putting a "wall" up in the squad room. This was a collection of photographs of victims and their families, and key witnesses, if there were any, along with a timeline, maps, connections and any other pieces of useful information. He was adding several printouts to the wall, including a picture of Mick Waterson, when Pope's phone rang. She answered and moved away, listening intently.

Brody watched as she frowned and asked questions he couldn't hear. Her look darkened.

'What's up?' asked Brody, after she hung up.

'That was Alex. Chloe hasn't come back from school.' She looked at her watch.

'She's probably at a friend's house. Has Alex called her?'

'Yes, but she's not answering. We had a big argument last because she wanted to go to a party tonight and stay over. Alex told her she couldn't. He's really worried.'

'I'm sure it's just teenage girl stuff,' said Brody.

'I hope so,' she said. 'But it doesn't feel right. Chloe will at least usually pick up the phone.'

She paced around, seemingly unable to stop herself moving.

'You don't think . . .' she said at last. 'You don't think this is connected to the case?' She shook her head.

It was unthinkable.

'No, I'm sure you're right and it's just teenage girl stuff,' said Pope.

But Brody was already putting on his jacket.

'I'm coming with you.'

* * *

Pope drove fast through the dregs of the rush hour. She ran through the door, followed by Brody. In the living room, Alex was on the phone, talking to one of Chloe's friends.

'Call me if you hear anything,' he finished as he saw her come in.

He hugged Pope close.

'Brody,' he said tightly, over her shoulder.

'Alex.'

'Where is she, Bec?' asked Alex, turning to Pope. 'She didn't come back from school and won't answer her phone. She always answers the phone. I've called all the friends I know. I've even called Tyler, who isn't answering, the little shit. But I can't get hold of her. Where the hell is she?'

'Almost certainly keeping away from us so she can go to that party. We'll find her. Don't worry.'

'Don't worry? You're hunting a bloody serial killer, who seems to be killing women every day, and my daughter is out, God knows where with God knows who!'

Alex was usually calm and resourceful. He could handle most things. But she understood. He had tried everything he could think of and although the "killing women every day" was hyperbole after only two victims, she too was concerned, although she couldn't tell him the full extent of her worry.

'Who's most likely among her friends to know where she is?' asked Pope.

Alex thought for a moment. 'I've called everyone I know. Maybe Charlie. Charlotte Bates. Chloe seems to be hanging around with her a lot at the moment. Well, when she isn't with Tyler. But I don't have her number.'

Pope had heard the name.

'OK, we'll start with her. Brody, can you find out where Charlotte Bates lives?' Brody took out his phone, dialled a number and walked out into the hall.

'You stay here in case she comes back. In the meantime, keep calling her friends. Try Tyler again. Let me know if you hear anything.' She put her arms around Alex, trying to reassure him. 'Her phone might have run out of battery. She may be on her way home now.'

'I've got an address for Charlotte Bates.' Brody was standing in the doorway.

Alex looked at her, his expression a mixture of scepticism and hope. He nodded.

'I'll let you know when we get anything,' she said. 'We'll go find Charlie and see what she can tell us. And don't worry. We see this kind of thing all the time and it invariably sorts itself out.'

Pope kissed Alex before they left.

Pope drove as Brody gave directions. Neither of them said what they were thinking. But each of them was thinking the same: that almost certainly Chloe Regis was getting ready to go to a party with her boyfriend and was prepared to accept the consequences when she got home rather than miss the party. Almost certainly.

When they arrived at the Bates house, all seemed perfectly normal. No loud music, no teenagers falling out of the front door, passed out on the lawn. They walked to the front door and rang the doorbell.

A middle-aged man came to the door. He was dressed in jeans and a sweater, with a business shirt underneath, and wore a pair of slippers. He was clearly relaxing into the weekend and had settled down for a quiet night in.

'Detectives Bec Pope and James Brody, Metropolitan Police,' Pope said, holding up her warrant badge. 'Is Charlotte Bates at home?'

The man looked predictably shocked. 'What's this about? I'm her father. Is everything OK?'

'I'm Chloe's stepmum. We can't get hold of her, she's . . . Your daughter might be able to help. Is she in?'

'Yes, she's upstairs. I'll get her.' He walked briskly to the bottom of the stairs and called her. No answer, so he called again. This time a reply.

Without any undue haste, a sixteen-year-old girl came down the stairs. She looked put out to have been disturbed by her father, but when she saw Pope and Brody's warrant cards, she suddenly lost that expression and looked nervous, as most people did when confronted by detectives.

'We're looking for Chloe Regis. You're a friend, right?' asked Pope.

'Yes, I know Chloe. We're in the same tutor group at school. Has something happened to her?' asked the girl.

'When did you last see her?' asked Pope, ignoring the question.

'Today at school.'

At least she's been to school, thought Pope. 'Do you have any idea where she might be now?'

'Not really.'

'What does "not really" mean?' asked Pope.

She hesitated. 'She said something about going to Tyler's house after school. That's her boyfriend, Tyler Watts,' she added.

'OK. Do you know what they were planning to do afterwards? Did she say anything about where they might be going?'

'No. I just know that she was meeting Tyler.' Pope looked at her and decided that she was telling the truth.

'Right. Thanks very much,' she said, and they departed, leaving Charlotte's father looking angrily at his daughter for bringing the police to their door.

Brody drove now, while Pope simultaneously directed him to Tyler Watts's house, and called Alex to update him and tell him where she was going.

They pulled up outside the house. 'Shall I handle this one?' asked Brody. 'You're a bit close, and he might respond better to me.'

Pope agreed. Although she wanted to be the one to talk to Tyler, she knew he was right.

Tyler Watts lived with his mother and younger sister in the ground-floor flat of a large Victorian house set back from the main road. It had obviously been something of a grand residence in former times, but there had been a trend in London in the 1980s to convert these kinds of houses into smaller units, to maximize revenue for landlords looking to buy and rent to young couples and students.

Tyler and Chloe had been together for six months now, and Pope had picked her up from here on a number of occasions. She liked Tyler better than Alex did, but that wasn't saying much.

Tyler's mother answered the front door and after brief greetings and explanations, she led them to Tyler's room, knocked and opened the door. Tyler was sitting on his bed, reading a magazine and listening to Jimi Hendrix on his laptop. There was an unmistakable haze in the room and a sweet smell that both Pope and Brody instantly recognized. He looked up when they walked in.

'Oh, hi, Mrs Pope,' said Tyler, looking immediately uncomfortable. 'How are you doing?' He shuffled on the bed, then got up and awkwardly shook Pope's hand.

Brody showed his warrant ID. 'We're looking for Chloe. Is she here?'

'Um, no. She was earlier, but we had a bit of an argument and she took off,' said Watts.

Pope wanted to grab him by the scruff of the neck and shake the information out of him.

'What did you argue about?' asked Brody, his voice calm.

'Oh. . .' Pause. He seemed to be collecting his thoughts. 'She wanted to go to this party tonight, but I wanted to chill. We had, like, an argument.'

'So, where is she now?' asked Brody patiently.

'She said she was going to the party anyway. I told her to stay here, but she just left. She said she might be back later.'

'So you let her go out on her own?' asked Pope.

'Yeah, I guess,' said Tyler.

'Where's the party?' asked Brody.

'I don't know,' he said. The hesitation showed that his loyalty to Chloe was still intact, despite the argument.

Brody moved towards Tyler. He was now uncomfortably close, but when Tyler tried to back away, he hit the wall.

'That smell in the room, Tyler. What is that? Is that incense or something? I know it from somewhere.' Brody waited, while Tyler looked at his shoes, around the room, then back to him. 'I'll tell you what, Tyler. I'll call my Forensics team to come and check the place over, and then we can see what it is. How about that? We could talk about it back at the station.'

Tyler Watts wasn't a bad kid, and just a small threat from Brody did the trick.

'I think the party's in Ladbroke Grove.'

'Where in Ladbroke Grove?' asked Brody.

Tyler had to think for a moment. 'I dunno. Portland Street, maybe? I don't know the number.'

'We'll find it. How long ago did she leave?'

Tyler checked the time on his phone. 'About two hours ago.'

Brody held his gaze and judged that Tyler was telling them the truth.

'Thanks for your help. Keep out of trouble.'

Tyler nodded.

Pope glared at him as she left.

Back in the car she called Alex and told him where they thought they would find Chloe. She told him that she would let him know as soon as they had her. She ended the call.

'Thanks, Brody,' she said.

'No problem. He wasn't exactly the hardened criminal.'

'Yeah, that's true. But I mean for coming with me to look for Chloe. Above and beyond the call of duty.'

'We haven't found her yet,' he reminded her.

* * *

Ladbroke Grove sat between Shepherd's Bush and Notting Hill in West London. Pope remembered that Chloe had said the party was north of the river, but had expected Islington or Finsbury Park. As they turned into the street, it was obvious which house was holding the party. It was in a terrace of tall and wide Georgian houses, much larger than they needed to be and probably very expensive. The road was full of high-end cars, including a light blue Mercedes 280 SE, probably from the early 1970s. The kind of car you had if you didn't really need to drive very far and had a lot of money. The insurance alone would have cost more than Pope's car. She wondered how Chloe had been invited to a party somewhere like this.

The windows of the house were closed, but the music still pounded out into the street.

'I wonder how many calls the local station has had about this so far?' said Brody as he pulled the car into the side of the road and opened the door.

Pope looked at her watch. It was eleven thirty. 'Plenty, but they're probably all on call queuing at this time of night. I'm guessing the parents are away and the kids are taking advantage of an empty house.'

As they walked up the steps to the entrance, the door opened and a guy and two young women stumbled out of the house. They almost bumped into Brody who was in front. One of the women mumbled a half-apology and then they all burst out laughing as they left. They linked arms and swayed as they walked down the street, one holding a bottle of whisky in her hand.

The party was in full swing. Loud music, a smell of alcohol, with a much stronger smell of cannabis permeating the hallway. Everywhere they looked there were groups of young people, drinking, smoking and dancing. They walked into the first room they came to, a living room, on the left of the hall. Nobody seemed to be worried about who was coming or going, and no one seemed to care that two strangers some twenty years older than them had wandered into the milieu.

In the middle of the room there was a large group of mainly young women, a few years older than Chloe, dancing. Spread around the edges were smaller groups, most with a drink in their hand, and some holding a spliff. A young man stood at a turntable, looking through an extensive vinyl collection in search of the next tune. He was wearing headphones. Pope wondered who lived here, and whether they knew about the party.

They split up to search the other rooms downstairs, and met back at the bottom of the stairs by the front door.

'Any sign?' she asked.

'Not of Chloe.' There were lots of things they could have taken issue with as police officers, but they chose to ignore them for the moment.

Brody looked at Pope.

'Better go upstairs, I guess? Want me to check?' said Brody.

'No, it's fine. Let's go,' she replied, despite a sinking feeling in her gut.

They weaved up the stairs, avoiding a couple having an earnest chat, fuelled in equal measure by teenage angst and alcohol. When they got to the top, Brody stopped and looked around. There were several doors but only one was pulled closed. Brody peered in through the open doors, but the rooms were empty. So he headed to the closed door, shouldered it open and walked in, Pope on his heels.

It was a teenager's room. Cluttered, covered in posters and with a few signs of the occupant's younger days. Sitting on the bed was Chloe, kissing a boy. Then she saw who had walked into the room. They immediately broke apart and Pope could see that the young man was several years older than Chloe. She had on a great deal of make-up, clearly trying to make herself look older than she was. She looked at Brody, then at Pope. Her expression was a mixture of fear, loathing and, overwhelmingly, embarrassment.

'Bec. What the hell are you doing here?' she yelled.

'Get your things, Chloe. We're leaving,' said Pope.

Chloe looked at her, but didn't move.

'Now,' said Pope, and this time there was no mistaking her authority.

Chloe's companion stood up and took a step forwards. 'Who are you?' he asked. 'You can't talk to her like that.' He was trying to impress Chloe.

Pope was furious, anger boiling up inside her.

Brody stepped between them. He held out his warrant card and held it in his face. 'You've got ten seconds to get out of here, or I'll take you and the spliff in the ashtray over there to the station and we can call your parents.'

He looked at the boy. This was the second time he'd made that threat this evening.

'Get out,' he repeated.

The boy's chivalry evaporated in the face of the threat to his liberty. He looked at the ashtray, then at Chloe, then at Pope. Finally, back to Brody. Then he left. It didn't take him ten seconds.

'What are you doing? I'm nearly an adult,' screamed Chloe.

'Nearly, but not quite. Let's go,' said Pope. She grabbed Chloe's arm, pulled her off the bed and guided her to the door. Pope was now clearly not in the mood to take any of her protestations and Chloe sensed that leaving was non-negotiable.

The three of them stormed down the stairs, passing the other partygoers. Chloe hid behind her hair. It was the ultimate humiliation.

In the car, there was silence for a while, as Brody drove them back through West London and crossed the Thames over Vauxhall Bridge. It was almost midnight. Pope texted Alex. *I've got her. On our way home.*

She looked at Chloe in the back seat. 'Why didn't you call us, Chloe? Your dad's been worried sick. You can't just go off like that.'

She didn't look up. Pope was expecting fireworks. Expecting high drama. But instead, Chloe said quietly, 'You had no right to come in there and take me out like that.'

Pope looked at her. She knew that it was probably all over social media by now. She would have to face that, as well as her dad, and Tyler.

'I had every right, Chloe, and you know that. You're only just sixteen.'

Chloe looked at her. 'What are you going to tell Dad?' she asked.

Despite Pope's anger and irritation, she felt for Chloe. She wanted to make it all right, to ease Chloe's torment in some way.

'Who was smoking the spliff, Chloe? Did you have any?' she asked, avoiding Chloe's question.

Chloe sat forward. 'No, Bec, I didn't. I promise. It was him and I told him to put it down before we . . .' She stopped. Pope didn't entirely believe her, but didn't press the issue.

'OK, I'll make a deal with you. I won't mention exactly where I found you, or the questionable substance your friend was choosing to smoke. But you never do that again. Disappear on your dad. I mean it. You need to be honest with us if we're going to trust you.'

Chloe looked very relieved. 'Yes, it won't happen again. Thanks, Bec.' She almost smiled. Pope sensed that out of this there might be a breakthrough in their relationship and for that she was willing to bend the truth a little with Alex. Out of the corner of her eye, she could see Brody raising his eyebrows, silently advising her against making these kinds of deals.

'And please don't say anything to Tyler. I've messed up and it won't happen again,' Chloe repeated.

Pope turned back around. She took out her phone as she said to Brody, 'I'll sort a car to get you from mine so you can get home. I'll need the car in the morning.'

'No problem. Thanks.'

When they arrived home, Pope told Chloe to go ahead. She watched as her stepdaughter let herself into the house. Pope looked at Brody.

'Thanks for this,' she said. 'I really appreciate you coming with me tonight. Yet again you've saved my sanity.'

'And saved you whacking that trustafarian stoner in front of Chloe,' he smiled.

'Yes, and that,' she said. The squad car pulled up outside the house. 'See you in the morning.'

She watched him get in and turned, steeling herself for whatever scene would greet her inside.

To her surprise, Chloe had already gone upstairs to bed, promising to talk about what had happened tomorrow. Alex was angry, but this was countered by a sense of relief, and he stayed with that for the moment.

Alex looked at Pope. 'Thank you, Bec.'

'No problem. Took us a while to find her, but no harm done.'

Alex was relieved, but she sensed a cloud.

'Why did Brody go with you?' he asked finally.

'We were just leaving the station when I got your call. He thought he might be able to help find Chloe. I'm glad he was there. He stopped me losing my temper with her.' The half-lie was acceptable under the circumstances.

Alex moved on. 'Had Chloe been drinking?'

'I don't think so. I didn't notice a smell or any slurring of words. She seemed OK as far as I could—'

Her phone trilled.

'What now?' she muttered, part to herself and part to Alex.

She pulled out her phone. Adam Miller. It was just after 1 a.m. She wondered what Miller would want at this time of night. It was unlikely to be good news.

Alex looked at her in disbelief.

'Are you answering that now?' he asked.

'I have to, it's work.' She pressed the button. 'Miller, what is it?'

She listened, exchanged a few words. 'I'll meet you there. Give me twenty minutes.'

She looked at Alex, who looked ready to tell her what he thought about her answering work calls at one o'clock in the morning.

'A woman has just walked into King's College Hospital. She says she was attacked by a man who tried to strangle her, but she escaped and went straight there. Miller thinks it might be our guy.'

CHAPTER 13

It was 1.30 a.m. The streets were quiet and Pope drove quickly.

She couldn't get ahead of herself. It could just be a domestic dispute, a date gone wrong. But if there was a chance that this was a potential witness, a possible lead in the case, she wanted to be there fast. This was one of those cases where sheer dogged police work wasn't going to cut it. She needed some luck. *He*, whoever "he" was, was too careful, too clever, too organized. This could be the break Pope needed. She really hoped so. Because she felt the pressure increasing minute by minute.

She pulled into the emergency bays in front of King's Hospital on Denmark Hill and placed her "Police on call" sign on the dashboard. She walked quickly into the A & E, flashing her warrant card at the security guard on duty.

'Pope,' Miller's voice called from down the corridor.

'Up here, fourth floor,' he said, motioning towards the lift. Pope followed and Miller punched the call button.

They got in and the doors closed.

'The victim's name is Karen Tarling. Twenty-seven years old, an accountant who works for a company called Cromwell and Shore Financial, based in Moorgate. She lives just round the corner. Bavent Road. She was sedated by the time we arrived, so we haven't been able to question her yet, but she said some things to the doctor who saw her. We found the other information in documents in her handbag: driving licence, credit card and work ID.'

'Is it him?' Pope asked.

'It looks like it could be. I've called Brody, he's on his way to Tarling's flat. Fletcher is also in the loop, he wants you to call him when you've spoken to the doctor. Doctor is a Jane Leigh, she'll be able to tell you the rest. But it all points to our guy.'

Pope felt her heart rate quicken as they got out of the lift. She followed Miller down a brightly lit corridor. She assumed that this was the private wing of the hospital. They stopped outside a small room in which Pope could see a doctor and several nurses looking at an X-ray on a slim screen mounted on the wall. The doctor was peering closely, tracing her finger around a part of the image.

'Dr Leigh,' interrupted Miller. Leigh looked away from her work. She left what she was doing and came towards them.

'This is DCI Pope, she's leading the investigation that we think might be related to your patient,' said Miller.

Leigh outstretched her hand and gave Pope a very confident handshake. This was no doubt perfected over the years as a means of denoting control and authority. *Don't worry, I'm in charge and I know what I'm doing*, it said.

Jane Leigh was forty-four years old. She was an imposing figure. Almost six foot, with long, thick ginger hair. She had unusually bright blue eyes, the type people often describe as "piercing". She wore tailored black trousers and a dark blue Oxford shirt, with brown, well-shined brogues. Expensive. Regulation stethoscope around her neck. She carried herself with the arrogance that can only be acceptable for doctors.

'What can you tell us, Dr Leigh?' asked Pope.

Leigh retrieved her clipboard and patient notes from the room behind her and walked back out looking over them.

'Karen Tarling arrived in A & E earlier this evening. She arrived on foot. She ran from her house, right next to the hospital, she said,' Leigh added, looking at Pope. She nodded for the doctor to continue.

'She was disorientated and extremely distressed, hence the sedation being necessary.'

'Can I talk to her?' asked Pope.

'Not yet, I'm afraid. I wouldn't recommend it anyway, but she's asleep and is unlikely to wake for ten to twelve hours.'

Pope was frustrated. 'Well, then can you tell me what she told you?'

'She was fairly incoherent when she came in and got progressively more so. She had been attacked, that was clear, and she needed immediate attention. I wrote down what she said, as I thought it might be useful for the police.' She checked her notes. 'Yes, here it is. She said that she had been out for the evening after work and got back late. There had been a knock on the door, and when she answered it, she had been physically attacked. He — she said it was a he — punched her and put his hands around her neck trying to strangle her.'

'Did she give you any description of her attacker?' asked Pope.

'No, sorry. That's more your territory, not ours. Our focus was on calming her down and treating her injuries.'

'Did she say how she managed to escape?' asked Pope.

'She remembered her self-defence training. Punched him in the throat, kicked him in the balls and fled. She came straight here. Nearer than the police station, I suppose. Left him in the flat.'

'Have we collected trace evidence?'

'Forensics are on the way,' said Miller.

'What were her injuries?'

'She had a cut and bruising on the left side of her face, consistent with having been punched by her attacker. She also had bruising around her neck. Again, consistent with what she told us about her attacker attempting to strangle her. She's in bad shape, but it sounds like it could have been much worse.'

'I really need to talk to her as soon as possible,' Pope said.

'I know. She's not going anywhere at the moment, and as I said, she'll be out until the morning. You should be able to talk to her then. I don't think there will be any lasting damage. Not physical, at least.' The doctor put down her notes.

'We really need to know as soon as possible when she wakes up,' said Pope. 'It's vitally important that we question her as soon as we can. This is a potential murder suspect here, and Karen Tarling might be our only shot at identifying him.'

'I'll let you know as soon as there's any change. I promise.'

'Thanks,' said Pope. 'I appreciate you noting all that down for us. Any chance you can give a copy of that to my sergeant?'

'That shouldn't be a problem. I'll make a copy.' Leigh looked at Pope. 'You look tired, DCI Pope. Why don't you go home and get some rest? There's nothing you can do here.'

'Thanks for the advice, Doc,' said Pope. 'I might just do that.'

* * *

Pope and Miller walked a couple of doors down to the room where Karen Tarling was recovering. She looked peaceful now, in bed with the lights on very low.

'What do you think?' asked Miller.

'It would be one hell of a coincidence if it was someone else. Not far from the first victim, young woman alone, punches her then tries to strangle her. It has to be him.'

Miller thought. 'There's a team at her flat now, and Forensics are trying to see if there's anything useful. But given how careful he's been previously, we can't hold out much hope.'

'True,' said Pope. 'But if he was caught off guard when she hit him, as Dr Leigh suggested, we might get lucky.'

110

Miller nodded. He said again, more to himself than Pope, 'Brody's on his way there.' He looked at his watch. 'In fact, he's probably there already. He's going to let us know if they find anything.'

Pope looked around and noticed there was no CCTV in the corridor. 'I want a guard outside this room. All night. I don't want him coming back to finish off the job.'

Miller called up a number on his mobile and had a quick conversation. Within a couple of minutes, a police constable in uniform arrived in the elevator. He walked towards Pope and Miller.

'Hi, Phil,' said Miller. He turned to Pope. 'This is PC Davies. He's going to be on duty tonight.'

Pope had not seen the officer before, and supposed he must be from a different station. She was too tired to ask for details.

'Keep her safe,' said Pope. 'Only medical personnel in and out, and let me know if there are any changes.'

'Got it.' Davies found a chair and sat down outside the room.

'Go home and rest,' said Miller. 'Doctor's orders.' He smiled at Pope.

Pope considered. She was reluctant to go home, bearing in mind the potential breakthrough in the case. But she also knew that without sleep she would be inefficient and tomorrow was going to be a long day. Miller was here. Brody was at the victim's flat. She made the decision, told Miller to make sure that she was immediately informed of anything, anything at all. Miller assured her that he would. Pope said she'd be back early in the morning and took the lift to the ground floor.

CHAPTER 14

Pope had arrived home at 3 a.m. Everyone was asleep when she let herself in, and Alex had not woken up when she eventually crawled into bed sometime after 4 a.m. The intervening hour had been spent drinking whisky and listening to John Coltrane on headphones. She needed to listen, but rather than helping her sleep, the soaring, kinetic tenor saxophone of "Giant Steps" had merely boosted her adrenaline, and she had taken too long to get to sleep. Waking at 7 a.m., she also regretted the amount of whisky she had drunk in such a short space of time. Her head was still pounding when she walked in to find an empty office.

Of course, Miller was at the hospital and Brody had probably been up late at the apartment, overseeing the forensic examination. She checked her phone. There was a message from Darke saying he would be at King's College this morning, so he would drop by the station straight afterwards.

Pope was making a cup of coffee when the door opened and Richard Fletcher walked in.

'Morning, Bec. Where are we with Karen Tarling?' Straight to business.

'Morning,' said Pope, gesturing for him to join her in her office. 'She's in King's. She had to be heavily sedated.

Miller's there now, and there's a guard on the door. He'll call as soon as she wakes up and then I'll go over and talk to her.'

'Is it our guy?' The same question Pope had asked.

'We don't know for sure yet. I guess we won't until she wakes up. But if it isn't, it's an incredible coincidence.'

'What do you think?' asked Fletcher. He wanted good news.

Pope hesitated. She didn't want to give her boss anything he could take to the media that would alleviate their hysteria, not if she wasn't absolutely certain.

'I think we need to wait and see. But it looks likely that it's him at this stage. Tobias Darke is coming in to see me later this morning. If it's our guy, or even if it isn't, I need his expertise so we have a better idea of who, or what, we're dealing with,' said Pope.

'Where's Brody?'

'He'll be on his way. He was at Karen Tarling's apartment last night with the forensic team. He'll brief us when he gets in,' said Pope.

Fletcher looked at his watch. 'OK. Let me know the moment you have anything. My phone won't stop ringing until we do.' He left the office.

Pope drank her coffee and thought. A bit of peace and quiet in which to think was rare, and always welcome. She was fired up about the prospect of a description or, better yet, an identification. She looked at her watch again. Patience was not her strong suit.

She didn't have to wait long before Brody walked into the office. He looked remarkably fresh for someone who had had only a few hours' sleep. Pope thought about her own dishevelled appearance in the mirror this morning.

'Hi, Bec,' said Brody as he fixed himself a coffee. 'How's Chloe this morning?'

'Chloe?' The incident with Chloe seemed a very long time ago. 'Oh, fine. I think. Still asleep when I left. How did it go last night? Anything interesting?'

Brody sat down at his desk and took a sip of coffee.

'Karen Tarling's flat is on the ground floor. She's right around the corner from King's Hospital, which I guess is why she ended up there. Probably seemed the safest place. One flat above, but the occupants are away for the weekend. Looks like she opened the door, there was no sign of forced entry. The state of the hallway corroborates her statement to the doctor that he punched her first and she fell over. There is evidence of a struggle just inside the door, but no signs anywhere else in the flat. Things had been knocked over and there was a small amount of blood on the wooden floor, just by the entrance to the living room. According to Miller, he tried to strangle her.'

Pope nodded, encouraging him to go on.

'Apart from the signs of the struggle, the only physical evidence Forensics found was the blood and some fingerprints. Forensics will have to take Karen Tarling's prints when she wakes up for elimination. But from a preliminary visual inspection, they all seem similar, and the sheer number of them suggests that they are probably hers. We checked the surrounding properties, but no one saw or heard anything. The perpetrator seems to have got away without anyone noticing him.' He paused. 'How is she doing?'

'Should still be knocked out from the sedative. It's going to be a while before she can talk to us. Miller's at the hospital. Tobias Darke is coming in soon.'

'Good. I've got a few questions for him.'

'Can you arrange for a couple of uniforms to pick up Mick Waterson? I think it's time we had a more formal conversation.'

'Do you think it's a bit early for that?'

Pope raised her eyebrows.

'I mean, what's his motive?'

Pope said nothing, forcing Brody to fill the space.

'Should we wait for the forensics report?'

'I know Mick Waterson much better than you do. He's capable of this. And what might not seem like much of a motive to you, absolutely will do to him.' She paused, looking directly at him. 'Get him in.'

The conversation was over. Brody nodded and made a call.

* * *

The phone on Pope's desk rang at just past 11 a.m. It was the officer on reception telling her that she had a visitor: Tobias Darke. Pope asked for him to be sent up to her office.

'Bec, James,' he said as he strode through the door minutes later. His confidence and presence reminded Pope of the doctor she had spoken to at King's last night.

'How are you both?' asked Darke as he removed his scarf and coat, hung them up on the coat rack and sat down opposite Pope. 'I've just come from a lecture at King's.' King's College was on the Strand, only a ten-minute walk from Charing Cross Police Station. 'A group of first-year medical students who wanted to know about my work at Broadmoor. Ghoulish, really. Wanted all the gory details on the most violent criminals I'd worked with. So I'm in the mood to talk about serial killers!' Darke laughed. Pope had got used to Darke's gallows humour over the years.

Darke opened his bag and got out his notebook and some loose sheets of A4 paper, and retrieved a pen from his jacket pocket. Brody updated Darke on the incident with Karen Tarling. He listened intently, making notes as Brody spoke. He was meticulous, and Pope knew that he would review them later. They would probably find their way into a research paper or academic publication once this was all over.

'Have you had any more thoughts since our conversation? Anything you think might help us at this stage?' asked Pope.

Darke finished what he was writing, then scanned his notes.

'Well, first, it's good news about your potential witness. You might be lucky and she might give you a decent description.' Pope nodded her agreement. 'However, if we assume that's not guaranteed, we need to think about how you might try to understand this type of killer a little better.' Darke flipped through the sheaf of notes, landing on a page scribbled in small print.

'The areas we discussed previously are still key. Particularly the use of the camera and the cards. Many killers prepare carefully, and a number over the years have been known to stage their victims for those who discover them. However, the camera. . . that's altogether a different thing.'

Pope could see he was considering how best to put what came next. 'That could suggest a number of things. I'm not sure they'll help you find him on their own, but it speaks to possible personality traits. Killers, and serial killers in particular, often suffer clinical personality disorders. One of these can be pathological narcissism, which is well documented in a number of serial killer cases. Ted Bundy is an obvious example. The camera could suggest a desire to spend longer with the victim, or to admire his own work from afar. In the first murder, he may have wanted to watch the family return home and enjoy their suffering. Bundy returned to the scenes of some of his crimes, but of course remotely accessing a camera is a much safer method of achieving this. Again, this suggests a high level of intelligence and premeditation at work here.'

Pope nodded. She had dealt with enough serial attackers in her time, and most of them were narcissists.

'He could also just be toying with you, of course,' Darke continued, 'which again suggests a level of narcissism, and a belief that he won't get caught. But either way, my advice would be to concentrate on the camera initially. This is the most unusual aspect of his behaviour, I think.'

'What's his next move?' asked Brody. 'I mean, the camera is proving difficult to get any leads from. So, what is this guy going to do next?'

'That, of course, is the million-dollar question, James.' Darke deliberated for a moment. 'He is moving very fast, that's obvious. Much faster than most serial killers. The definition of a serial killer is generally someone who kills three or more victims over a long period of time. Most serial killers fit that description. Yours doesn't. He's compressing the timescale and that's what's really interesting here. Why so quick? The time between attacks makes it seem like he's out of control, unable to moderate his impulses. But the careful preparation and the way he carries out his murders suggest that this is not the case. Serial murder is often about control, and I think what you have here is someone who is very controlled in his actions. So the question is, why has he suddenly started now? What's the trigger, and why is he acting so rapidly?'

'How might the failed attempt to kill Karen Tarling affect him, do you think?' asked Pope. 'If we are assuming it's our guy.'

'Difficult to predict. If this is about control, this could make him very angry. He will have planned the murder, and if he is as organized and controlling as we think, he's not going to like his plans being derailed. He may seek out another victim quickly. If that does happen, you may find that this one is attacked more brutally. That is not uncommon with serial killers when things don't go their way, I'm afraid.'

'Do you think he'll stop?' asked Pope. 'I mean, some serial killers do, don't they? They just seem to stop killing for no apparent reason.'

'Some do,' replied Darke. 'But that is typically when the murders happen over a longer period of time. However, I get the sense your perpetrator is only just getting started. I wouldn't expect him to stop. Remember, serial killers often enjoy what they do. They enjoy killing, enjoy the control. Why would he stop unless he is forced to? There are a number of high-profile serial killers who have never been caught, and who appeared to have just stopped killing.'

Darke was warming to his subject now, leaning forward in his chair.

'But it's difficult to be certain that they stopped. They could have simply moved location, altered their method, or geographical cross-referencing between law enforcement agencies may have not been effective. Remember, most serial killer cases we know of are from the United States, and there's a big area in which to lose yourself and become anonymous if you want to. Those who haven't been caught often kill a large number of victims. Jack the Ripper, probably the most famous serial killer of all time, is credited with five murders over a relatively short period of time. But many think he actually killed far more. The infamous Zodiac Killer had seven confirmed victims in the late 1960s and seventies in California. But he claimed thirty-seven victims in his letters to the newspapers. There are others, but not with only two victims.'

'So, what's his motivation? What's his endgame, Tobias?' asked Pope. 'What can we expect?'

'His motivation? That's a good question. There have been a number of research studies done into exactly this subject. Unfortunately, the general consensus of these studies is that the majority of serial killers are troubled, psychotic individuals who kill because they derive great enjoyment from killing people.' Darke paused as he reflected on what he was about to say. 'It's true that financial gain can also be a factor in some cases, as can fury, rage, you know, a jilted lover or similar. But in this case, I think we're looking at someone who enjoys killing and enjoys the attention. The camera would suggest that, as would the cards. Have you got anywhere in trying to ascertain if he has killed before? Anywhere else?'

'Not yet,' replied Brody. 'We've sent the details, but we haven't got anything yet.'

Darke considered this. 'As I said before, I don't think these are his first murders.'

'Nor do I,' said Pope.

'As to his endgame, that rather depends,' continued Darke. 'If he is killing simply because he enjoys, he won't stop until someone stops him. But if he's doing this to get your attention, there's a good chance he'll escalate until you eventually find him. The fact that he watches you arrive on the scene and has watched your initial investigation of the crime scenes indicates the possibility that this could be about one of the team. Most likely you, Bec, as you're the one in charge. And the cards? Well, they confirm the theory, I'm afraid. Yes, this is very much about you. He wants your attention specifically.'

Pope thought about what Darke had said for a minute. 'What do you mean by "escalate"?'

'Well, it would be difficult for him to escalate the frequency of his attacks. So, he may escalate in terms of the brutality or nature of his attacks, or make them more public. There is one more possibility.'

For the first time, Darke looked troubled.

'If your killer is trying not just to gain attention generally, but get your attention specifically, there is always the chance that he will pick a target who means something to you personally. A family member, friend, or colleague,' he added.

Pope thought about those who were closest to her. She didn't have many close friends, not in London. But Alex, Chloe, Hannah. . . Their faces flashed through her head.

'Right. Thanks,' she said.

'I don't want to be alarmist, Bec. But I think you do have to consider that possibility.'

'I understand,' said Pope. 'I appreciate your time and energy on this, Tobias, I really do.'

'No problem at all. Let me know if you get anything from the latest victim, and if there's anything more I can do to help. In the meantime, I've brought you some bedtime reading.' Darke pulled a hardback book out of his briefcase and handed it to Pope. She looked at the cover. *Inside the Mind of the Serial Killer* by Michael Elliott.

'It's a fairly psychiatric approach to the subject, but it doesn't get hysterical and you might find some of the information useful. Required reading if you're studying serial killers.'

'Thanks,' said Pope. It sounded sarcastic, but it wasn't meant to.

Darke got up to leave, but then paused. He looked like he was deciding whether to bring something up.

'What is it, Tobias?' asked Pope.

He hesitated. 'One thought struck me, as I was rereading the notes I made when we last met. Do you remember a character called Edward Boyd? Long time ago?'

'There is no way I could forget Edward Boyd,' said Pope.

'Who's Edward Boyd?' asked Brody. He'd never heard the name.

Darke answered. 'He was an early case of Bec's. Well before she joined Homicide. Almost sixteen years ago now.'

Pope frowned. *Was it that long ago?*

'Edward Boyd killed a middle-aged woman in Woolwich,' explained Darke to Brody. 'Strangled her and then wrote all over the walls in her lipstick. Elementary devil worship stuff. He served fifteen years, and was released four months ago.'

'Released already?' Pope raised her eyebrows.

'Yes. I was surprised too.'

'Why do you mention Boyd?' asked Brody.

'Well, he was an unusual case. I interviewed him at Broadmoor to assess his competence to stand trial. His defence lawyers were trying to construct an argument that he was mentally incapacitated and was not responsible for his actions. He certainly played up to it. But it was clear that it was an act. He was certainly a psychopath, but he knew exactly what he was doing. Highly intelligent, very organized.'

'You think he could be involved in this case?' asked Brody.

'Well, not necessarily. But Boyd developed an unhealthy obsession with Bec. He blamed her for his situation as it was Bec who eventually arrested him. He talked incessantly about her while I was meeting with him and wrote to her from prison for several years after he was incarcerated. Isn't that right, Bec?'

'Yes. I stopped opening his letters after a while. Put them straight in the bin.'

'What kind of stuff was he writing?' asked Brody.

'He told me he was in love with me, what he wanted to do to me, that kind of stuff.'

Brody grimaced. 'So why bring him up now?'

'It strikes me that there are similarities in the murders,' said Darke, 'but also he is absolutely the kind of psychopath who would fixate on you fifteen years later. The cards, the photo . . . it just seemed like his way of working.'

Pope nodded. 'I'll check it out.'

'Just be careful getting involved with him again, Bec,' said Darke as he put on his coat.

They said their goodbyes, and Darke saw himself out. Pope sat down and began to leaf through the book. She considered Darke's warnings about Boyd, and the killer going after someone close to her.

Brody could see that she was slightly thrown off balance. 'Do you think he's right?' he asked. 'About a victim with a personal connection to you? About Boyd?'

'I don't know what to think,' replied Pope.

'What are you going to do?' asked Brody.

They were interrupted by the phone on her desk.

'They've brought in Mick Waterson. He's on his way to Interview One. Shall we have a chat?'

'Love to,' replied Brody, getting up and putting on his jacket. 'Should be fun!'

* * *

Interview Room One — as it was unimaginatively named — was small and claustrophobic. Pope had never really known if this was a conscious, rather sadistic design feature or a result of cost-cutting. Either way, it served to disorientate interviewees and could be used to the interviewer's advantage if they knew what they were doing. Equally, however, once you'd been interviewed a number of times, you began to understand and recognize these psychological techniques. Mick Waterson had been interviewed a number of times.

'I'll lead,' said Pope as they approached. 'I want you to observe him very closely. He'll deny everything and in my experience he's not easy to rattle. So, we'll need to be a bit clever in what we're looking for. I don't think he'll give much away voluntarily.'

Brody nodded. Pope opened the door.

Mick Waterson was a big guy. Six feet two inches, broad, muscular. The crew cut and the black Fred Perry polo shirt lent him the air of a 1970s National Front supporter. Tattoos on his forearms scrolled the names of his wife, son and daughter. Pope tried not to flinch when she saw the final name indelibly inked on Tina Waterson's father. He sat upright in the chair, two officers stood behind him at an appropriate distance. From the look of apprehension on their faces, Pope guessed that it had not been the easiest of jobs to bring him in today. Waterson looked completely unfazed by the whole thing.

Pope and Brody both sat down opposite Mick Waterson. There was an empty chair next to him.

Pope started. 'Hello, Mick.'

No response. He merely stared at her.

'You don't have legal representation here. Have you called a lawyer?'

'Don't need one.'

'Are you sure? We can arrange one if you want.'

'I don't need one.'

'Why do you think you don't need a lawyer?' asked Pope, although she knew what he was going to say.

'I haven't done anything. Why would I need a lawyer?'

'OK. That's fine. We just need to ask you a few questions. Shouldn't take long. If at any point you change your mind about legal representation, just let me know.'

He continued to stare at her, said nothing. Pope thought that he was attempting to intimidate her, a common strategy of male suspects when faced with female detectives. He still assumed that she was the inexperienced detective of seven years ago. She considered how best she could use that to her advantage.

She started the tape, went through the preliminaries, including explaining his rights and listing the people present in the room. Then she opened a file containing a number of sheets of loose paper and began to read. The intention was to irritate him by making him wait in silence, but he didn't react.

After a while, she began. 'Mick. According to your record, you were arrested for driving while under the influence of alcohol, er, let's see, four years ago.' Her intonation at the end of the sentence indicated that it was a question.

'You already know that.'

'Just clarifying. I want to make sure we've got the facts right here,' she said, indicating the folder on the desk in front of her.

He raised his eyebrows, knew exactly what she was doing.

'Do you want to explain what happened?'

'Explain? Driving after a few beers? Does it need to be explained? What don't you understand?'

'Why did you choose to drive after you'd been drinking?'

'Why not?' he replied.

'Well, you lost your licence for eighteen months, so I guess that's one reason.'

His look turned darker. Irritated at last.

'That must have been difficult, with you being a mechanic. Tricky for test drives, I would imagine.'

'I survived.'

'Yes, I can see that. Survived well enough to be arrested for GBH last year. What happened?'

'You have the file in front of you. Read it.'

'OK, Mick. I'll do that.' She leafed through the records, the silence in the room growing larger, more uncomfortable. As she attempted to unsettle him, he attempted to resist it.

Waterson turned to look at Brody as Pope was looking down at her notes. Brody stared back.

'You're not taking notes, Officer Broadly? You get paid for this. Shouldn't you be earning your money?'

123

'It's Brody. Detective Inspector Brody. Thanks for your concern.'

Waterson grinned.

Pope glanced up, ignoring the exchange. 'Right, I think I get the picture. You were in a pub, after a few drinks.' Waterson had turned his attention back to her now. 'Recurring theme, eh? You unable to control yourself after a few drinks.'

He intensified his stare, but said nothing. Pope knew he was trying to control his temper.

'You beat up a guy for reasons that you chose not to reveal at the time. Care to enlighten us now?'

'He said something that annoyed me,' replied Waterson.

'What did he say?'

'Ask him.'

'I'm asking you.'

'And I'm telling you to ask him.'

'My guess is that he won't tell us.'

'Maybe.'

'Why do you think that is, Mick? Did you threaten him?'

'No. Think he just changed his mind.'

'OK. Only background, really, so it's fine. Tells us a bit about your character, though.' She left that hanging. He didn't respond.

'Now. You've had time to think about the questions I asked you at the garage. Had any thoughts about either Susan Harper or Linda Wilson? Do the names ring any bells?'

'I told you. No.'

'You've never heard of either woman, never met either of them?'

'No. Again.'

'Are you sure, Mick?'

'Yes. I'm sure.'

'How about Karen Tarling? Do you recognize that name?'

'No. Never heard of her.' Quick response.

'You didn't really think too hard about that one, Mick.'

'I don't need to think too hard about whether I know someone. I either do or I don't. I don't know her.'

'Right.' She checked her notes again. 'Where were you last night, Mick?'

'Last night?'

Pope knew he was buying a moment to think. 'Yes, last night.'

'At the garage.'

'Until what time?'

'About eleven thirty, 12 a.m.'

'You were at the garage until midnight last night?' said Pope, unable to keep the disbelief from her voice.

'Yup.'

'Seriously? Why so late?'

'Because you'd pissed me off and I needed to work off some anger. I thought of you while I was panel-beating an old Vauxhall.'

She looked at him, glanced at Brody.

'Anyone verify that? Where you were?'

'No.'

'You were on your own at the garage?'

'Yeah. I told you, I work alone.'

'Not much of alibi, is it, Mick?'

He shrugged. 'That's where I was.'

Pope paused. She didn't have anything, no evidence to hold him. But he was clearly a suspect now. She needed more time. Pope decided to bluff, unsure of exactly what this might achieve.

'I've got two murders and an attempted murder, Mick. And I'm inclined to hold you until we can arrange a line-up. I've got a victim in hospital who I'm certain will be able to pick out her attacker.'

She saw something, a reaction, a small loss of composure. His expression changed. Almost imperceptible, but it was there. She decided to push.

'You see, our attacker was incompetent last night. He messed up. Too arrogant and was outplayed by a young woman. He must be feeling pretty pathetic right now.'

But it was too late. The moment was gone as he realized she was bluffing.

'What have you got to hold me on? What evidence? What are you charging me with? You have to charge me, or let me go, right?'

Pope stood up, this time she was buying herself a few moments.

Waterson watched her and his demeanour suddenly changed. He addressed Brody, a renewed aggression appearing in his voice, in his body language.

'Did your boss tell you what happened to Tina, my daughter? Did she tell you?'

Brody looked at him, then at Pope.

'No, I bet she didn't. Murdered by some psychopath. He murdered three other girls as well. They never found the killer. Did she tell you that?'

Brody said nothing.

'Do you know why? Because her twat of a boss decided it was me. Her fucking father! Spent all his time chasing me. And little princess over there was too wet behind the ears to know one end of a murder investigation from another. Fucking joke, the lot of you. Seven years ago and you still have nothing. You've given up.'

He slumped, at last some genuine emotion.

Pope concluded the interview and switched off the tape. She asked the two officers in the room to escort Mick Waterson out of the building.

'We're letting you go for the moment, Mick. But don't go too far. We'll need to talk to you again.'

He stood up and walked towards the door, guided by one of the officers with their hand on his arm. He shrugged it off and glared back at Pope.

'Seven years. Seven years. Do your fucking job.' He stalked out of the interview room.

Brody walked over to Pope. 'I was right. That was fun.'
'Wasn't it?'
'What do you think?'

'I think he's proved that he's aggressive, and we know he's capable of violence. I'm pretty sure that he threatened the guy he beat up last year so that he wouldn't talk. And the lawyer stunt concerns me. It's a double bluff. *I'm going to make like I don't need a lawyer, to suggest innocence.*'

'Yeah, that was odd, given the circumstances and his history with you. Most people would want someone in there with them. What about motive?' said Brody.

Pope thought for a moment. 'No obvious motive, but he hates me and the personal nature of this, the cards. . . the photograph. It's a pretty extreme form of revenge. . . but he's got to be in the frame at the moment.'

Brody didn't look entirely convinced.

'Miller's looking deeper into him. We'll wait and see what comes up. In the meantime, get a car outside his house and watch him. I want to know everywhere he goes, who he sees.'

'Will do.'

'Christ,' said Pope. 'Let's go and get a cup of coffee. A strong one.'

CHAPTER 15

Pope poured herself a coffee and sat down behind her desk. She checked her phone again. Still nothing from Miller. She texted him to do a check on Edward Boyd and to send a couple of officers round to see what Boyd was up to. Then she opened the book that Darke had given her. She needed to learn a little more about what she was dealing with.

She was just about to start reading the chapter outlining the sheer enjoyment some people get out of killing another human being when her mobile phone started to ring. She saw that it was Miller and pushed the answer button.

'Miller,' said Pope.

'We've got a problem,' said the voice on the other end.

* * *

Pope pulled up at the entrance to King's Hospital, jumped out of the car and walked quickly to the reception desk. It was just past 2 p.m. She checked in and took the stairs two at a time to the fourth floor, where she found Miller and a new officer outside Karen Tarling's empty hospital room.

'Where is she?' asked Pope.

'She's been taken into surgery,' replied Miller.

'What happened, exactly?'

'She began to come round from the sedative, but as she started to wake up she had difficulty breathing. She used the emergency cord to call the nurses, that's the first anybody knew of it. Dr Leigh said it appeared that her breathing was getting worse, a result of the injuries she sustained during the attack. They rushed her into surgery. She says she'll let us know as soon as they know anything for sure.'

Pope's frustration was palpable. 'I really need to talk to her. This is our one break so far. Our one possible lead. Did they say how long she'd be in theatre?'

'No,' replied Miller. 'But Leigh suggested it could be a while.'

Pope took a deep breath. She sat down on one of the grey plastic chairs provided for relatives. Uncomfortable and miserable. *Fitting*, she thought.

Miller looked at Pope. 'Do you want to go back to the station? I can wait here.'

'I'm staying.' It didn't invite discussion. She looked at her watch and sighed. Took out her phone and sent several messages to Brody, Fletcher and Alex, in that order. It was Saturday afternoon, and she was outside an empty room in a hospital, waiting to find out if her only witness in a multiple murder case would actually be able to tell her anything. Her head throbbed. She closed her eyes.

It was over an hour before Leigh appeared in the corridor.

'DCI Pope, DS Miller,' she said. No handshake this time.

'How is she?' asked Pope.

'Her internal injuries are more serious than our initial examination suggested. The fact that she was sedated means that we didn't catch this as early as we might otherwise have done. When she woke up from the sedation, she clearly had trouble breathing unaided and was unable to speak. We've now X-rayed her and she has a fractured hyoid bone and her larynx is also damaged. In addition, she's suffered a pulmonary oedema. The injuries have caused a build-up of fluid in the lungs. The surgeon has operated on the fracture and that went well. However, the pulmonary oedema left her with acute difficulty breathing. He's had to intubate her and give her further sedation for the fluid to drain fully and give her time for her breathing to return to normal.'

Pope was worried both for Karen Tarling the person, and for Karen Tarling the witness. 'Will she be OK?'

'She should make a full recovery, but that will need a little time.'

'How long until I can talk to her?'

'She's in the postoperative intensive care unit at the moment. Once she's stronger, we'll bring her back up here. After that, it's difficult to be specific as it largely depends on how well she responds to the treatment. But I'd guess at least twenty-four to thirty-six hours before we can remove the tube and then we'll have to see how she is.' Leigh left them with this and hurried off to continue with her rounds.

'What next?' said Miller.

Pope thought about what Leigh had said. Twenty-four to thirty-six hours, and then no guarantee that Karen Tarling would be in a fit state to answer any questions. Just then, she felt her phone vibrate in her pocket.

'Fletcher,' she said to Miller. 'Give me a minute.'

'I've organized for us to be interviewed by the local news media for the evening bulletin,' he told her after he was caught up to speed.

'As the senior supervising officer on the case,' he said, cutting off her protests, 'it would be useful to have you there to reassure the public that everything possible was being done to find the killer. I also want your assistance in quashing this ridiculous nickname: the Cameraman.' This particularly seemed to annoy Fletcher. 'You can emphasize the other aspects of the case and play down that one.'

Reluctantly, Pope agreed.

'Be at the station by five thirty.' Fletcher hung up and Pope looked at her watch. She texted Alex to tell him roughly what time she would likely get home. Then she called Brody. She told him about Karen Tarling.

'What are you working on?' she asked.

'I'm trying to get some background on her. At the moment I can't find anything that links her with Susan Harper or Linda Wilson. They all existed in totally separate work and social circles. I'm not sure there really is a link. It looks more and more like he chose his victims at random. Which begs the question, how did he choose them? I'm having trouble finding any common denominators whatsoever.'

'There must be something,' said Pope. 'Something which connects the three of them.'

'Maybe,' said Brody. 'I'll keep looking.'

'You should go home, Brody. Go for a drink or something. Relax and take your mind off the case.'

'Is that what you're going to do?' he asked.

'I wish. I've got the excitement of an interview with Fletcher and the local TV news. And then I need to get home and see if World War Three has broken out between Alex and Chloe.'

Brody laughed. 'Maybe I'll go home and watch the local news,' he said.

This time it was her turn to laugh. 'I'm headed back now. You need to go home. Seriously. Haven't you got a documentary on JFK you could obsess over?'

She ended the call and put on her jacket.

'Miller, can you organize an officer to be outside Karen Tarling's room for the night? And did you get my message about Edward Boyd?'

'Yes and yes. I already have a team in place to check up on him and pay him a visit.'

'Good work. In that case, go home and enjoy what is left of your Saturday afternoon,' said Pope.

Miller looked pleased. He would call his long-suffering girlfriend and hope that she was free this evening. They would go for a drink, maybe the cinema and a good meal.

Pope called the lift and waited for it to arrive. She saw a vague resemblance to herself in the brushed-steel doors. She hoped she didn't look as dishevelled as the fractured reflection made her appear. She wondered if that made her vain.

The lift arrived and the doors opened. A middle-aged male doctor and a younger female nurse got out, laughing about a joke they'd shared on the way up. As she got in and waited for the doors to close, her mind flashed to what Tobias Darke had said about the possibility of the killer targeting someone close to her. She felt a rising knot of tension. As soon as the interview was finished, she would go straight back home to Alex and the girls.

CHAPTER 16

Pope felt exhausted. The interview had been delayed thanks to a technical fault with one of the cameras. The crew had attempted to repair it onsite, but eventually decided they had to send for a replacement. All this took over an hour, and by the time they had finished, it was past 7 p.m. The interview had taken too long. And she hadn't eaten.

Now she just wanted to be home.

At last she pulled up outside her front door. Was it too much to hope Alex and Chloe had sorted out what happened last night without her? *Selfish*, she admonished herself, and got out of the car.

Alex and Hannah were watching the final of *Strictly Come Dancing*. One of Pope's least favourite shows. It was designed specifically for a demographic that was supposed to, but did not, include her.

'Hi,' she said to Hannah, as she kissed Alex hello. She went into the kitchen and found a beer in the fridge. She drank it standing at the countertop, while the other two watched the show.

'Where's Chloe?' asked Pope.

'She's upstairs with Tyler. The door's open,' he added, looking at Pope. 'I've told her he's got to be out by 11 p.m.'

Alex got up from the sofa and came over, refilled his glass of wine. He spoke in hushed tones, so as not to be overheard by Hannah, who was deep into the realms of ballroom dancing.

'We had a long chat this morning. I told her I was angry, worried and that this must not happen again. I was going to ground her, but she seemed genuinely sorry and so amenable, that I relented. Hence Tyler's visit.' Pope listened and nodded.

'Thanks again for going to get her last night. I wouldn't have known where to start looking. I was so relieved when she came home. Perhaps that's why I was a bit easy on her. From what she said, I think she's learned her lesson. Time will tell, I guess.'

'She started off pretty belligerent in the car,' said Pope, although she instantly regretted saying it when she saw Alex's reaction, adding, 'But she soon saw that she'd made an error of judgement. I've seen a lot worse.'

He put his arm around her waist. 'How was your day?'

'Long, tedious, frustrating.' She explained in broad terms how the case was going and about the setback with their witness, and described the debacle of the TV interview.

'Bec is on the ten o' clock news later,' Alex called over to Hannah. 'We'll have to gather round for a family viewing,' he said, smiling and giving Pope a squeeze.

'Great, thanks,' she said, without enthusiasm.

Alex looked at her. 'It's Sunday tomorrow. Will you be at home? It would be good to have a family day. We haven't had one of those for a while.'

Pope hesitated. 'I hope so, but I may have to go in for a few hours. This case is in its early stages, so it kind of depends on any developments, and how our witness is doing in hospital. But I'll try.'

'Will Fletcher be at work tomorrow?'

She knew what he was getting at. 'I doubt it. But his job and mine are very different. He deals with public relations and administrative work, resources. I'm the one actually in charge of the team, in charge of the case. I have to find this guy before he kills again. It's difficult to take days off at this stage.' She kept her voice low.

Alex looked exasperated. 'I understand that. I know someone has to do that part of the job. But does it always have to be you?'

'Alex. . .'

'You should take the promotion Fletcher offered you.'

Pope started to protest, but he kept talking.

'It would mean more money, regular hours and no calls at 1 a.m. where you have to leap out of bed and rush to a horrific crime scene.' He'd clearly had a couple of glasses of wine and was telling it as he saw it.

'You've been playing the hero for twenty years, Bec. Maybe it's time for someone else to have a go. You can still do a lot of good in the new role.'

"The new role", as if it were already in place, as if she'd already agreed to take the job.

'Maybe I like playing the hero.' Pope said, with a smile.

He took his arm away from her waist and took a step back. 'This isn't only about you.'

'Alex. I understand what you're saying. And of course it isn't only about me. But can you really see me behind a desk? I'd be bored rigid. I'm a Homicide detective, and that's what I like being. I'd hate senior management.' Just saying it sounded ridiculous.

He looked away, focused on the TV. Pope went to him and this time put her arm around his waist.

'I'll tell you what,' she said. He looked at her. 'Let me work this case. I can't do anything until this is all over anyway. After we've caught this guy, we'll sit down and talk properly. How does that sound?' She kissed him, and he let her.

She knew he had a pretty good idea that he was being played, and that she was simply buying time. He seemed to let it go for the moment. A battle for another day.

'Let's go and watch your star turn on the BBC.'

Pope groaned and allowed herself be pulled to the sofa.

They watched the end of the dance show, with Alex and Hannah discussing the merits of the various performances and disagreeing with the judges' decisions, discussing technique and application like experienced critics. Pope found her thoughts wandering back to the case, how she might make progress in the investigation while they waited for Karen Tarling to recover and speak to them. She knew she'd be at work tomorrow. Sunday.

She was brought back by the theme music and saw the credits roll.

'Bec, you're on next,' Hannah said with a level of excitement Pope didn't feel was warranted.

'It's only brief, and pretty dull,' she said. 'It might not even be on if they haven't got it ready for broadcast.'

'Don't be a killjoy, Bec. We like to see you up on the screen,' said Alex.

They watched the first story, about an impending strike on the London train network, including the underground. The management company had announced plans to cut jobs and make remaining drivers work longer hours, including nights and weekends. The train drivers were protesting. The second story was about the weather expected in London overnight. A hurricane that had wreaked havoc in the Caribbean and southern Florida had crossed the Atlantic and some of the winds were still blowing. It wasn't strictly still a hurricane, but the winds remained powerful and were predicted to cause some disruption to trees and buildings. People were warned to take precautions. Pope was glad there were other stories deemed more important than her murder case. The more this was played down the better.

Then the newsreader introduced the story. Alex and Hannah seemed excited for her, but when the details were explained, their enthusiasm subsided somewhat. Hannah, in particular, looked nervous. The footage cut to a reporter outside Linda Wilson's house.

'This is where the serial killer, known as "the Cameraman", struck three nights ago.' The report described how the killer had attacked his victim, and linked it to Karen Tarling's attack and subsequent escape. Her current location was given only as 'a London hospital'. The reporter spoke with a sensationalist tone, more tabloid than broadsheet. There were some details, but this time only those that Pope and Fletcher had agreed to release. No evidence of a leak. Then it cut to the interview with Pope and Fletcher. She looked tired and drawn. More than tired — fatigued. Fletcher looked smart and well coiffed, sat upright, had just the right expression and body language. The non-verbal communication training course she had avoided. Fletcher did most of the talking. Then a question to Pope.

'DCI Pope, what can you tell us about how the investigation is progressing?'

She cleared her throat. 'There's not much I can add to what Superintendent Fletcher has told you. Except to say that we are pursuing a number of leads at this point.'

'Has the latest victim been able to tell you anything so far?' the interviewer asked.

'Not yet. She's still not in a condition to answer questions, but we hope to be able to talk to her very soon. I'd ask you to respect her privacy at this time. She's been through a great deal,' said Pope.

'Should the public be concerned?'

'I think Londoners should exercise the usual caution they do at any time. We live in a big city. Try not to travel alone, check who's at the door before you open it, the kind of precautions we all normally follow. As ever, if you're unsure about anything, call the police immediately.'

The report cut back to the newsreader, who wrapped up the segment and moved on to the next story.

Hannah looked at Pope. 'Is the Cameraman near us?' she asked. 'I mean, have any of his victims been anywhere near here?'

'No, Hannah, don't worry. He's not coming anywhere near us.'

'Are you going to catch him?' she asked, hope and concern mixed equally in her voice.

'Yes, I hope so. We've got a witness, and there's a very good chance that we'll be able to get a description from her. Hopefully then we can find him quickly. You've got absolutely nothing to worry about,' Pope reassured her.

They moved the conversation on, and it wasn't long before Hannah was engrossed in another TV programme, an American crime drama that bore very little relation to reality.

'Good job,' said Alex. She wasn't sure whether he was talking about the TV interview or her reassurance of Hannah. He handed her his empty wine glass.

'Any chance of a refill?'

Pope took his glass into the kitchen and uncorked the bottle. Outside the wind was becoming stronger and she moved to the window to take a look. The less substantial trees were swaying, and leaves were gusting along the ground. Something caught her eye. A bright flash of light floating in the darkness. She blinked and it disappeared. *Reflection of a headlight*, she thought. All this talk of Londoners keeping their eyes open must be getting inside her head.

She poured the wine and took the glass back to Alex. Sitting down next to him, she attempted to lose herself on the fictional, crime-ridden streets of New York.

* * *

He stood under the shadow of a large London plane tree. He held a mobile phone in one hand, the other thrust in his coat pocket as some protection against the increasingly fierce wind. The figure switched his gaze between the house and the screen in front of him. On that screen, he could see three figures sitting in their living room. The man and the woman were drinking wine, sitting on the sofa, watching TV. Next to them was a young girl. They were all absorbed in what they were watching, although he couldn't see what that was. There was one missing, he thought. He wondered where she might be.

He shifted from one foot to the other and leaned against the thick trunk of the tree. He watched for some time. At one point the woman disappeared from the screen and appeared in the window at the front of the house. He thrust the glowing phone into his coat. Had the light of it given him away? But the woman disappeared from the window, and looking back at the screen, he saw that she had sat down again. Oblivious.

He watched the scene. Happy family, *he thought. He would have to do something about that. He had one more thing to do, and then he would turn his attention to Bec Pope's happy family.*

* * *

It was 11 p.m. Pope was tired. She'd worked too hard, slept too little, drunk too much wine. Alex sensed it. He told Hannah to go upstairs and get ready for bed, then he called up for Chloe and reminded her that it was time for Tyler to go home. Some minutes later, Tyler popped his head around the door, said goodbye and left. Chloe didn't come down.

When they eventually got into bed, Alex moved close to Pope and put his arm on her stomach, tracing circles with his fingers. Neither of them spoke. His hand moved slowly downwards, continued past her waist. She was tired, but she was unable to resist him.

Afterwards, when Alex was asleep next to her, she lay thinking, listening to the howling wind outside. It was very much a city storm, the sound of the wind punctuated with car alarms and large plastic rubbish bins being blown over. She thought of all the horrific things she had read earlier in the book she had been given by Tobias Darke, and the raging winds outside seemed a poetic background. She tried to push out of her head the two thoughts that she sensed were keeping her from sleep. First, would he be one of the serial killers Pope had read about who are never caught? Second, was Darke right about the killer escalating?

It was after 2 a.m. when Bec Pope finally found sleep.

CHAPTER 17

Pope was walking towards a warehouse. A storm was raging.
The winds screamed, an impression of wolves howling. She
looked around but couldn't see anything except the warehouse. The rain fell out of the sky and although the wind
was strong, the rain fell completely vertically, in huge quanti-
ties. Pools of water were gathering on the ground, wet, black
gravel giving beneath her feet.

She was aware that the storm seemed to have no end.
The sky was inky black, the night mixing with the rain to
obscure any light from celestial bodies. The roar was all she
could hear, although she was aware of her own heartbeat:
powerful, fast, erratic.

Then she was at the warehouse door. Rusted steel and
timber, with the wooden supports rotting away. She reached
out to open it. The handle felt sticky to the touch, a gelati-
nous slime that had been made viscous by the falling water.
She pulled the door towards her and hesitated. She could
hear something else now. Screaming, mixed with the howls
from outside. Human? Animal? Something else? She couldn't
tell. She listened, inched forward.

Pope was sweating now, had to wipe her forehead to
keep the salt from entering her eyes. Her vision now blurred,

she was vaguely aware of someone over her, but that was impossible. She looked up, but could only see the sky above. There was no roof, although the rain was not coming into the building.

Then she saw where the screaming was coming from. Tina Waterson was lying on the floor, her hands and feet bound by waxed rope. She sounded like a wild animal. The screams were not human, not like any human Pope had ever heard.

Standing over Waterson was a figure she couldn't make out. Tall, strong, with an animalistic presence. The figure had his hands around Tina Waterson's neck. She was trying to scream, but there was no sound.

Pope tried to call out, but was unable to make any sound either. She tried to walk towards Waterson, but could not move. It was as if her feet were cemented to the floor. The figure then seemed to become aware of her presence. Turned and looked straight at her, although Pope couldn't make out his features. Then he let his hands fall from Tina Waterson's neck and he turned towards Pope. He started walking in her direction. She saw the figure take something out of his pocket. A gun. Pope put her hand in her own pocket, reached for the gun she thought she had. It wasn't there. She frantically searched each pocket in turn, as the man walked inexorably forward. He sped up. Pope couldn't move, couldn't turn away. The gun was drawn, lifted, pointed at her chest. Nearer, faster. He was so close now that Pope saw him curl his finger around the trigger, saw him position the gun between his eye and Pope's heart. She couldn't explain how, but she felt the force being applied to the trigger. Then there was a flash and she saw the bullet leave the barrel.

She was woken by a loud bang. She sat up immediately.

'Jesus!' exclaimed Pope, looking around the room wildly, expecting to see a figure in the dark pointing a gun at her. When she realized she had been dreaming, she let her body relax a little, although she could feel her heart racing. It had been one of the most vivid, disturbing dreams she had experienced in a long time. She thought about what she'd dreamed. Pope didn't need Freud to work it out.

Then she heard the bang again. She realized that the noise she had first heard had not been simply in her dream. It was coming from downstairs.

She looked at the clock. 3 a.m. She looked over at Alex, who was sleeping deeply. She got out of bed, pulled on the nearest shirt she could find, and silently crept out of the bedroom.

She padded to the top of the stairs. A light was coming from below. Had they left the light on last night? Slowly, all senses heightened, she stole down the stairs. One step at a time, listening. At the bottom of the staircase she hesitated. Nothing. She walked into the open-plan kitchen/living room, ready for something, although she had no idea what. She scanned the room. Nothing out of the ordinary. She left and walked into the dining room. Again nothing. She checked the front door. It was firmly closed, with the bolt, attached to the inside of the frame, drawn across.

Pope exhaled, felt she hadn't taken a breath since she walked out of the bedroom. Then she heard the noise again. This time close. In the living room.

She picked up a large umbrella from the corner of the hall. She wasn't sure exactly what she'd do with it, but it was all she had. She lunged into the room, brandishing the umbrella. There was jolt of movement in the corner of the room. She spun round, held the umbrella out in front of her and braced herself, tensed and ready.

It was the curtain blowing into the room. She walked over and drew it back.

The French doors to the garden had blown open in the strong wind. There was a lock, but it had obviously been left undone recently and worked itself loose in the storm. She looked outside, into the rear garden, but saw nothing unusual. She closed the door, making a mental note to fit a more secure lock.

Pope looked down at the umbrella in her hand and felt very foolish. She replaced it where she had found it, glad that

142

no one had seen her. She went back upstairs. She checked in both Chloe and Hannah's rooms. Both of them were asleep, getting a far better night's sleep than she was going to have. She longed for the days before responsibility when she had been able to sleep through the night. When was the last time she had woken feeling refreshed and ready for the day? She got back into bed and pulled the covers over herself. She listened to the howls of the wind outside and closed her eyes.

* * *

That had been close. A little too close. He reminded himself that was what happened if you were spontaneous, if you didn't plan carefully enough. He had been watching the house from outside. But then he was overtaken with an intense desire to go inside. To breathe the same air, to see the house for real, not simply on a screen. To sit in their chairs and look where they looked.

He waited until the lights had gone out, and then he waited some more. His patience meant he had been able to do exactly what he had wanted for so many years, without impediment or discovery. So, he waited.

The screen showed two people asleep. It had taken a while, particularly for her to go to sleep, but he assumed Bec Pope had a few things on her mind. He hadn't watched them make love. His personal moral code deemed that unacceptable.

He left it some time, until he was sure they were both asleep, and then he walked around the back of the house. French windows. He was not particularly experienced in breaking and entering, but he knew what he was doing, and he thought French windows were relatively easy to open. And indeed they were. Slipping the latch, he stepped inside the house. He gently closed the door behind him and looked around the room. He recognized it from viewing them. But of course, he had been in here before. Left the cameras. They had been out that day. But being here while they were upstairs made the hairs on the back of his neck stand up. He felt bold enough to switch on a lamp in the corner of the room.

He treaded silently around the room. He opened cupboards, looked inside. He walked over to the sofa and sat down. This is where Bec Pope had sat earlier. Where Alex and Hannah had also sat, as they watched TV. He inhaled deeply. He could smell them, smell the family, the contentment they felt in one another, the ease with which they navigated through their world.

He got up and went to a dresser placed by the wall on one side of the room. There was a picture in a frame: four people, two adults and two children, girls. They were on holiday somewhere hot and sunny, the picture taken in a rustic restaurant with red-and-white-checked table-cloths. They were all raising a glass to the camera. It was probably taken by the waiter. He picked it up and ran his fingers over the figures in the picture. He wished he had not been wearing gloves, so he could really feel the photograph. Really feel the family. His finger moved over the picture, first to the woman, then he moved to the man, and to the younger girl. Finally, he let his finger rest on the older girl.

Suddenly there was a loud bang. He turned to see the door to the garden had been buffeted by the wind and had crashed against the door frame.

He replaced the photograph and moved silently to the door. He slipped out, drew the curtains back into position, and pulled the door to, leaving it slightly ajar, to account for the noise.

As he crept through the garden, he realized that he had left the light on. There was no time to go back. He climbed over the wall of the garden and then was hurrying away from the house.

Now, back in the safety of his car, he took his mobile phone out of his pocket. On the screen, Bec Pope was walking around the room he had just been in, holding an umbrella. He continued to watch until she left and went back upstairs.

He put the phone back in his pocket. His breathing had returned to normal now. He knew they would meet for real next time.

CHAPTER 18

Sunday. Early. Pope was woken by Alex curling his arm around her and burying his head in the crook of her neck. *Not a bad way to start the day*, she thought. They lay for a while, Pope slowly waking up as she recalled the vivid dream she had last night, and her adventure downstairs armed with an umbrella. She decided not to mention either to Alex.

'Coffee?' she asked.

'Mmmm, yes please.'

As Pope disentangled herself from Alex, he turned over and pulled the covers over his head. Pope looked at the clock. 7.30 a.m. A lie-in, for her.

She walked downstairs, opened the curtains and filled the coffee maker with water and ground coffee beans. As it went to work, she instinctively walked to the French doors on to the garden and checked the lock. All fine. There was something nagging her about last night. The doors coming open. It had never happened before. On the other hand, there had been no one there, nothing missing, nothing disturbed.

Her thoughts were interrupted by the machine buzzing to tell her the coffee was ready. She poured two cups and took them upstairs. She placed one on the table beside Alex's side of the bed and climbed back under the covers with her cup.

The coffee tasted good, and she was almost able to relax.

Pope checked her phone. No messages. That was good. She knew she would have to go into work at some point today, but she had been hoping for a couple of hours of respite, and this seemed now to be within the realms of possibility.

She opened the news app on her phone and tapped the section for local news. The first item was her case. It had obviously been bumped up now the weather had calmed down and nobody would be quite so interested in the train strike on a Sunday. She read the article. It was brief, but had the relevant facts. She was mentioned by name, as was Fletcher and the other victims. Something positive.

She put the phone down and folded herself into Alex's arms. She was just drifting back to sleep when she was disturbed by the ringtone from her mobile phone. Alex looked out from under the covers and his expression said enough. Pope picked up her phone and checked the caller ID. It was Adam Miller. Karen Tarling must be awake. She answered quickly.

'Hi, Adam. Is she awake?'

'No. I'm phoning about something else,' said Miller, his voice hesitant.

'What is it?' asked Pope.

'It's your father. He's been admitted to hospital. I think you need to get down here.'

* * *

She drove up to the front of the hospital and parked for the third time in two days. She knew her father was ill, knew he was keeping something from her. At least now she might find out what was going on.

Pope entered King's Hospital through the main doors and went to the reception desk, and was directed to a ward on the third floor. It was mercifully quiet at this time on a Sunday. She texted Miller that she had arrived and would find him to see how Karen Tarling was later.

Exiting the lift on the third floor, Pope followed the signs to a large ward on the left-hand side of the corridor. A rather severe sister at the nurses' station informed her that visiting hours began at 2 p.m. Pope showed her warrant card, explained that she was busy investigating a serial murderer, so she couldn't come back at 2 p.m. to see her father. Her dramatic explanation seemed to do the trick and the nurse led her to bed fourteen.

John Pope didn't look particularly ill. He looked his usual self. She sat down on the chair next to the bed.

'Hello, Dad.'

'Bec. What on earth are you doing here? I told them not to bother you.' Her father looked genuinely concerned to see her. 'You should be at home on a Sunday morning with the family, not in this godforsaken place.'

'For God's sake. You're in hospital, I've no idea why. Of course I'm going to be here. There isn't exactly any other family to visit you, is there?' Pope took a breath and bit back her emotions. She tried again. 'So, what's going on?'

'Nothing serious,' said her father, brushing Pope's concern aside. 'They're simply doing some tests. Probably worrying over nothing.'

'If it's nothing, why were you brought in early on a Sunday morning as an emergency?' asked Pope, her frustration mounting. 'Just give me a straight answer. Why are you in here?'

He looked at her. They hadn't been close, nothing like it, for many years. Her father leaving when Pope was twelve years old had pretty much sealed the deal for their relationship. Still, outside Alex and the girls, he was the only real family she had left. Pope was sure that she detected some genuine emotion in her father's eyes.

'Bec. You shouldn't keep pushing me about this.'

'Dad. I'm forty-one years old. I've been a police officer for almost twenty years. I'm a detective chief inspector and I investigate homicides. I don't think I need protecting.' She softened a little. 'Just tell me.'

John Pope paused. He seemed to be making a decision, calculating how much longer he could avoid telling his daughter. He evidently decided that he had run out of time.

'I've been feeling unwell for a while,' he admitted. 'I've had chest pains a few times in the last couple of months and a cough I can't get rid of.' Another pause. 'Bec, you remember that I used to smoke when you were younger? When I was living at home?'

Pope's heartbeat quickened with an immediacy that surprised her. She felt suddenly nervous. She knew what her father was going to say. She nodded.

John Pope continued. 'Last night the chest pains got worse, and I was finding it difficult to breathe, so I called an ambulance.'

'Why didn't you call me?' Pope asked.

Her father brushed aside her protests with a dismissive wave of his hand. The John Pope she remembered.

'They brought me in here, but by the time I got here I felt much better. They gave me some oxygen in the ambulance and that did the trick. I could do with some of that at home.' He smiled.

Pope wasn't in the mood for jokes. 'What do the tests say?'

'They think I've got something wrong with my lungs,' he said.

It was like pulling teeth. 'Either tell me what they think it is, or I'll go and ask the doctor right now.'

It seemed difficult for her father, but Pope had to know.

'They're investigating several possibilities,' he said.

Pope sighed and got up as if to leave.

'Bec, sit down. OK. They think, but they're not sure, it might be lung cancer.' Her father seemed to sag a little after telling her. The act of saying it out loud made it something different, something real.

Pope looked at him. 'Christ, Dad. How long have you known?'

'I had an idea. But I didn't know for sure. I had some tests last week. They seem to have confirmed it.'

148

Pope wasn't sure how to react. She wasn't close enough to her father to break down, to be overwhelmed. But he was still her father.

They talked for a while, Pope navigating her feelings, trying to talk to her father and process how she felt at the same time. She was somewhat relieved to be interrupted by a doctor walking towards them. She held a clipboard and had a cheerful expression on her face.

'Mr Pope. How are you today?' she asked, smiling. She looked at Pope, waited for her to introduce herself.

'I'm Bec Pope,' she said.

'My daughter,' explained her father, when she offered no further explanation. 'She's come here to worry for the two of us.'

'Hello, Ms Pope. I'm Dr Hopkins. It's not really visiting hours, but Nurse Andrews explained your situation. Actually, it's quite good timing. Are you happy for your daughter to stay while we talk, Mr Pope?'

'Yes, it's fine,' he said, although Pope got the strong impression that he would much prefer her not to be there.

'Right. As the doctor discussed with you last week, there does seem to be something on your lung.' She flicked between the pages on the clipboard. 'It appears as a shadow on the X-ray. It's not very large, but it's definitely there.' She had a good, business-like manner, thought Pope. Straight talking without being patronizing.

'We're going to do a biopsy, in order to establish exactly what we're dealing with. Then we'll have a much clearer picture of what this is and how we can treat it.'

'My father said you thought it was lung cancer . . .' said Pope. She hadn't meant to be so direct.

'The tests last week and the X-ray we've taken suggest that might be a possibility. We'll know for sure when we've carried out the biopsy,' replied Hopkins.

'When will that be?' asked Pope. Her father didn't seem to be saying anything, so she took over, almost without thinking.

'Not until tomorrow or the next day, I'm afraid.' Hopkins turned to her patient. 'We're going to keep you in until then, to ensure your breathing has stabilized. Also, if you're already here, it's likely that it will happen sooner. As soon as we can fit you in.'

'I hope the food's good,' said her father.

'It could be worse,' said Hopkins cheerfully, as she wrote something down on his charts. She placed the clipboard into a basket at the bottom of his bed. He thanked her, and she left to continue her rounds. Pope watched her go, thinking she looked hassled and overworked.

Pope looked at her father, unsure what to say. She had a sense of her life changing. One of those moments where, afterwards, nothing would be the same. The need to be there for her father tugged at the reality that he had never been there for her. At least not in the last thirty years. *Thirty years.* Had it been that long ago that her father had left? He had more or less absented himself from her life, despite the fact that they had lived in the same city. He had lived just over the river from her when her mother had been admitted into a hospital ward not unlike this one. Just over the river, but always too busy to be by his daughter's side. And yet. Loyalty crashing up against a sense of betrayal and abandonment.

It was her mobile phone ringing that brought her back from these thoughts. With the disapproving looks of the nursing staff and other patients directed at her with full force, she checked the screen. It was Miller. She answered. One of the nurses turned to her colleague and said something seemingly conspiratorial, looking over at Pope.

'I can't really talk now,' she said.

'It's Karen Tarling. She's awake.'

CHAPTER 19

Pope jogged up the stairs to the fourth floor and pushed open the large double doors leading on to the wards. She hesitated, until she saw a sign to the ward she was looking for. It struck her that such a labyrinthine system was a particularly unnecessary obstacle for those who were ill, or who were desperately worried about their loved ones being ill. She eventually found the room. Miller and another officer in uniform were standing outside. Miller came forward to meet her.

'How's your dad?' asked Miller.

'A conversation for another time. How's she doing?'

'She's just woken up. They're about to remove the tube from her mouth. We can't talk to her yet, but the doctor says that if it goes well, she should be able to speak after the tube's out.' Miller was breathless, expectant. He was delivering important news.

'So, she hasn't said anything yet?' clarified Pope.

'No. Nothing,' said Miller.

Dr Leigh was inside Karen Tarling's room as Pope and Miller waited outside. Pope watched a nurse change the pack attached to her intravenous drip, a clear liquid, which was attached to a holder at about head height. It was too slow and Pope was desperate to get in and talk to Karen Tarling, the anticipation fizzing. The nurse squeezed the bag gently, followed the liquid passing down the tube, and Leigh seemed to be giving the nurse in the room instructions, and once satisfied, eventually came outside.

Pope looked expectantly at Leigh when she came out.

'Hello, DCI Pope. Good to see you again.' She had a good memory for names, thought Pope.

'Dr Leigh. How's she doing?'

'Well, she's not bad under the circumstances. She'll be in pain for a while, as a result of the tube that was in her throat, but I've given her some painkillers and hopefully they will kick in soon. She's been through a great deal, with one thing and another,' she added.

'Can I speak to her?'

'You can try. It'll be very uncomfortable for her to talk for a while and she can only talk in a whisper. You might find it difficult to understand what she's saying. I had a hard time in there with that just now. The damage to her larynx means that her voice will take some time to recover properly. But you have to remember what she's been through. She's quite traumatized.'

Pope looked at Leigh, raised her eyebrows.

'OK, I know you get all this, DCI Pope. But I'm just looking after my patient. I'm sure you'll be sensitive,' said Leigh. She wasn't sure, Pope could tell. She knew this was Leigh's way of telling her to be careful, without using so many words.

'That's fine, Dr Leigh. I'll take it slowly. Thanks for your help,' said Pope.

'The nurse is in there if you need anything.'

Karen Tarling looked awful. She had bruising around her throat, large dark circles under her eyes and her lips were dry and cracked. She looked like she had been punched several times. There was a cut above her forehead and she looked like her nose had been broken. Her breathing was laboured and each time she breathed in, she winced. She was clearly in a lot of pain.

Pope pulled up a chair next to Tarling's bed and introduced herself, as Miller pulled out his notebook and a black pen and settled himself by the wall.

'Ms Tarling. I'm DCI Rebecca Pope, this is Sergeant Adam Miller.' She spoke quietly, gently, but with authority. 'I'm very sorry about what happened. I'd just like to ask you a few questions, if that's OK with you. We want to try and find this guy as quickly as possible.'

Karen Tarling looked away, a tear rolling down her cheek. Pope noticed there was a box of tissues on the table by the bed, so offered the box to her. Karen shook her head and wiped the tear away with the back of her right hand, the one that didn't have the drip attached to it.

'Are you OK, Ms Tarling?' asked Pope.

She said something. It was almost inaudible and Pope had no idea what she had said. She leaned forward.

'Sorry, I didn't catch that,' she said.

'Karen.'

'How are you feeling, Karen?' said Pope.

'Terrible.' This time she heard her, just.

'Sorry to hear that. I wonder if you could tell us what happened. Just before you came to the hospital.'

Karen hesitated, looked at Pope. It was a lot to ask of her. But Pope had no choice.

Tarling seemed to summon up her reserves of energy.

'There's not much I can tell you.' Slowly, quietly, painfully. 'There was a knock at the door. . . a man. When I opened the door, he punched me. . . I was on the floor and he was standing over me. He kneeled down and hit me again.' She took a long time to form her words. Now she stopped, clearly distressed.

'I know this is really hard, Karen,' said Pope sympathetically. 'Do you need a drink of water?'

Karen nodded, and Pope passed her some water. She winced as she drank, but the relief of the drink was stronger than the pain of drinking. She placed the cup on the tray and leaned back against her pillows.

'What happened then, Karen? What do you remember?' asked Pope.

'His hands around my neck. . . strong. . . hands around my throat. I tried to push him off. I couldn't.' She wiped her eyes again but was determined to go on. Pope wasn't sure whether it was the pain or the memory that provoked the tears. Maybe both.

'But I'd done self-defence. . . at work. I punched him in the throat as hard as I could and he let go. I got up and kicked him in the balls and ran out. I thought he would be right behind me, but he wasn't.' She shrank down.

The nurse stepped in from the doorway. 'I think Karen's had enough questions for now. She needs some rest.'

'Just one more question.' Pope looked appealingly at the nurse, who hesitated then nodded.

'Did you get a good look at this man, Karen? Can you describe him?'

'He was wearing a balaclava. I'm sorry.'

Her key witness hadn't seen the killer's face. Pope thought she visibly deflated. She was sure Karen Tarling must have noticed. She tried to be upbeat.

'What about the rest of him? Was he tall? White? Black? Well built or slim? Anything else you noticed?' asked Pope.

Tarling thought for a bit. 'Quite tall, taller than me. White, I think. I could see his eyes, his neck. He was strong. Sorry, I didn't see much. It was so quick.' She looked exhausted, and started coughing again. Pope knew one thing: Mick Waterson matched the description.

'OK, DCI Pope, time to go. Karen needs some peace and quiet.' The nurse was firm now.

'That's fine,' said Pope. 'Thank you, Karen. I hope you recover swiftly. There will be an officer outside your room until you're discharged, in case you remember anything else. Any detail, no matter how small.'

The nurse refilled Karen Tarling's water and helped her to settle back in her bed. Then she ushered Pope and Miller out of the room like troublesome children. As Pope reached the door, she heard Karen say something. She turned back.

'I was lucky, wasn't I?'

'Yes, Karen. Very lucky.'

'Let's get a coffee,' said Pope to Miller, once they were out in the hallway.

They found the cafeteria on the ground floor. It was a large area, with a long metal serving counter along one edge. There were two people behind the counter, busy preparing the area. It was still early, well before general visiting hours, so the place was almost empty.

Pope walked up to one of the members of staff and ordered two coffees. She paid and joined Miller at a table by the window overlooking a bedraggled flowerbed on the far side of the cafeteria where they would not be disturbed or overheard.

Outside it was starting to rain. The drops were heavy, and Pope noticed a few leaves begin to sag under the weight of the water. Beyond the flowerbeds stood a small plastic shelter for those who wished to smoke. There were more people crammed in there than there were in the large cafeteria. Pope thought that probably told her something about the human condition, but she wasn't quite sure what it was. She took a sip of her coffee and screwed up her face. Why did hospitals always serve such terrible coffee?

'What do you think?' asked Miller.

'Awful coffee.'

He smiled. 'What Karen Tarling had to say. It doesn't give us much to go on.'

'No, it doesn't. She's in shock, but she seems pretty lucid. There is always the possibility that she'll remember something else once she starts to feel a bit better, but I'm not holding out much hope. I didn't get the feeling that she was vague or disorientated. I think she's fairly tough,' said Pope.

Miller took out his notebook and leafed to the page where he had taken notes of their interview. 'Tall. White, athletic build. Wearing a balaclava,' he read aloud. 'That's about it. Doesn't narrow it down much, but do you think it matches Mick Waterson?'

Pope looked out of the window. 'We know more than we knew before. Send a car to pick up Waterson. We'll need to push him harder and see what he has to say. I need to get back to my father for a while. You go back to the station and I'll meet you there. Can you call Brody and let him know?'

'I spoke to Brody earlier. He's already at the station. I'll let him know we're on the way and fill him in on Karen Tarling, sort out a car for Waterson. What's going on with your father?' asked Miller.

'He's downstairs on the third floor. They've got him in for tests but won't know much for a couple of days. Should know more then.' Pope didn't really want to get into her father's illness, certainly not before she had had time to process the information herself. Besides she didn't need any distractions at the moment. Her focus had to be on finding the man who had attacked Karen Tarling.

Miller sensed that his boss didn't want to talk about that anymore, so he changed the subject.

'I'm going to get this information out to everybody,' he said, getting up from his chair. Just then his phone rang. He answered, listened.

'It's Edward Boyd,' he said to Pope. 'He's entering St Paul's church in Deptford, where Susan Harper was found. We've got eyes on him now.'

Pope was stunned for a moment. Was this a coincidence? 'OK. Keep with him, see what he does, where he goes. We'll pay him a visit at home, catch him off guard.'

Miller relayed the instructions into his phone and ended the call.

'Christ! What's going on with him?'

'I think that's what we need to find out,' replied Pope.

Miller left. Pope looked down at the cup of coffee she had barely touched and prepared herself to see her father. She headed out of the cafeteria and walked down the stairs to the third floor and back to his ward. The nurse she had spoken to earlier watched her, but didn't say anything. Pope's father was reading the paper. He smiled when he saw her.

'How are you feeling?' Pope asked, as she sat down.

'Fine,' said her father. 'I really don't think I need to be in here. I should just leave and come back when they're ready to do the tests. This all seems like a waste of time.'

'You can't do that,' replied Pope. 'The doctor thinks you should be here for observation. Chest pains and difficulty breathing are not minor symptoms. Besides, the doctor said you were more likely to get the tests earlier if you were already in the hospital. You need to stay,' she added emphatically.

Her father looked like he was about to argue, but relented. 'OK, Bec. Have it your way. I'll stay here. But I'm bored. Tell me about your case. How did your interview with your witness go?'

Pope didn't want to talk about it with her father, but he had folded away his newspaper and was looking expectantly at her, and she didn't really have anything else to talk to him about.

'She's in bad shape. She's been attacked.'

'By the guy you're after? The Cameraman?' He indicated the newspaper he'd just been reading. 'It's all over the paper,' he added.

Pope attempted to conceal her irritation. 'Yes, we think it's the same guy. I don't really want to go into the details.'

'Oh, come on, Bec. Who am I going to tell in here? I need something to keep me from dying of boredom. They wake you up at 6 a.m., then leave you all day with nothing to do.'

'The MO of this attack has similarities with the other two murders we're investigating,' Pope relented stiffly. 'The way in which he attacked her suggests that it's the same guy.'

'Poor girl,' said her father. He seemed melancholy, thoughtful, as if the misfortune of Karen Tarling had reminded him of his own precarious position. 'You should go, Bec. Go home and be with the family.'

'I will later, but I'll stay for a while.'

'No, I insist. There's nothing you can do here, and you've got other, more important things to attend to. They're not going to be able to tell me anything useful for a couple of days. You need to have some time to relax, otherwise you won't have the reserves of energy you need to catch your killer.'

"My" killer, thought Pope.

It was a novelty to have her father take any real interest in her life, her work, even if it was only out of sheer boredom. She felt obliged to stay, but she did need to get back to the station, and then get home at some point today. In addition, if she was being honest with herself, she didn't really want to be in the hospital with her father. She needed a bit of space from this.

'OK. I've got to go into work for a little while actually,' said Pope.

'All work and no play,' said her father.

'You sound just like Alex.'

They said their goodbyes, a little stilted, a little too formal. Pope told him she would check in with the hospital and either visit him later today or tomorrow. He said tomorrow would be fine. Pope was relieved and tried not to show it.

She left the ward and went back up to Karen Tarling's room on the fourth floor. Outside stood Mike Hawley.

'PC Hawley. Your turn, eh?'

'Yes, ma'am. Sunday morning duty. Nothing better,' replied Hawley with a smile.

'Well, she's been through a lot,' said Pope. 'Keep an eye out. Don't leave until you get relieved, OK?' said Pope.

'DS Miller briefed me before he left. No problem.'

Pope looked around, looked in on Karen Tarling. She appeared to be asleep, a brief respite from the things she would remember the instant she woke up.

Pope left the hospital, again. She would drive to work and think about where the investigation needed to go next. Then she would go home and spend some time with Alex and the girls. Yes. That was her plan for the day.

The wind was strong and drove the rain into her face as she hurried across the tarmac. The trees were starting to bend as the wind increased and the leaves swirled across the car park and around her legs as she tried to avoid the pooling water. Pope reached her car and cursed when she couldn't immediately locate her car keys. She found them in her jacket pocket and climbed quickly into the car, shaking the water from her hair and drying her hands on her trousers. The sky was growing darker, an impending storm. She hoped she would get to the station before the weather became even more inhospitable.

Pope started the car and waited for the heater to bring some warmth. She felt chilled to the bone, damp, weary. She thought of Karen Tarling and the lack of the breakthrough evidence she had been counting on, of her father and the knot of complex emotions that his current situation brought up. Then of Edward Boyd showing up at the first crime scene.

Too much, Pope thought to herself. *Too much*.

CHAPTER 20

Pope drove through the driving rain, covered by a ceiling of thick, low, dark cloud. Ahead of her the high rises climbed, and there seemed to be no distinction between the buildings and the sky. It was one huge sheet of grey.

She pulled into the underground car park below Charing Cross Police Station, glad to be out of the storm. One inhospitable, gloomy environment replacing another, but at least this one was dry.

When she arrived at her office the first person she saw was Miller.

'Mick Waterson isn't at home or at the garage.'

'Where is he, then? Is Trish at home?'

'No. We've put out an APB on both of them.'

'Shit. We need to find him fast,' said Pope, more to herself than to Miller.

'I'm on it,' he said. 'Edward Boyd is at home.'

'Where's home?' asked Pope.

'Covent Garden. Just off Seven Dials.'

'Right. Let's see what he has to say. We can walk from here.'

Pope and Miller grabbed umbrellas, left the station and headed along St Martin's Lane. Pope briefed Miller on Boyd's history and the connection to her.

When they arrived at the smart apartment block in which Boyd's flat was situated, Miller looked up and let out a whistle.

'Serious money. How can he afford to live here after fifteen years in prison?'

'There's a lot about Edward Boyd that's difficult to explain. I think it's family money, but I'm not sure.'

Pope rang the bell. After a brief wait, a familiar voice came over the intercom.

'Rebecca Pope. What a surprise! Come on up.'

Miller looked in surprise at Pope, who pointed to the camera above their heads. They pushed open the door, heavy with dark oak and ornate iron bars. The residents wanted security, but they wanted it to look like decoration. They climbed four flights of stairs until they reached Boyd's door, which was slightly ajar. Pope knocked and they entered.

The flat was spotless. Modern, minimalist, expensive. Everything placed very carefully and designed for effect. This was a statement about the owner, and it said control.

As she walked into the living room, Pope felt a chill run through her when she saw Edward Boyd. She seemed to be making a habit of meeting ghosts from her past these days, and here was a particularly unpleasant one.

Boyd was standing by the floor-to-ceiling windows, his hands in his pockets, turned to them when they walked towards him. He was still a striking figure, despite the years in prison, though Pope supposed they were about the same age. The first thing she noticed was his eyes. Bright blue, unnaturally so. Similar to Jane Leigh's, but with a completely different effect. Boyd's had the ability to unsettle you. He was handsome, but the eyes betrayed the rest of his benign appearance. The eyes of a psychopath.

He wore a navy blue three-piece suit, the jacket unbuttoned, the bottom button of the waistcoat undone. Black brogues. Gold-rimmed circular glasses sat beneath his fine blond hair, shoulder length, almost girlish. He looked like a lawyer or a financial trader.

'Rebecca.' Boyd looked her up and down. She thought she could put him and Mick Waterson in a cell together and they could swap notes.

'How lovely to see you.' He emphasized the word "lovely". 'You look ravishing. "Age cannot wither her, nor custom stale her infinite variety".' He stared into her eyes.

'*Anthony and Cleopatra*,' she said, then wished she hadn't. Don't play his games.

'Very good. Act two, scene two. Most people think it's Anthony who says this, but it's actually Enobarbus. I've always thought of you as a Cleopatra.'

'Is that right?'

He appraised her. 'You do look good, Rebecca. How long has it been? Oh, that's right, a little over fifteen years.' He seemed to be thinking back. 'I thought about you a great deal in prison, you know.'

She didn't reply.

'You got me through many a long, cold night.' He smiled.

'That's good to know.'

He laughed. 'Ah, the old Detective Pope distancing technique. Did they teach you that at police college?'

'All self-taught, Mr Boyd.'

'Oh, come now. Edward, please. We've known each other long enough and intimately enough to be on first-name terms, Rebecca.'

'Hardly intimately, but Edward if you want.'

'Oh, I do. I do.' He smiled at her again. Old friends catching up. 'Shall we sit?' he asked, indicating a pair of black leather sofas facing each other. The large room was easily big enough to accommodate both without breaking a sweat. Pope and Miller sat on one, Boyd then sat facing them on the other. He leaned back and crossed his legs.

'This is DS Adam Miller,' said Pope. Boyd glanced at him and nodded politely.

'Did you enjoy reading the letters I sent you? They stopped sending them after a while, I was most put out. I must apologize. No manners, no class, some of the guards in that place.'

'I didn't read them.'

He looked at her carefully. 'I can see you're lying, Rebecca. Maybe we'll get together and discuss them a little more. . . informally next time.'

'I don't think so,' she said.

He let that go without reacting. 'How's Tobias Darke these days? I haven't seen him in a while.'

'He's fine.'

'Do send him my regards. I must pay him a visit. We had some good conversations. He's a big fan of Shakespeare. I enjoyed discussing some of his plays with Tobias, although he's not quite as well read as he ought to be.' Boyd looked out of the window on to the street below.

'Is that right?'

'Yes. Better than most, though. Appreciates the value of a classical education. All too rare, these days.'

Pope redirected the conversation.

'I need to ask you a few questions about a case we're currently working. Is that OK with you?'

He turned back to look at her. 'Yes. Ask away.'

Pope noted he didn't ask which case.

'You were seen this morning at St Paul's church in Deptford, Edward. Can you tell us why you were there?'

'Have you been following me, Rebecca?'

'No, just a lucky strike.'

He smiled again. A lot of smiling.

'What do you think I was doing there?'

'Don't play games with me, Edward. Just answer the question, please.'

'You always did have impeccable manners, Rebecca. One of the things I always liked about you. OK. I was just having a look around. It's a beautiful building, you now. Something of a hidden gem in that part of London.'

'You just happened to wander into that church. Of all the churches in London?'

He smiled. 'Ah, well. You've got me. I may have read a report about your case and how you were there a couple of days ago. Thought I'd visit, walk in your footsteps, see what I could see.'

She tried to work out whether to lean into the very weird vibe she was getting from him.

'Have you ever been there before?'

'To St Paul's?'

'Yes.'

'No, never.' He stared at her for a moment too long. 'First time. Maybe we could go back together at some point?'

'I don't think so.'

'Hmm. I suppose it's not the most romantic of locations.'

He waited for a reaction, which she chose not to give.

'What have you been doing since your release, Edward?'

'Oh, this and that. Reacquainting myself with outside life, enjoying the delights that London has to offer. I visited Paris for a few days. Now that is a romantic city. It's a cliché, but it's a cliché for a reason.'

She knew he was trying to get inside her head, show her that he wasn't fazed by the questions or the situation.

'Where were you on Tuesday morning. Up until about midday?'

'Tuesday morning,' he repeated. Made a show of thinking about it. 'Tuesday, yes. I was at home. I got up late — one of the luxuries one is not afforded in prison — then I read and listened to some music. Wagner's *Siegfried*, the third part of the *Ring* cycle. Wonderful stuff. Are you familiar with it, Rebecca?'

'No, I'm not.'

'Oh, you should listen. Do you know it took him twenty-six years to complete the *Ring* cycle? Outstanding work. I'll get you a copy.'

'No, it's fine. Was anyone at home with you?'

'No. I'm enjoying being alone at the moment. I only need female company rarely.' He looked at her with an intensity when he said this. She held his stare.

'What about Wednesday evening? Where were you?'

'Wednesday evening I was at St Martin-in-the-Fields. Attending a concert.'

'So you will have been seen there?'

'There were lots of people. Whether anyone can recall seeing me, I couldn't tell you.'

Pope was pretty sure he'd be remembered.

'Would you be happy if we sent some officers round to search your flat, Edward?'

'Will it be you doing the searching, Rebecca?'

'No, it won't be me. I'll send a specialist forensic team.'

'Do you have a warrant?'

'We don't have a warrant yet. Do we need one?'

'If you don't have a warrant. . . Then no, sorry, you'll need to get a warrant.'

'OK, Edward. I'll do that. Expect a visit very soon.'

Pope got up to leave. Miller followed suit. Boyd walked them to the door.

'It's great that we're back in touch. I'll be seeing you soon, Rebecca. Take care of yourself.'

Pope didn't respond. As the door closed gently behind them, she and Miller walked down the stairs and out into the bustle of the street. They headed back in the direction of the station.

'Did we just interview Hannibal Lecter?' asked Miller.

'Something like that.'

* * *

It was 6 p.m. before Pope began to consider whether she should visit her father in hospital or go home. She decided to go home. She really wanted to see Alex.

As she drove over Waterloo Bridge her phone rang. She answered.

'Brody?'

She listened to his voice on the other end of the line.

'No,' was all she said.

CHAPTER 21

Police Constable Mike Hawley was twenty-two years old. He had been a police officer for three years. He enjoyed the job most of the time. He was a big guy, so he didn't get much trouble he couldn't handle. He enjoyed the sense of doing something useful, something that contributed to society. He wasn't stupid. He was aware of the problems in the force. But he knew it could do enormous good.

He was also aware of the weather today. Which was why, although he usually enjoyed being out on the beat, today he was very happy to be standing outside Karen Tarling's room in King's Hospital. He had pulled a double shift. It was Sunday, and they were short-staffed, so he'd been asked if he could stay on longer than usual. A warm, easy shift on a stormy Sunday in southeast London.

Right now, Hawley was trying not to feel bored. There were very few people around now. Tarling was asleep. The doctors were not on their rounds until later, and the limited supply of nursing staff were seeing to other patients elsewhere on other wards. He wasn't complaining. But easy though this was, it was a little boring. Hawley walked up and down the corridor, looking down at his black Dr Martens shoes. He'd give those a polish when he got home tonight. He leaned against the window, staring out at the rain. His girl-friend, Kerry, would be cooking dinner right about now and it would be ready when he got home. He wondered what film they might watch after they had eaten. Then he thought about what he might spend this month's overtime payment on. It would be quite a good amount.

The next thing Mike Hawley thought about was the crushing, searing pain on the back of his head, before everything went black.

Then he thought about nothing.

* * *

He opened the door to Karen Tarling's room slowly, quietly. He had seen that she was asleep, seen the officer staring cluelessly out the window. It had been perfect timing.

He walked carefully into her room, closing the door behind him. It was just the two of them now. He could see the shape of her body beneath the covers, still. Both arms lay outside the sheet, a cannula attached to the wrist of her left hand. This led up to a tube, which in turn led up to a transparent plastic pouch containing clear liquid. The amount administered was controlled and monitored by a small, rectangular machine on a stand next to the patient. A regular blue flash, a constant orange glow behind it.

He had needed to be extremely careful finding his way to this room. CCTV in many areas of the hospital. But he was used to being careful, used to planning, had understood the zoning and placement of cameras. He saw that there were blind spots, spaces that went unmonitored. He had checked the route carefully, walked with confidence when he passed others, who would assume he was a member of staff, belonged there. Baseball cap, a nondescript jacket and, underneath, scrubs. Head down, feigning absorption in his phone when he couldn't avoid a camera. People everywhere, blending in, hiding in plain sight. It had been challenging, but he knew they would focus on the entrances and exits. Finding the right corridor turned out to be easier than anticipated. He slipped into the staff lift, flashing a grin at the two nurses as they walked out talking about the secure patient on the fourth floor, oblivious to who was listening behind them. There was no camera outside this room. He had been lucky.

He looked at her, let his eyes move up and down her body. But he knew that time was limited. This was not like usual. Normally he planned, made sure that he had plenty of time. Time to take things slowly. To enjoy the process. He would still enjoy it. But it would be different. His pulse quickened, and he felt almost lightheaded.

He checked through the window. There was no one there. He leaned over her, close now, close enough to feel her light breaths against his face. He would have liked to spend longer. Not this time.

He flexed his gloved hands, pulled his shoulders back. He found her larynx and hyoid bone with his fingers, closed his hands around her neck and squeezed with all his considerable strength.

With a start she woke. She tried to scream, absolute horror in her eyes. But there was no sound. Only the crack as her bone fractured further. She arched her back and the two locked eyes, predator and prey. He felt the connection, the power, the control that could only be felt taking another human being's life. He imagined the pain that would be searing through Karen Tarling's body. But only briefly, for she fell unconscious almost immediately. He continued the pressure, the unrelenting force, until he knew she had no more life left in her.

She looked calm now, serene in her bed. He straightened her up, arranged the pillow neatly behind her head. He flattened the sheets and tucked one loose corner underneath the mattress. Then he slipped a white envelope from his inside pocket and laid it carefully, almost reverently, on her chest. He stood back and looked. Perfect. Like a well-composed photograph or a still life painted by a master. Quickly he looked around the room, then opened the door and left quietly. He closed it behind him and glanced over to the police officer lying prostrate on the floor. He took one last look at his work through the large glass window, then walked away.

CHAPTER 22

Panic coursed through the building. The staff at King's were used to death, but they were not used to murder in their own hospital. The scene was discovered by Rachel Fraser, a young nurse arriving to carry out a routine check on Karen Tarling. Only eight months as a qualified nurse, she was already very good at her job: calm, level-headed, unflappable in a crisis. This was her first full-time job, and what happened that day was something that she would never forget. Entering the room, in a state of some agitation, she looked at Karen Tarling. Ironically, although she wouldn't know it, Fraser's heart was beating at almost exactly the same elevated rate as the previous visitor to Tarling's bedside.

The door to the corridor banged open as Pope rushed in. There were police officers and security guards outside Tarling's room.

'Where's Hawley? How the hell did this happen?' she demanded as she strode towards the open door.

No one answered her. She looked into Karen's room. The body had not been moved and remained just as it had been found. She took a deep breath. Despite the turbulence around her, Pope had to keep calm, had to be seen to keep calm.

She went quietly inside. Karen looked peaceful, but Pope thought of what she must have gone through just before she had died. The sheer terror and horror as she realized what was happening, realized that the same man who had attacked her before had returned to finish the job.

The last thing she had said to Pope was that she had been very lucky. The previous two victims had been killed, but she had escaped. She had felt safe in this room, with a police officer on duty outside, and doctors and nurses ready to support her recovery. That confidence and feeling of security had been misplaced.

Pope felt desperately sad. Karen had been through an experience that would scar her emotionally, if not physically, for life, but she had thought it was over. Thought she had made it. But they had failed to protect her. And now she was dead.

Then Pope noticed the envelope on the floor. She knew immediately what it was, that it was for her. She took a pair of latex gloves from her pocket and slid them on. She bent down and picked it up. On the front was printed *DCI Pope*, just like the others. Her heart beat faster as she slowly, carefully opened the envelope. Again, a single sheet, white, the highest quality paper. Blank on one side. She turned it over. *So close, Bec, so close* printed on the reverse. She stared at the envelope, willed it to say something else, to explain, to offer a clue. The use of her abbreviated first name once again a shock. Bringing the case yet another step closer to her.

Pope's thoughts were interrupted by the arrival of Brody and Miller. They all stood for a minute, respectful in their silence.

'And there was this,' said Pope eventually. She showed them the envelope and its contents. Miller held out an evidence bag into which she placed the envelope. He sealed the bag.

'Let's talk to Jane Leigh,' said Pope. 'See what she can tell us.'

They left the room and asked the nurse outside where to find Leigh.

'I just paged her,' she said. 'She'll be here in a minute or two.'

'Thanks,' said Pope, then turned back to her team. 'We can check on Hawley and look at the CCTV.'

'Yes,' said Brody. 'There are cameras at all the entrances and exits. They must have picked up something. He must have used one of the main entrances. We could get lucky,' he added. Pope wasn't sure if it was expectation or hope.

Jane Leigh approached, looking considerably less confident and in control than she had on the previous occasions Pope had met her. The death of Karen Tarling had affected both of them. Both were used to dealing with death, but this was different. Pope considered that she and Leigh were the two people who had been ultimately responsible for keeping Karen Tarling safe and well. Both had been found wanting in that task. Sometimes it was all too easy to take responsibility for the things you could do nothing about. But she wondered if there was anything else either of them could have done.

'DCI Pope,' said Leigh.

'Dr Leigh.'

'The circumstances in which we keep meeting are becoming more and more grave,' said Leigh.

'How is Hawley?' asked Pope.

'He's still unconscious. He received a nasty blow to the head, we think from the fire extinguisher over there,' said Leigh, indicating the red cylinder standing against the wall at the end of the corridor. 'But your guys will check if that's the case, I'm sure.'

All of them looked at the extinguisher, noticing its solid construction, assessing the damage it could do if it came into contact with the human skull. It wasn't where it should be, instead sitting slightly away from its wall bracket.

'His vital signs are there, but are weak. We took him straight down to A & E and then he'll probably be taken to Intensive Care.'

'Is he going to be OK?' asked Brody.

'He's still being assessed at the moment. We'll know more after that. I'll take you down there in a minute and we'll see how they're getting on with him.'

'What about Karen Tarling?' said Pope. 'What happened?'

'The first thing we knew was when one of the nurses on duty, Rachel Fraser, came to carry out a routine check on her. She saw that Constable Hawley had been attacked. He was lying on the floor just over there.' Leigh pointed to a spot further along the corridor. 'She checked him, saw that he was still alive, and called for assistance.'

'We'll need to talk to Ms Fraser,' said Pope.

'She's downstairs at the moment. She knew you'd want to talk to her. She tried to resuscitate Karen Tarling, but she was already dead. When I arrived I took over, but it was no use. She'd been strangled. Due to her previous injuries, I doubt she was able to put up much of a fight. I'll page Rachel,' said Leigh. 'She can meet us at A & E.'

Then she led the way to the second floor.

The room was large in comparison to Karen Tarling's room and held four beds. Three of them were occupied. Pope saw Mike Hawley lying in the bed furthest from the door.

Hawley had lost a lot of blood and he looked ghostly white. A web of wires connected him to a bank of machines, giving the room a sense of quiet gravity. A number of nurses were checking on the progress of their patients. A tall man standing by Hawley's bedside seemed to be writing in the notes attached to a clipboard. Pope watched for any signs that might offer some insight into the officer's condition.

Finally the man noticed Dr Leigh, who gestured for him to join them.

'Mr Patterson, these are Mr Hawley's colleagues. DCI Pope, this is Mr Patterson, the consultant looking after your PC.'

'What can you tell us?' asked Pope.

'He's had a serious hit on the head,' said the consultant. 'There may be a fracture, and quite possibly some bleeding, but we won't know for sure until we've taken him for X-rays.'

'When will that be?' asked Brody.

'Soon. I'm waiting for Radiography to confirm when we can get him in.'

'Will he be OK?' asked Pope. She knew the doctor wouldn't be able to answer the question, but equally she knew that she had to ask.

'Too soon to tell,' replied Patterson. 'Head injuries can be unpredictable. This particular injury is serious and he's lost some blood. It really depends on what the X-ray shows. Once we've seen that, we'll know how to proceed. But he's in the best place now and we'll look after him.'

Pope recognized the cliché. She had used it many times herself with concerned relatives.

Pope thanked him, and as she turned back to Leigh, she became aware of a young woman standing just behind the doctor. She hadn't noticed her arrive.

'DCI Pope, this is Rachel Fraser, the nurse who found Karen Tarling and your constable,' said Leigh, indicating the woman.

She stepped forward. She looked like she had not slept for days and was on the brink of collapse. She was young, early twenties, and Pope imagined that what she had gone through this evening had taken its toll on her.

Pope asked Miller to call Mike Hawley's girlfriend and his parents, while she and Brody went with Rachel Fraser to the cafeteria for a coffee and to see if there was anything she could add to what Leigh had told them.

They ordered three cups of coffee and sat down at a table. It was busier than it had been earlier. Pope assumed most visitors had left quickly after seeing their loved ones, choosing not to spend any more time than was necessary in King's Hospital on a Sunday evening. She thought of her father and promised herself that she would go up and visit him when she was done here.

Rachel Fraser sipped her coffee, grimaced at the taste.

'It's not the best coffee I've ever had,' said Brody, smiling.

'It's awful,' said Fraser. She took another sip.

Brody led. 'Is there anything you can tell us about earlier, Rachel? Anything that you think might be important or useful in finding the killer?'

Rachel Fraser looked scared, like she had been trying not to think about it too much. 'Do you think it's the man who attacked her before?' she asked. 'The one who killed those other two women?'

'We think it's a strong possibility, yes,' said Brody. 'That's what we're trying to confirm.'

Fraser paused. 'You know what happened, right?' she asked.

'Yes,' said Brody. 'Dr Leigh told us. But we just want to know if there's anything you might remember that you didn't mention to her. Was there anything odd? Anything that struck you as unusual?'

'The only thing, well, apart from a patient getting attacked in the hospital — the only thing was I noticed how neat and tidy her room looked when I arrived.'

'In what way?' prompted Brody.

'Well, it was all a bit surreal. I walked in and nothing seemed out of place. The bed was made neatly, her arms were by her sides, all the machines were hooked up as usual. It seemed odd, because I assumed there must have been a struggle. Maybe not much of one, but she probably would have woken up, so there would have been a struggle,' Fraser repeated. She was thinking it through as she spoke, clarifying what she meant in her mind.

Brody looked at Pope. The killer had tidied up, had neatly arranged Karen Tarling's body after he had killed her. Another staged murder scene.

Brody thanked her for her help, and for looking after Mike Hawley, and told her that she would need to remain in the hospital for a formal statement to be taken. Rachel Fraser told them where to find her and left.

Pope looked out of the window. 'I told him where she was.'

Brody frowned.

'I told Waterson that we had a witness who had survived the attack and who would probably pick a suspect out of a line-up. I even told him she was in hospital. I might as well have given him a map. And now he's disappeared.'

'You didn't tell him which hospital. There's no way he could have known where she was,' said Brody.

'It wouldn't be hard to find out. There's only so many big hospitals in London. In this area. King's is the first place I'd look.'

Brody looked like he was about to argue, but seemed to change his mind. 'We'll find him. He can't have gone far.'

'We need to look at the CCTV footage,' said Pope. Brody called Miller and asked him to meet them at the security desk.

Down in the main reception, a woman directed them to the security office, and they found it near the main entrance. Years of coming to this hospital, and neither Pope nor Brody had ever had cause to seek out this office. When needed, security had always come to them. Pope knocked on the door, and they were greeted by a young man in a dark grey uniform with *King's Hospital Security* written neatly on the chest. His ID badge hung around his neck and identified him as Geoffrey Smith. 'You can call me Geoff,' he told them, more perhaps to Pope than to Brody. Brody smiled. Pope didn't.

They explained who they were, showed their ID badges, and were let into the office just as Miller arrived. The security guard made a point of checking Miller's ID also. Pope got the impression that he was quite pleased with the power and authority his uniform afforded him. Pope told him what they wanted. He had been one of the guards who had attended when Rachel Fraser had alerted security, so he was aware of the circumstances of their visit. He had shown some initiative and had already downloaded and prepared the CCTV footage for each entrance and the area surrounding Karen Tarling's room, anticipating a visit from the police.

There were three chairs in the office. Geoffrey Smith sat on one, Pope and Brody took one each, pulled them closer to the monitor and sat down. Miller stood.

'What time frame are we looking at?' asked Smith, his hand hovering over the controls.

Brody checked his notebook and told him the time when Rachel Fraser had last checked on Karen Tarling before the attack. Then the time when the body was discovered. They gave it fifteen minutes either side of that.

'Luckily, we can watch on fast-forward, at double the speed. Otherwise we'd be here for hours,' laughed Smith, directing both his humour and his look in Pope's direction. She smiled but indicated that he needed to get on with looking at the tapes.

'I've got the footage for the entrances and exits, so we can start with those. The corridors around her room are downloading now. We can look at them next,' said Smith.

They scrolled through footage of one entrance, then another, then another. There was one more recording to look through. As figures moved in and out of the automatic doors, Smith would slow the recording down and check the person involved. Each time the other three would involuntarily lean a little forward, to get a good look at each person, trying to find someone who looked like they didn't belong.

Eventually, after what seemed like hours, they finished the final tape.

'That's it for the entrances,' said Smith. 'No more footage of those areas, unless you want to extend the time frame.'

Brody thought. 'No, he wouldn't have hung around. He would have come in quickly and left quickly. There's nothing to be gained by waiting in the hospital.'

'Unless he knew we'd be looking at the tapes,' suggested Miller. 'He may have deliberately waited in order to skew the time frame. He knows we'll check, so he waits until he thinks we won't be looking at it anymore.'

'I don't think so,' said Pope. 'He wouldn't have had the time to think this through. This isn't like his previous kills.

He planned those meticulously, probably over weeks. This was quick and spontaneous. I think Brody's right. He's long gone, and he's somewhere on that footage.'

They watched elderly patients and visitors as they came and went. Casualties brought into A & E by friends and family, children, doctors and nurses, porters, ambulance crews, and discounted them all. They didn't see anyone fitting the admittedly sketchy description that Karen Tarling had given them enter or leave the hospital during the time frame they had estimated.

They moved on to the footage from the cameras in corridors around Karen Tarling's room. Smith explained that there wasn't CCTV outside her room, in that corridor. A bad break. But the adjacent corridors. Pope thought that had to show something.

'He must be on there somewhere,' said Pope again, more to herself than to anyone else in the room. 'He must be.'

'What if he was dressed as a doctor or a porter,' said Brody. 'He could have used a uniform. No one would bat an eye if a guy in a white lab coat walked past them in a hospital.'

They looked carefully at the tapes. Smith worked in a methodical pattern out from the corridors nearest Tarling's room, first one corridor, then the next. It was Brody who spotted it first.

'There,' said Brody, suddenly leaning forward and pointing at the screen. 'Hold it there.'

Pope and Smith also leaned in, Miller took a step forward. There on the screen, frozen in grainy black and white, a tall figure. Dressed in scrubs, wearing a dark jacket and a baseball cap. Facing away from the camera, walking towards the corridor that led to Karen Tarling's room. Pope checked the timestamp.

'What do you think?' asked Brody.

Pope studied the frozen image. 'Could be. He's certainly not behaving like a doctor. Seems to be attempting to look away from the camera. That looks odd.'

'How tall do you think he is?'

Pope looked carefully. 'Difficult to tell. Maybe six foot, give or take. Same as Mick Waterson.'

'And Edward Boyd,' said Brody.

Pope turned to Smith. 'Can you isolate this and keep looking? See if you can find this guy anywhere else?'

Smith nodded and started the process.

'Do you have photo ID for all members of hospital staff?' Pope asked him.

'Yes. I've got access to it here.'

'I need you to assemble your security team and go through the footage again, and this time I want you to check anyone dressed as hospital staff against their ID. Can you do that?' Pope knew it would go more smoothly with the security guard's cooperation, but she needed results and she needed them now.

Smith nodded. Pope could see that he had worked out how long this would take. She wondered when his shift would finish.

'It's a lot of material to get through. I'm sure you'll have no objection to one of our techs coming down to help.'

Smith seemed to be weighing up the suggestion that he and his team needed outside help with the fact that he wanted to get home at some point before midnight. 'That's fine,' he said.

'Great,' said Pope, already dialling Stephen Thompson's number.

'OK,' she said a few minutes later. 'Geoff, you can expect Stephen Thompson from Technical Support in about twenty minutes. He'll come straight here. Thanks for your work on this so far. It could really help us in catching this guy.'

Geoffrey Smith smiled with pride. 'Happy to help, DCI Pope.'

Brody held the door for Pope and they headed for the exit.

'I think you have an admirer there, boss,' he said. 'You should have got his number.'

She punched him so hard in the arm that he was glad to be within reach of a doctor if he needed it.

The three of them, Pope, Brody and Miller, stood outside in the main reception area. Around them were the ill, injured and those who looked after them.

'I'm going to go up and see my dad. See how he's getting on,' said Pope.

The other two both nodded.

'I hope it goes OK,' said Brody. 'We'll go to check on Hawley. Meet back at the security office in half an hour?'

But instead of moving, they all stood still, rooted to the spot. The magnitude of events momentarily overwhelming. Another possible lead that had come to nothing. Another dead end.

'It's like he's some kind of a ghost,' said Brody at last. 'No one sees him, hears him. He's almost invisible to the cameras here. How can he come and go as he pleases?'

Miller said nothing, nor did Pope. They had no answer to give. Pope turned and walked away, to see her father. To face the other crisis she was currently having to deal with.

CHAPTER 23

When Pope arrived at the ward on the third floor, she walked unhindered to her father's bedside. The nurses seemed to have given up questioning her erratic visiting hours.

There had been police searching the ward earlier and her father had seen frequent patrols outside in the hospital corridors. Pope had arranged for a thorough sweep of the whole hospital, top to bottom, as soon as possible after being notified of the attacks. Needless to say, many of the patients had been agitated by the sight of police officers on their wards. But they had found nothing: no traces, no signs.

Pope sat down on the chair next to her father's bed.

'What's going on, Bec? There are police everywhere. Has something happened?'

Pope sighed. 'There was an incident in the hospital.' She kept her voice low, so the patients in the neighbouring beds wouldn't hear their conversation.

Her father looked at her, waited for her to continue.

'There was an incident. . .' she repeated. She really didn't want to go over it with her father. She decided to try to keep it brief.

'Someone attacked a patient upstairs, and the police officer outside the room as well.'

'Police officer? Who was attacked? Was it your witness?' he asked.

'Yes.'

'Are they OK? Are they hurt?'

'No, they're not OK. Our witness has . . . has been killed. The officer is in Intensive Care.'

Her father looked shocked.

'I'm sorry, Bec. That must be very hard for you. Is the officer going to be OK?'

She was surprised at his empathy. 'We don't know yet. They're doing tests. He was hit pretty hard.'

Her father looked at the floor.

Pope realized that she ought to change the topic. 'How are you feeling? What have the doctors said?'

'Apparently they're going to do the tests first thing tomorrow morning, then I can go home after that,' he said.

'OK. I'll pick you up and drive you home when you're done.'

'No, no, you don't need to do that. I can make my own way home.'

'No, you can't. I'll be here in the morning anyway. Give me a call when you're all finished.'

'Bec, you really don't—'

'I insist. You can't go home on your own after all this,' she said.

He half nodded his agreement.

'I need to go.' She got up. 'I just wanted to check everything was OK. I'll see you in the morning.'

'Yes, see you then,' he said.

'Don't forget to call me as soon as they've finished the tests.' She made a mental note to check with the doctors in the morning, fully expecting her father not to call.

When she arrived at the security office, Stephen Thompson was already there, talking to Brody and Miller.

'Stephen, thanks for coming in. Sorry it's so late,' she said.

He nodded, a resigned and weary smile.

Brody continued. 'So, if you can work with Mr Smith on the CCTV footage, see if you can do anything? Let me know the moment you have something.'

Smith and Thompson shook hands formally, then disappeared into a world of technical jargon. Pope, Brody and Miller stepped outside the security office and closed the door. There was little more any of them could do until the CCTV footage had been examined more closely.

'You two should go home and get some rest. It's been a long day and it looks like it'll be the same tomorrow,' she said.

Brody nodded. 'What about you?'

'I need some sleep,' said Pope. 'I'll see you back here in the morning.'

'I'm going to hang around for a bit,' said Miller. Pope and Brody looked at him. 'Mike's girlfriend is going to be here soon. I've met her a few times. I thought it would be good for her to see a friendly face when she gets here.'

'OK, that sounds good,' said Pope. 'But make sure you get home at some point. I need you fresh tomorrow.'

Miller nodded. Pope opened the door to the security office.

'We're off now,' she said to Thompson and Smith. 'But I want to know as soon as you've got anything. Anything,' she repeated.

They both nodded and she closed the door again.

Miller headed to Intensive Care and Pope and Brody left through the main entrance. The air outside was fresh and cool, a breeze blowing. A welcome antidote to the sterile, still nature of the hospital environment.

'I'll see you in the morning,' said Pope.

'Yeah, OK,' replied Brody.

There wasn't anything else to say.

* * *

Pope woke early, showered and gave Alex a guilty kiss before leaving the house. He hadn't said anything last night, but she could sense an argument was brewing. He was caught, like the partners of most police officers, between understanding of, and respect for, what she did, and a desperate desire for it not to destroy their home and family life. They didn't argue, but she knew it was there. Pope could see it in Alex's face as she described her day. She wondered what it would take to push him over the edge.

It was a little after 7 a.m. as she joined the early tide of traffic heading towards Central London. By the time she arrived at the hospital, rush hour was in full swing.

Brody arrived soon afterwards. Miller had been there until late, so Pope assumed he was still at home asleep. She was wrong: Miller arrived only a few minutes later. Pope wondered how Miller's fledgling relationship was surviving the strain of a major homicide case. She didn't know much about his new girlfriend, but she could remember the strained reassurances, in the early days of being with Alex, that 'it was fine' when she had to rush out. Those three words only seemed to get more frequent.

Brody had spoken to Stephen Thompson on the phone. Thompson and Geoffrey Smith had come up with nothing that was particularly useful. They had scoured the tapes, relying on old-fashioned visual matching to try to find anyone who looked out of place coming into, or leaving, the hospital. It had taken them hours. But everyone had checked out. They had found the suspicious guy in the hoodie on two other corridors. In each case, he averted his face from the camera and lost himself with other people nearby. Thompson isolated each part of the tape, so he could continue work on it back at the station. He had got home sometime after 4 a.m. Smith had left six hours after his shift should have ended.

'I think you two need to go back to the station. Get on to Thompson when he gets in and see what he can do with the images he's isolated,' said Pope. 'Brody, I want four officers in the hospital today. I want them visible to patients and staff. And tell them to keep their eyes open.'

'Do you think he'll be back?' asked Miller.

'I doubt it,' replied Pope. 'But I don't want to take any chances and I want the people here reassured. My father is being discharged today so I'm going to run him home then I'll be back. Keep me informed of anything.' She tapped her phone in her pocket. Brody and Miller nodded.

Pope walked into the ward and was greeted by the sight of an empty bed.

'Shit,' she said, immediately fearing the worst. She'd seen enough movies to know what an empty hospital bed meant.

'What's the matter?' said a voice from behind her.

'Dad.' Pope felt a rush of relief. 'Where were you?'

'I just had my X-ray. They say I can go home now, thank God.'

'How long do you have to wait for the results?'

'They'll contact me to make an appointment once they've had a look,' he replied.

He seemed pretty upbeat, considering his situation.

Pope waited outside while her father got dressed and gathered his belongings. He thanked the nurses on duty, without mentioning his daughter's complete disregard for the visiting schedule laid down by the hospital.

Driving to her father's flat in Finsbury Park took over an hour. Crossing London Bridge, the route took them through the heart of the City of London, near Whitechapel and Shoreditch. They didn't speak much. Neither of them wanted to discuss the obvious topic of conversation. The test results would be ready in a few days, and there wasn't much they could do about it in the meantime.

Pope pulled the car up in front of her father's building. He took off his seat belt and opened the car door. Pope reached down to release her belt.

'No, don't come in, Bec. I know you've got an important case and you need to get on with that.'

'It's fine, I can at least see you in.'

'No. You're busy. I'm fine. Thanks for the lift.'

Pope's father climbed out of the car and closed the door behind him. He turned and walked up the stairs, found his keys and let himself in the front door, closing it without looking back. Pope wasn't sure whether to feel offended or relieved.

She drove back to the police station, parked her car and went up to her office. She was frustrated and wanted to get at this case, wanted to find the one thing that would tear it wide open and prevent another murder. The frequency of attacks meant that she was permanently aware of a ticking clock.

As she entered the Homicide squad offices she heard the sound of officers all talking at the same time, the raised voices of excitement. Gathered around the computer on Miller's desk were Miller, Brody, Ana McEwan and Stephen Thompson. Thompson was sitting in Miller's seat and pointing at the top of the screen, as they peered closely to see.

'I think we may have something,' said Miller when Pope entered the room.

Her pulse immediately quickened. She stepped closer to the desk.

Stephen Thompson took over. He showed Pope the screen. 'We've been searching the shops where you can buy that type of camera, including online. You know, the camera the killer used?' he added.

Pope nodded.

'Well, we came up with nothing. We checked all the outlets in the UK, but no luck. So then we broadened the search and moved further afield, outside the UK, in case he bought them abroad, maybe online,' said Thompson.

'It would make sense,' said Brody. 'If you buy them in a shop, you risk being identified, being caught on CCTV. But not if you bought it mail order from abroad. You could use any name you liked, a PO box, and it would be harder to trace. Certainly not as quick.'

'And . . .?' Pope said to Thompson.

'So we started widening our search to online suppliers of surveillance equipment that were based abroad, but shipped to the UK. We started in Europe, with France, Germany, Italy and Spain,' continued Thompson, looking at Pope, clearly revelling in his story.

'And what have you found?' asked Pope, her impatience growing.

'We got a hit,' he said triumphantly. 'Rive Électronique in Paris. They are an actual store, but they also ship world-wide. They specialize in all types of cameras, you know, DSLRs, GoPro, video cameras, lenses. But they also carry surveillance and espionage equipment.'

'Espionage equipment?'

'Yes. Like pens that are also cameras, briefcases that contain cameras. Real James Bond stuff.' Thompson was clearly enthusiastic about the concept. 'But they also stock the exact mini-camera that we found at the first two scenes. We checked with them, and they sent an order of six of them to an address in South London two months ago.' He handed a piece of paper to Pope with a name and address printed on it. Michael Brooks. The address was in Greenwich, southeast London.

Not far from my house, thought Pope.

She stood and looked at the piece of paper, hardly able to believe what she was holding. 'How do we know this is our guy?' she asked Thompson.

'We don't. Not for sure. But it's a hell of a coincidence, don't you think?'

Pope looked at the name and address again. Michael Brooks. Could this be him? The killer? Was this the break they were searching for? She looked up at Brody, then at the others. They were all staring at her, waiting for her instructions.

'Good work. OK. Check out the address. And check out Michael Brooks. It'll be a false name. But see if you can find anything. I'm going to see Fletcher.'

* * *

'We're going to need Armed Response,' said Pope.

'How sure are we?' Fletcher asked, mulling over everything she'd told him.

'We're not sure. Not at all. But it's a bloody big coincidence. Six cameras, of the exact type found at the houses of the first two victims, bought together, in the last two months. It's got to be him,' added Pope.

'Do you really need Armed Response?' He was hedging.

'This isn't the time to be saving money,' said Pope, trying to control her irritation. 'I'm not putting my team in there, into an unknown situation, without armed backup. It's just not happening. Yes, I need Armed Response.'

'How many?'

'Four armed, four of us and four extra officers.'

Fletcher thought for a moment. 'When?'

'As soon as possible. Have them meet in my office for a briefing at 5 p.m. We'll leave at 6 p.m.,' said Pope. 'I don't want any chance that he'll get away or find another victim.'

'OK. I'll make a call.'

Pope turned to leave the room.

'And, Bec.' She looked back at Fletcher. 'Everyone's watching. Don't screw it up.'

'Yeah,' she said, as she hurried out.

* * *

When she got back to the office, Brody filled her in on what they had discovered. The address was about forty-five minutes' drive at this time of day. Looking online at street photographs, it appeared to be a detached house, small, at the end of a terrace, separated somewhat from the other houses on the street. Close to the River Thames. A large, disused industrial complex behind. Semi-isolated, yet close to escape routes if needed. There were two means of access by road, one from the north and one from the south. They would need four vehicles. One to approach the address from either direction, and one each side to block the road further up. They would also need officers at the rear of the property, which was flanked by a path that ran behind all the houses on the block and opened near the industrial estate.

Pope went down to Resources and Equipment to get the Kevlar bulletproof vests for her team. These offered more protection than the standard stab vests commonly issued to officers. She needed vests that were resistant to handgun bullets, the type issued to Armed Response officers. She had no idea what they were walking into and she wanted to check each one personally before issuing them to the others.

Once she'd handed out the body armour to her officers, she set about planning the detail of the operation with Brody, Miller, Thompson and McEwan. Thompson found the best images of the property, got copies, and coordinated with the other officers involved. Just before 5 p.m., as promised, the Armed Response team arrived. These were officers from SCO19, the elite Metropolitan Police firearms unit. They routinely carried Glock 17 pistols and tasers, but due to the nature of the operation tonight they would also be issued with Heckler & Koch 9 mm automatic rifles. They cut imposing figures as they entered the room. One female and three male officers, they carried an air of quiet professionalism and determination.

Once Pope had explained the operation and answered all the questions that arose, she told them that they would all meet downstairs in reception at 5.55 p.m. She knew they'd be precisely on time.

Once everyone had disbanded, only Pope and Brody remained in the office.

'How are you feeling?' he asked her.

'I've got so much adrenaline flying around I think I could run to Greenwich faster than we can drive,' Pope replied.

* * *

Brody left to get some water from the vending machine outside. Pope was alone in the office. She considered what they were about to do. She was responsible for the operation and knew they had to get it right. If the killer was there, he would be dangerous. A cornered killer with nothing to lose was potentially the most difficult situation a police officer could face. Add heavily armed officers into the equation, well . . . she didn't want to think about it.

Pope looked at her watch. 5.45 p.m. Ten minutes. She decided to call Alex. Just in case.

She kept it light. She said they were going on an operation, told him she couldn't say too much about it, just that it was routine. She'd be back later. After she had hung up she thought that she should have said something else, told him she loved him, said something about what they'd do at the weekend.

But it was too late now.

She pushed the thought aside.

CHAPTER 24

They drove in convoy out of the garage, and once they had crossed Waterloo Bridge they headed for the Old Kent Road en route to Greenwich. Pope was driving, focused on the road. Whenever guns were involved, there was always the question of personal security. Pope thought of her father, thought of Alex, Hannah and Chloe.

As they approached Greenwich, Pope pulled herself out of her thoughts and checked with the others that they were all clear on what they were doing.

'McEwan, when we get there, we're meeting at the northern end of Montague Street. You and one of the armed officers will move to the back of the property as discussed.'

McEwan nodded.

'We'll give you time to get in place while the two uniform cars position themselves at each end of the road. They'll need to make sure it's clear before we proceed, so you'll have plenty of time. Make sure you've got the whole of the back wall covered.'

'OK.'

'Brody, Miller, we'll be with the other armed officers. Once everyone is in place and we're sure the area is clear, we'll go in. Nice and quick. SCO19 will lead. We go in behind. Right?'

Both detectives acknowledged Pope's instructions.

'What are we expecting?' asked Miller. 'I mean, when we get in there?'

'Good question.' Pope was a vastly more experienced officer, but even she had no real idea of what they were going to encounter once they entered the house. 'It may be a red herring, but I don't think so. It's too much of a coincidence. The cameras, six of them, two months ago. It's got to be him. Whether he's there or not, that's the question.'

'And if he is inside. . .?' asked Miller.

'If he's there, we take him by whatever means necessary,' said Pope firmly. 'He won't get away. With luck he'll come quietly, but if we need them, SCO19 will shoot to kill. I hope it won't come to that.'

Pope was aware that Adam Miller had not been on an operation with Armed Response before. Pope could sense that the anticipation was working hard on his nerves. She willed him to stay calm. He had to.

Pope guided the car through Greenwich, the two Armed Response vehicles ahead of her, and once they had passed through the centre, leaving the *Cutty Sark* and Old Royal Naval College behind them, they turned left into St Asaph Road. At the end of the road the four vehicles quietly and carefully pulled over to the side of the road. While the others in her car checked their tasers, batons and bulletproof vests, she went to each car in turn, checking that they knew exactly what they were doing. They already knew what they were going to do, but as the one in charge of the operation, she was determined it was going to go smoothly.

Then Pope signalled McEwan and one of the armed officers to walk around to the next road and find the back of the house. The two pairs of officers positioned themselves at either end of Montague Street, placing their cars across the road to ensure that no one could pass. Pope checked walkie-talkies and made sure everyone had communication. They would wait exactly ten minutes, to ensure that no members of the public were around, and so that her team, going in through the front, could get themselves in position and get eyes on the entrance to the property.

With the other teams in position, Pope indicated to the SCO19 officers to lead as they moved towards the house. They walked quickly, quietly along the street. It was dark, cold, damp, but none of them felt the light drizzle. All they felt was adrenaline. Miller was sweating, pulled his sleeve across his face to clear his vision. The streetlamps poured a solemn, off-white light over them. The emptiness echoed. When they got to the end of the terrace just before the property, they stopped, shielding themselves from view by the left-hand wall of the house.

The house itself was Victorian, two-storey, detached. It was small, two up, two down, guessed Pope. The exterior was exposed red brick, the front door painted black. Unobtrusive, separated. Just the kind of place to find some privacy. There were no lights on. Pope's pulse started to run, she could feel her heart beat in her chest. She had to remain as calm as possible, had to be able to make lightning-fast decisions and the right call.

She looked at her watch, then looked at each of her team in turn. Each nodded to her, indicating that they were ready.

Pope lifted her walkie-talkie. 'One minute,' she said.

She looked across at Brody. Like Pope, he had his baton drawn. An instinctive action, perhaps. With the firepower going in ahead of them, their batons were unlikely to be needed. But the nature of their adversary, the things he had done, the ferocity of the attacks, insisted that they didn't go unarmed.

Pope checked her watch. 'Thirty seconds,' she called quietly into the walkie-talkie. She looked at the house in front of them. No signs of activity. Curtains drawn, so it was impossible to see anything inside. This worried her. She preferred to at least have some form of visual cues before she gave an operation the green light. They were going in blind.

She looked at her watch again. She held the walkie-talkie up close, pressed the button to communicate. 'Ten seconds,' she said. She realized her mouth was dry. Her heart pounding. She indicated ten to Brody, although he'd already heard it. Then, time seemed to move incredibly slowly. The second hand on her watch seemed to be moving in slow motion. She had time to consider what they were doing, who they were looking for, what he'd done. Various scenarios played through her mind. Then the second hand reached zero.

'We're going in.'

The SCO19 officers moved quickly to the front door, their Heckler & Koch 9 mms ready. The door splintered as the steel battering ram cracked it down the middle, the two officers with rifles behind it shouting, screaming, warning any occupants who they were and what they were doing. They moved quickly and with absolute authority into the house.

Pope followed, and saw the first room was to the left as they entered. Two officers ran in, shouting, making as much noise as possible to disorientate any occupants. The third, rifle now drawn, stayed outside to cover them.

'Clear,' one of them shouted. The officer outside the room repeated the word for others to hear.

Withdrawing from the room, they moved quickly and efficiently to the next room. Two inside, one outside. Clear again. Then the room at the back. Pope could see this was a kitchen. It was empty.

Then the next wave of danger. Upstairs. Whoever was up there knew they were here and exactly where they were.

One of the SCO19 officers signalled for Pope and Brody to stay downstairs while they went up. Pope held her breath as the three cautiously ascended the stairs, rifles pointed in front of them, fingers on the triggers. They were intensely alert, eyes rapidly searching left to right and back again. Highly trained, for exactly this type of situation. Pope was glad they were here. Was glad they were walking up the stairs first.

As the first officer got to the top of the stairs he stopped. Looked around. Signalled it was clear to the other two, but this time silently. The dynamic had shifted and now they wanted silence, so they could listen for movement. They had the disadvantage visually, so other senses had to come in to play. He listened again, then quietly turned the corner and disappeared out of Pope's view. Pope could see Brody intently watching the top of the stairs. She looked behind them, checked the front door. Nothing. She turned back, listened. The sound of boots on the floorboards above. She looked straight up and followed the sounds above her head. She heard them go into the first room. Pause. Pope's heart raced. She could see the light bulb, suspended on a thin cord above her, swaying gently. They were right overhead. Then they exited, and along the corridor. Then into the next room. Another pause. Then more movement, out of that room, and further along the corridor. Now the sound was different. Louder footsteps. Pope thought they were checking the bathroom, the tiled floor failing to absorb the sound of footsteps like the carpeted rooms had done. Then nothing.

After what seemed like an eternity, the lead officer called down. 'All clear. The premises is cleared.'

Then: 'DCI Pope. You might want to come up and have a look at this.'

CHAPTER 25

Pope started walking upstairs, Brody behind her. They reached the top, where the team were standing outside one of the rooms.

'There's nobody here. But you need to see this.' The team leader indicated the doorway in front of him, and stepped aside to let them in.

They walked in through the door, cast their eyes around the room. A fairly large room, bigger than you might expect from looking at the outside of the house. Painted an off white. A bedroom with no bed.

But across one wall were four large TV monitors, side by side. All were switched off. In the middle of these was what looked like an electronic controller. A rectangular metal box full of buttons, sliders and dials. Like the mixing desks in recording studios, but with fewer channels. Next to the controller was a small pack of white envelopes, open with what looked like several missing. She silently indicated to Brody, who nodded.

On the wall to the left of this was a collage that covered around three quarters of the wall. Photographs and articles, pieces of text, diagrams. Pope took a closer look, Brody beside her. It was difficult to take in immediately. There were pictures of Susan Harper, Linda Wilson and Karen Tarling. Candid photographs, clearly taken at long range and without the subjects' knowledge. Some on their own, some with other people. In the case of Susan Harper, with her family. Then Pope's eyes cast over the rest. There was a photograph of herself. Leaving her house, on the way to work. Recent. But then another one, and more. Many more. And of Brody, Miller and even Tobias Darke outside his house in Richmond. *How the hell. . .?*

Then Pope froze. Alex opening their front door with a bag of shopping. Next to that more images of him, and of Chloe laughing with a friend, Hannah in her school uniform. Then one of the four of them, taken through the window of her house.

'Jesus Christ,' said Brody. 'This is. . .'

Pope didn't reply. She looked at the rest of the wall. Articles about the case, about Pope herself. All connected to either the victims, the case, her team, or her family. The headlines: "Another London Woman Murdered", "The Female Cop Hunting London Killer", "Serial Killer Terrorises London".

Darke had been right. He had predicted that the killer must have a personal interest in Pope, that she might connect these seemingly unconnected people. By leading the investigation, she had provided a link to the victims. But it was more than that. The cards the killer had left, these photographs. This was personal.

'What does all this mean?' asked Brody. 'Is he coming after us? After Alex and the girls?'

Past victims and future victims? Was that what this wall was all about? By far the most common photograph was of her, or of her and Brody, or of her and Alex. The common denominator.

She broke away from her thoughts. Saw that the SCO19 officers were also looking at the wall, looking at her.

She took out her walkie-talkie. 'All clear. Miller, come in. McEwan, stay where you are and make sure no one comes in or out. Hawley, organize a house-to-house along Montague Street.'

Pope took out her mobile phone to call Fletcher. She gave him a brief summary of what had happened. 'I need as many officers as available to conduct a house-to-house. And I want Forensics and Tech Support, specifically Stephen Thompson, down here as soon as possible.'

She paused, not wanting to say the next part out loud.

'And we're going to need to talk about arranging protection details for my family and Tobias Darke. I think you should come to Greenwich to see this for yourself.'

When she had finished organizing the resources and people she needed on the scene, Pope turned to Brody.

'Could this be Mick Waterson? Edward Boyd? Someone else?' he asked. 'Who could do all this?'

'That's a question I can't answer yet. Let's look around the rest of the house, then we'll come back to this,' she said, indicating the wall and the monitors.

The two of them walked downstairs, pulling on gloves. They would have to go back to the case files, back even further. It had to be someone she had come into contact with through an old case. She searched for an idea, a suggestion of who it might be.

Miller met them coming in through the front door and joined them as they checked the downstairs of the house. Pope didn't say anything about the room upstairs yet. They entered the first room. This was the first that the SCO19 officers had gone into. It looked very ordinary. A small, tidy living room. A TV in the corner, next to a bay window that stretched across the entirety of the wall. Stripped floorboards, the walls painted a light blue. A sofa, two armchairs and a sideboard. Nothing on top. Finally, a low coffee table in the middle of the room. That was all.

Brody leaned down and opened one of the doors in the sideboard. He looked inside. Empty. The other door revealed the same.

'It doesn't look like anybody actually lives here,' he said. He looked around. 'There're no belongings, no clutter. No "stuff". It's like a show house.'

Brody's description only heightened Pope's sense of unease.

They left the room and went into the next door along the narrow hallway. A similar picture. This was notionally the dining room, although it was clear that no actual dining went on in here. There was a table, with four chairs around it, one on each edge. Again, a sideboard along one wall. Brody checked it. This time it wasn't empty. Plates, glasses, serving dishes and a tray full of cutlery, in their separate compartments. There were no pictures on the walls, no photographs on the sideboard or the mantelpiece above the fireplace, which was spotless and looked as if it hadn't held a real fire for many years. The floorboards also looked scrupulously clean.

'Nobody uses these rooms.' Brody was confirming his previous thoughts. 'They're maintained for appearances, there's no dust. But nobody eats in here. Either that, or they've got a serious cleaning fetish.'

Pope nodded.

'So who lives here, then? Do we know if it's his house?' asked Miller.

'Yes, we know it's his house. You'll see in a minute when we go upstairs,' said Brody. 'We're definitely in the right place.'

'Or one of the right places,' said Pope.

'What do you mean?' asked Miller.

'I don't think he lives here,' said Pope. 'I think he uses this place to plan. He surveils, collates information, prepares. But he lives somewhere else. This is his office. And I don't think he'll come back.'

'But we're going to keep the house under surveillance, right?' asked Brody.

'Yes, of course,' replied Pope. 'But he's been one step ahead of us so far. He watches everything.'

Miller looked at Pope. 'You'll see when we go upstairs. But I think he knows we're here.' They all involuntarily glanced around the room, looking for the signs of hidden cameras. 'He won't come back,' Pope repeated and left the room.

Brody and Miller followed her into the final room downstairs. It was a kitchen in name only, much like the other rooms. All the usual appliances were there; fridge, washing machine, oven, kettle. But when Pope opened the fridge, it was empty. When she opened the cooker door, it was spotlessly clean, unused. The eye-level cupboards were full of pristine new crockery.

'Let's go back upstairs,' said Pope, and led the way.

They first looked through the other rooms upstairs and it became clear that only one room in the entire house was in use.

Miller's jaw dropped when he entered the room. He looked around and took in the same scene as Pope and Brody had a few minutes before. Now he understood Pope's certainty that they were in the right place. Pope watched him go through the same process that she and Brody had been through. First the TV monitors and control equipment, then the montage on the wall, and finally the realization that some of the pictures were of them. Of Miller.

'What the. . .?' Miller trailed off, unable to articulate his thoughts.

After the initial shock had subsided, they began to look in more detail at the pictures and articles on the wall. Pope knew she wouldn't be able to do much with the audiovisual equipment until Stephen Thompson arrived, so she concentrated on the more analogue elements of the scene.

A number of articles were tacked on to the wall between the myriad photographs. They were from newspapers and online sources. Brody looked round the room, found a desktop computer sitting on a small table next to a printer. He walked over, took a pen from his pocket and used it to press one of the keys, preserving the integrity of any fingerprints that might have been left on the machine. The computer was on standby and the screen sprang to life. "Enter password" flashed up on to the screen, above a narrow, rectangular white box ready for the magic word. The cursor flashed. He returned to the wall.

'These are very recent. Some from yesterday,' said Miller, indicating two articles from online sources. 'He's been here in the last twenty-four hours.'

All the articles detailed either the murders of Susan Harper or Linda Wilson, or the attack on Karen Tarling. One was an account of the murder of Karen Tarling in King's Hospital. Pope frowned. The articles came from a wide variety of sources. A collector.

'What do we make of the photographs?' asked Pope. They began to search the images, looking carefully at each in turn.

Pope could see that the pictures of the three victims were taken at various locations, at different times of the day, apparently over a period of some time. Most were taken at their homes, through the windows, as they were leaving in the morning, returning in the evening. Each was a document of some part of the victims' daily lives, coming together to form a whole picture of their routines and lifestyles, their comings and goings, their social interactions. And the times they were alone. A shot of Susan Harper standing at the front door saying goodbye to her husband, another as she said goodbye to her son and daughter as she saw them off to school, maybe for the last time. Another from outside as she stood in her bedroom window, maybe checking the weather as she chose an outfit for the day. Shots of Linda Wilson leaving for work in the morning with her partner, returning late in the evening, always alone. Always in the dark — she started early, worked long hours. *Easy prey*, thought Pope. Then photographs of Karen Tarling, the same thing. Early, late, alone. Pope knew then that he was a hunter, a predator. He found women who were easy targets. Learned their routines, knew where they would be and when they would be alone.

He was a cold-blooded killer. No heat of the moment, no crimes of passion. All premeditated and carefully controlled. She understood the how. Now all she needed were the who and the why. And actually, she only needed one of those.

Finally, Pope examined the photos of herself, her team and her family. Telephoto shots of her walking out of the station with Brody. Her car driving into the underground police car park at Charing Cross, Pope clearly visible through the windscreen. Another shot of her leaving, late, dark. She looked tired, drawn. Then shots of Brody on his own. Not only arriving and leaving from work, but entering his apartment. Then a shock: a shot of Pope and Brody in a pub, the Coal Hole on the Strand. They were leaning into a conspiratorial-looking conversation. They looked like lovers sharing a secret thought, a moment. It seemed very intimate. Pope felt uncomfortable, wasn't quite sure why. And Pope with Alex. And Alex: on his own, with Chloe and Hannah, going to work, leaving for the cinema, going to school. And shots of their house, their home. From the front, from the back. Entrances and exits. A shot of the French windows from over the garden wall at the back of the house. Pope instinctively thought of the night she had heard a noise downstairs, had assumed it was the wind on that stormy night. Now she wasn't so sure. She knew she would have to talk to Fletcher as soon as he arrived to ensure an immediate protection detail for Alex and the girls.

From behind her, Miller said, 'This guy's been everywhere!' He looked at Pope. 'You, me, Brody, all the victims, everywhere.' He was scared. Pope hadn't seen him like this before. She knew as Miller's boss she needed to offer solace, calm him down. But she had no idea what to say. No words that could undo, or make right, what they were looking at.

Just then they heard sounds downstairs, followed by voices and footsteps coming up the stairs. Stephen Thompson appeared in the doorway. He was carrying an aluminium flight case: his travelling box of electronic tricks.

'Hi,' he said.

'Hi, Stephen,' said Brody. Then, as Thompson's eyes scanned the room, took in the electronic equipment, and then the contents of the montage on the wall behind the three officers, his expression changed. He opened his mouth to say something, but closed it again, saying nothing.

'Thompson,' said Pope. 'I need you to look at these screens and see if you can find anything. Bearing in mind the cameras at the first two crime scenes, it seems likely that this is where he watched the feed. See what you can do.'

'And the computer,' said Brody, indicating the machine in the corner. 'It's password protected.'

Thompson took in the equipment with a visual sweep, then set his case down on the floor and took out a number of items. He then turned his attention to the controller between the four screens. He pressed a button. The console hummed into life, blue and red lights flashing, peaking, and then set-tling down to a low level in front of him. He moved quickly, scanning for what he needed and soon the four screens came to life, each with its own electronic beep. But they showed nothing. He worked for a few minutes, examining the device, trying to find how to make something appear in front of them. Pope, Brody and Miller stood behind him, anxious to see some piece of conclusive evidence, some irrefutable clue to the identity of the killer suddenly appearing. The monitors remained dark. Thompson leaned over to see the back of the system, then climbed underneath the desk and checked the wiring and connections. He was following the cables, checking where they led and how they were interconnected. Eventually he came up for air. He sat back in the chair.

'I think this is certainly where he views the feeds from the cameras. These must go to a remote server that amplifies and relays the signal so he can receive it here. He knows what he's doing, or whoever installed this does, at least.'

'So why is there nothing on the screens at the moment?' asked Pope.

'Probably because there's currently no feed. The mon-itors show what's being picked up by the cameras. If there's nothing being broadcast, there's nothing to watch,' he explained simply.

'But does he not record the signals? Does he have to always watch them live?' asked Pope.

'Possibly yes. He's here, and he watches what's going on as it happens. The other possibility is that he stores recordings here,' said Thompson, indicating the computer to the right of the monitors. 'It is connected, and there's no other method of recording transmissions that I can see with this equipment, so he may have set it up through the computer. But it's password protected, so I don't know if we'll be able to access it. Certainly not immediately.'

Pope thought. 'OK. Keep working on it. I need to know as soon as possible if there's anything that can help us here.'

Thompson nodded.

As they were turning their attention back to the collage on the wall, Richard Fletcher walked in, two police officers behind him. He nodded to Pope and the others, then caught sight of the photographs. He scanned each element, skim-reading the headlines and first paragraphs of each article, then looking at each photograph in turn. No one spoke, allowing Fletcher time to process the scene and take in the implications of what he was seeing.

'So, no question that this is his place,' said Fletcher. This was clear to everyone in the room. He looked at Pope. 'Let's go next door.'

Pope nodded and followed Fletcher into the hallway. They walked downstairs and went into the staged dining room.

'What the fuck is going on?'

Pope saw that he was rattled, which was why he didn't want to have the conversation in front of the other officers.

'Good question,' said Pope. 'It looks like this is where he organizes, plans and controls the murders. You saw from the photographs that he keeps the victims under surveillance for some time before he acts, planning carefully and taking the time to learn their routines, their movements. Then we think he comes back here to watch the live feeds from the cameras he leaves at the crime scenes. Thompson is checking all that equipment now to see if it can tell us anything.'

Fletcher paused, looked at Pope. 'Why the pictures of you, Brody, Miller? Your family? Hell, there's even a picture of me on that wall. It centres on you.'

Pope felt uncomfortable, hearing it said out loud again. 'There're no links to the victims, except that I'm heading the investigation, which I guess creates a link in the killer's eyes. But the others. . .' She let the words hang in the air.

'Do you want me to take you off the case, Bec? I can reassign you if you want me to. . .'

'No.' Pope was emphatic. 'If this is about me, I need to find him. If I'm at the centre of this, I'm the one most likely to be able to figure it out. I need to find him now.'

Fletcher nodded.

'But I do need a protection detail for Alex and the kids,' said Pope. 'The pictures on the wall tell us that he's been to my house, taken photographs of all of us. I'll need to talk to Alex about taking the girls away somewhere, maybe to his parents. But in the meantime, I need immediate protection for them. Tonight.'

'Yes, no problem,' said Fletcher. 'I'll go back to the station now and get that sorted.'

'Thanks,' said Pope. 'I'll meet you there. I'm going to talk to Brody and Miller, tell them to wait until Forensics and the other officers get here. They can brief them and organize the house-to-house interviews. Then I'll come back to the station with Brody and we can work out how we proceed. How are you getting on with that warrant for Edward Boyd's apartment?'

'I'm working on it. There was some question of a lack of evidence initially, but after this. . .' He pointed, indicated the room they had just walked out of. 'Well, I don't think there'll be much of a problem.'

'I'm going to need that as soon as you can get it. And the same for Mick Waterson's house. He seems to have disappeared.'

'OK. I'll sort both of those ASAP.' Fletcher left the room and went towards the front door. Pope watched him leave, then walked back upstairs.

She explained to Brody and Miller what she wanted them to do.

Pope lowered her voice. 'I don't want either of you alone at any point. Miller, you'll be here with the rest of the officers. Brody, when you come back to the station, get a lift with one of the uniforms. Understand?' They both nodded. 'Our pictures are up there too. We need to take care. No mistakes.'

As Pope walked out on to the street, she was aware of the changing quality of the air. Gone was the claustrophobia of the scene she had just left. In its place a gusting wind pushing along the street. It felt good.

But as she searched for her car keys, she was thinking about only one thing. What the hell would she say to Alex?

* * *

He sat with his head in his hands, a low, guttural moan emanating from deep within his throat. He moved his fingers through his hair, across the top of his head and down to the base of his neck. He sat there for a long time, rubbing the back of his neck, trying to keep control, trying to think.

They'd found it. This wasn't the plan. Wasn't what he'd wanted. He knew he'd kept it clean, knew they wouldn't find any evidence to lead them to him before he was finished. But it wasn't in his plan. Not yet.

This was the second problem.

The first had been Karen Tarling's escape.

He had made an error. But he'd corrected that very quickly and very efficiently, and in many ways, returning to finish the job had been even more satisfying. He imagined how Pope must have felt. She had thought she was keeping her safe, thought that she was protecting her. Thought that maybe she'd lead her to a solution. And it had all been taken away under her nose.

He would fix this problem too.

205

He looked at the screen on his mobile phone. He could see them, looking at his work, looking at the photographs of themselves, trying to decipher his equipment. The guy sitting in his chair, looking at his monitors, trying to work out why he couldn't see anything. Trying to unlock his computer, see if he could find anything incriminating. He hated him.

This was his. His private place. But he knew that the guy wouldn't work it out, wouldn't find anything useful. Yes, they would trace the ownership of the house and that eventually something might lead back to him, once they had disentangled the web he had created to preserve his anonymity. It wouldn't last for ever.

He didn't have much time. Needed to act faster than he had planned. That's all right. Plans can be changed. Improved.

He watched the other two examining the wall he had created. He hadn't wanted anyone to see that. Not yet. This was for him, for him alone. But he suppressed his fury.

It was a negative and self-destructive emotion, one that prevented him from thinking clearly and accomplishing what needed to be accomplished. He now knew what he was going to do. Knew where he would go, and exactly how this would end.

He touched the screen on his phone, navigated to a virtual controller and pushed a button to take him to an alternative camera feed. In front of him on the screen was Bec Pope's living room. Alex Regis and Hannah Regis sitting on the sofa, drinking coffee, watching TV. Oblivious. Standing behind them, Chloe Regis, looking at her phone, tapping the keys. He used a dial to zoom in on her face. Watched her typing.

Time to end it.

CHAPTER 26

It had been a difficult telephone conversation with Alex. Pope had called him in the car, before she drove back to the station from the house in Greenwich. She had tried not to unduly alarm him, didn't want to cause him to panic. But at the same time she knew what this killer was capable of, and the pictures on the wall of the house told Pope that she had to warn her family.

She had explained as best she could what was going on and that there was a chance that Alex and the girls might be considered a target. She didn't tell him about the photographs, instead suggesting that her investigation of the case placed them in a vulnerable position.

'There'll be a protection detail outside any time now.' said Pope. 'Lock the front and back doors and don't open them for anyone. Just normal, sensible precautions,' she added, the conviction in her voice weak at best.

There was silence on the other end of the line.

'Alex . . . I'm so sorry about this. If it could be any other way. I'll be back as soon as I can and we can talk about getting the girls somewhere away from here.' She knew exactly what he would be thinking, and the silence was unbearable.

'Alex?'

'Yeah, I'm here. I need to go. I'll see you when you come back.'

She started to reply, unsure of what to say, but he had already ended the call.

He wasn't happy, she knew that, but there wasn't much he could do. It was too late to take the girls anywhere now. She would deal with the rest when she got home.

* * *

Once again, thought Alex, Pope's work was encroaching upon their personal life. He knew there was more to it, more than she had said. But he accepted that she had to get back to the station and that they would talk later. He drew the bolt across the bottom of the door, checked the main lock and returned to the living room. He'd talk to the girls about this in the morning, after he had talked to Bec. They were both here, weren't going anywhere. He had been just about to go to bed when he received her phone call. Now he felt wide awake. He poured himself a large glass of red wine, sat down on the sofa and took a long drink.

* * *

Pope was troubled on her drive back to Charing Cross. She felt uneasy about the call with Alex. She knew she could have told him more, could have really frightened him. But she couldn't do it. She felt that she had got it more or less right, but still it concerned her. Now she was away from the house in Montague Street, she had the time to reflect on what she had seen. The images and articles detailed every aspect of the case so far. This was obsessive detail, the work of a psychopath. She made a mental note to contact Tobias Darke and send him to have a look for himself, see what he could make of it.

But the thing that was really nagging away at Pope was the pictures of her, her family, the rest of her team. Why were

208

they there? The answer to that question was the real problem. They were all potential targets. Maybe one of them was the next target. Sooner or later, once he had finished playing his sick games, the killer would come for her. Pope couldn't see any other explanation for what she had seen in that house.

But what, Pope wondered, did he have in mind before that? How many of them would he go for, before his apparent endgame?

When she arrived at the station, she went straight to Richard Fletcher's office, knocked and walked in without waiting for an answer.

'Bec. Are you all right?' asked Fletcher. He was sitting behind his desk, had been typing an email on his computer.

'I'm fine. Brody just called. He and Miller have set up the house-to-house, they're doing that now. Forensics and Tech Support are working at the scene. They'll be there all night. Brody's on his way in, then the three of us should consider where we go now,' said Pope.

'Yes, I agree,' said Fletcher.

'Have you organized protection for Alex and the girls?' asked Pope. Her tone suggested that only one answer would be acceptable.

'I'm doing that now. I'm authorizing the operation and the overtime. There'll be a car there within the hour. Have you spoken to Alex?' asked Fletcher.

'Yes. I've given him an outline. I didn't want to worry him too much.' Pope was justifying her actions, to herself as much as anyone else. 'Once we've met with Brody I'm going to go home.'

'Good idea,' said Fletcher. 'I'm sure everything will be fine, but it's better to be safe than sorry.'

'I need to check on a few things. I'll let you know when Brody gets here,' said Pope, already halfway out of the door.

Pope walked along the corridor and into her office. She sat down at her desk and picked up the phone. Tobias Darke answered on the third ring.

'Hi, Tobias. It's Bec. I'm sorry to be ringing you so late.'

'Absolutely nothing to worry about, Bec. What can I do for you?'

How to explain this?

'We've found his house. Or one of them.'

'By "his", you mean your killer?' asked Darke.

'Yes. We think so.'

'Where?'

'In Greenwich. We found a connection to an electronics store that appears to have shipped the same type of cameras used at the crime scenes to this address,' replied Pope.

'Was he there? Have you got him?'

'Unfortunately not. But he's been there recently. Crime Scene are there at the moment. I was wondering if you'd like to take a look, see what you think?' asked Pope. 'Maybe first thing tomorrow?'

'What kind of thing are we talking about?'

'It's a lair, really. Photographs, newspaper clippings, computers. All kinds of stuff,' said Pope.

'Sounds fascinating. I'll be there early tomorrow. Send me the address.'

'I'll send a car for you. Say, 7 a.m.?'

'OK, I'll be ready.'

'I'll see you there. And Tobias,' she hesitated. 'Some of the pictures are of Alex and the girls. Of me and the team. There's one of you,' she added.

There was silence for a moment on the other end of the line.

'Right. Thanks for the warning. Are you OK? How are you feeling?'

He sounded concerned. 'I'm fine,' she said, although she was lying and she knew full well that he knew. 'We just need to catch this guy before. . .' She let the sentence trail off.

'I understand. Take care of yourself, Bec. See you in the morning.'

* * *

Approximately seven miles southeast from where Pope was talking to Tobias Darke on the telephone, Chloe Regis was startled by a knock at the front door. She had begun to feel drowsy, lying in bed messaging Tyler and continuing several text chains with her friends, and this made her jump. She looked at her clock. Late. Bec. She had come home late, couldn't find her keys. Chloe sighed, got out of bed and walked down the stairs. She looked in on her father as she walked past his room and saw that he was fast asleep.

How nice for him, thought Chloe. She walked to the door and looked through the spy hole. Frowning, she took a step back. Then she drew back the bolt and opened the door.

* * *

Just as her computer was coming to life, Brody arrived in the office.

'How'd it go?' asked Pope. 'Is everything underway?'

Brody took off his jacket, hung it up by the door and sat down opposite Pope. 'Yes, it's all being handled,' he replied. 'Miller and I briefed the officers regarding the house-to-house. They'll let him know if there's anything interesting. Miller will handle the follow-ups. Forensics are there. They're also looking at the computer and the other equipment with Thompson. I've asked Miller to let us know the moment he gets anything,' said Brody.

'Good. Tobias Darke is meeting me in Greenwich tomorrow morning. I'll go straight to the house and then come in after that.'

'What do you think about the electronics and the technical stuff, the surveillance? Does that strike you as something Mick Waterson would do? Would be capable of doing?'

That thought had struck Pope as they were looking at the set-up in the upstairs room. 'I don't know. It certainly isn't what I would have expected from him. But who knows what people are capable of, what talents they have?'

'What about Boyd?' Brody hadn't interviewed Edward Boyd.

'He certainly strikes me as the type of man who would have the financial resources and the patience to set something like that up. And the desire to photograph and observe is him all over. He loves to be in control. Although, talking about him as a "type of man" is pretty ridiculous. He's a one-off.'

'Have we found Waterson?' asked Brody.

'Not yet. APB out on him and Trish. Fletcher's sorting warrants for his house, and for Boyd's. Hopefully they'll be ready in the morning and we'll execute a search of both places early.'

'Did you talk to Alex?' asked Brody.

'Yeah. It was tough.' She leaned back in her chair and looked up at the ceiling.

'Did you tell him about the wall? About the photographs of him and the girls?'

'No,' said Pope. 'I thought I'd wait until I see him face to face. It's not really the kind of news that you want to deliver over the telephone. That a psychotic killer who has been strangling young women has your picture on the wall, next to his other victims. And those of your daughters,' she added.

'No,' said Brody. 'I see your point. What are you going to do? They can't stay in the house with the door locked indefinitely.'

'No, they can't,' agreed Pope. 'As soon as we've met with Fletcher I'm going to go home and suggest that he takes the girls away to his parents for a while.' She looked at Brody. 'He's going to go mad. He'll be furious at the threat to his family. But it has to be,' said Pope.

'That sounds like a good idea. Not easy though,' said Brody. 'Is there anything I can do?'

'Tell me the identity and whereabouts of "the Cameraman",' said Pope.

Brody smiled, knowing how much she hated the nickname, but it wasn't very funny.

'I'll call Fletcher,' said Pope, reaching for the phone on her desk. Just as she did so, her mobile rang. She saw it lying in front of her, saw it was Alex calling, the vibrating amplified by the cheap Formica of the desk. *Why is Alex calling so late?*

She reached for the phone and answered.

Then time froze. Alex was shouting. Brody could hear him on the other end of the line. Pope sat forward, tensed as she tried to calm him down, to get him to stop shouting. But he was hysterical, distraught.

'Alex. Alex. Stop shouting, tell me what happened.' Pope raised her voice, well-practised authority. 'Alex. Stop shouting and talk to me.'

This seemed to do the trick.

Alex had heard something and come downstairs. The bolt on the front door was drawn back, but he knew he had locked it. In the living room a table had been knocked over, cushions on the floor. He had run upstairs and checked on the girls. Hannah was asleep in her bed. Chloe was not.

'She's gone, Bec, she's gone,' he kept repeating.

'I'm coming now,' said Pope. 'I'm coming now.'

She put down the phone, looked at Brody.

'He's got Chloe. He's got her.'

* * *

Pope knew it was not a good idea for her to drive, but she was behind the wheel and revving the engine before Brody even reached the car. He had no choice but to jump in the passenger seat. Pope stepped on the accelerator and the car was already moving as his door slammed shut.

'Take it easy, Bec,' he said, but Pope wasn't listening. Her mind was flooded with guilt, terror, rage, frustration.

'Be careful,' said Brody, as she raced through a large roundabout, cutting in front of several cars, and sped on to the Old Kent Road, headed south. She was driving on the wrong side of the road, siren blaring and lights flashing, trusting that the cars coming in the opposite direction would get out of her way in time for her to pass. Mostly they did. Others were slow to realize and several times she slid between two cars, inches on either side.

Then she was pulling into her road, arriving at her house. The home that should have been a place of safety for Alex and the girls. Pope jumped out of the car. She was vaguely aware of the sound of sirens in the distance. Fletcher would have sent all available units to meet her.

She ran up to the front door, Brody behind her. It flung open as she tried to find her key. Alex was standing there, pale, terrified, in shock. Suddenly he slapped Pope hard across the side of her face. She felt a sharp, stinging pain, but stood still. He blamed her. She should have done more to protect them.

Brody flinched as the slap connected.

Then Alex put his arms around Pope. He leaned heavily on her as she held him tight. Then he looked her in the eye.

'He's got her, Bec. That bastard has got her, hasn't he? It's him.'

What could she say? She knew it was true but didn't want to say it. Instead she said, 'We'll get her back, Alex.'

Alex pulled away. She sensed a change in him, and suddenly the anger returned. He took a step back, distancing himself from her.

'How, Bec? How are you going to find her? How are you going to get her back?' he demanded, his voice raised and challenging.

'Alex. . .' she said, taking a step towards him. But Alex took another step backwards into the house.

'Don't, Bec. What are you going to do, exactly? You brought this fucking monster to us! You got involved in this, and now my daughter is paying for that. Paying for you being the detective hero.'

'Alex,' she repeated, but it was no use. The enormity of the situation was incomprehensible. His daughter had been taken by a sadistic serial killer of young women. How could you deal with that?

'If you'd done what I asked, taken the job you were offered, this wouldn't have happened. You're selfish, and this is the result. What are you going to do? Where is Chloe?' He stared at her, then at Brody, expecting some kind of answer.

Pope had absolutely no idea where she would find Chloe. Her stepdaughter. Suddenly Pope felt sick. Felt that knife that came when your kids were in trouble. She hadn't felt anything like this before.

She took a step towards Alex, and this time he didn't move away. They stood close, facing each other.

'I'm going to find her, Alex. I'm going to check the house, then I'm going to find where this son of a bitch is and get Chloe back.' She looked him in the eyes.

He simply said, 'Find her, Bec.'

She nodded. She had to hold it down. The rising panic. For now. For Alex.

She was taking it in, trying to evaluate the crime scene, as she had done so many times before. Trying to eliminate the context, the sense of a personal connection that was making it difficult to evaluate what she was seeing. She could hear Brody outside, briefing the officers who had just arrived. She was glad they hadn't witnessed the scene with Alex.

She saw the table that had been knocked over, the cushions on the floor, just as Alex had described on the phone. This had been the scene that had greeted him as he had come downstairs and it had been obvious that something was wrong. Looking at it, she knew exactly what had happened.

The killer had entered the house and then there had been a struggle with Chloe. He had overpowered her. Exactly the same as the previous three victims. This thought, this confirmation in her own mind, was like being punched in the stomach. Pope experienced a physical sensation of pain as she thought of Chloe fighting with him, her terror as she realized what was happening and then knew that he was too strong and she was not going to escape. Had he hurt her? Beaten her, punched her like he did the other women?

She walked over to Brody. He was looking at the front door carefully. She lowered her voice so that Alex wouldn't hear them.

'Where has he taken her?' she said. 'I mean, the other victims. . .' She paused, finding it difficult to say what she was thinking, not wanting to hear the words. 'With the other victims he killed them in their homes, or tried to. The same MO. So why didn't he do that with Chloe? Why has he taken her somewhere else?'

Brody thought about this. 'He has some other plan for her. But there's a good chance she's still alive, or why not just kill her immediately?'

It was very tough to hear this, but Pope knew he was right. It had been exactly what she was thinking.

'There's something else,' said Brody. He stepped close to the door, so he could examine the lock again. Pope leaned in and looked closely. 'There's no sign of forced entry. He didn't force the door. So Chloe must have let him in. Just like the others. Why would she do that so late at night?' he asked. 'What does he do that makes women open the door?'

Pope walked over to Alex. 'Was the front door locked? Was it bolted?' she asked.

'Yes, it was. You told me to lock and bolt the front door and to open it for no one except you. So, yes, I bolted it. Why?'

'I'm not sure,' said Pope. 'But if it was locked, Chloe must have opened the door to him. Why would she do that?' She asked the question, but knew there would be no answer.

'I don't know.' Alex looked confused.

She spoke quietly, attempting calm. 'Look, he's taken Chloe. He could have harmed her, but he took her instead. So he must have other plans for her.'

Alex started.

'No, no.' Pope reassured him, held his gaze. 'That's good, because it means he needs her for something. Maybe a bargaining chip if he thinks we're getting close.'

Alex looked dubious.

'I'm going back to the station. That's where I can be most effective. You stay here, in case she comes back.' She looked over his shoulder into the house. 'They'll be in the house for a while checking forensics, and there'll be a car outside.'

Alex nodded. She could see the pain. Pope knew he didn't want her to go, but this was what needed to happen.

'I promise I'll let you know the moment I know anything,' she said.

As she and Brody left the house, Alex called to her. She turned, as did Brody. 'Find my daughter,' he said.

'I will.'

CHAPTER 27

She felt pain all over her body. Her head, her wrists and ankles where she was tied, her throat, her upper body. She looked down at her T-shirt and saw the blood. She thought it must have been from when she was hit, or when she fell, and instinctively tried to lift her hand to her face to check the damage. But her arm wouldn't move. She tugged again against the ties and a sharp pain stung up through her elbow. Why could she remember being hit, but not who had done it? This she didn't understand. Now her thoughts were arriving quickly, jumbled and confused.

She could see that the building was some kind of warehouse. A long, wide space, hardly a room. Yes, a warehouse. Along one side were windows, boarded up. Only one was left open, a piece of chipboard leaned against the wall to the right of this one window. Obviously removed so there was some sight of the outside. The rest was old, dark, black. One light bulb at each end, attached to long, dirty cords and swinging just perceptibly in a breeze from somewhere. The floor was brick, but old, rutted, uncared for. It hadn't been cleaned for a very long time. She had no idea what this place had been used for in the past.

Her head ached all over, but particularly on the left. Then she remembered: she had been punched hard, had fallen, hit her head. That was all, and now she was here. Her first thought was to scream, but something stopped her. She couldn't decide whether she wanted to draw attention to herself or not. Something told her not. She couldn't tell if it was night or day. The small amount of light that entered through the one available window could be daylight or street light. Impossible to tell from this distance.

She was beginning to feel panic welling up inside her now. She looked down. She was sitting on a tubular metal chair, maybe brown or red? She couldn't tell, partly because of the lack of natural light and partly because her vision was still blurred and she couldn't trust the colours. Her hands were tied tightly to the steel arms of the chair with black nylon cable ties. She tried to wrestle them free, but they were held firm. The ties were strong, she could feel that. They cut into her wrists and the more she tried to move the more they hurt. Her feet felt like they were bound by the same ties, also too tight.

Suddenly she was aware of her heart beating in her chest and she felt sweat on her forehead. A drop fell into her eye, but she had nothing to brush it away with. Survival instinct took over.

'Help!' she shouted. Her throat hurt. 'Help. Somebody help! Can anyone hear me? Help!'

She listened, but after the faint echo of her final word, she heard nothing. Just the sound of rain on the corrugated roof above her head.

She tried to piece together what had happened, but her memory wouldn't oblige. She had no recollection of who had hit her, or how she had got here. Again, she was aware of the power and speed of her heartbeat and the panic rising inside her. She called again, as loud as she could, but as before there was no reply.

Where was she? Who had brought her here? Why was she tied up?

She thought of her dad, and of Bec. Surely Bec would find her, be searching now. Her mind skipped back to her heartbeat. The combination of pain and fear was making it difficult to think clearly. She felt disorientated and afraid. And now she was about to vomit.

Then her thoughts were interrupted by a noise at the far end of the large space. She looked up. The door, old, metal, grey, was scraping along the floor at the bottom, opening.

Someone was coming.

* * *

Fletcher was there to meet them as Pope and Brody hurried into their office. Pope flung her coat on to a chair.

'How's Alex?' asked Fletcher as soon as Pope had come in.

'Um. . . as expected,' replied Pope. 'Have we got anything yet?'

'Not yet. Miller and Thompson are downstairs checking if there's anything useful from the house in Greenwich. Forensics are still working on it but they'll let us know as soon as they have anything. There are two units outside your house, they'll be relieved by two more in the morning.'

'Thanks.'

'We've got units at both Mick Waterson's and Edward Boyd's registered addresses. Nothing, both empty, no sign of either of them. Forensics are working at both locations and at your house now,' said Fletcher.

'He left nothing at the other crime scenes, he won't have left anything.' It felt unreal to describe her own house as a crime scene. 'We need something else.' Pope was now pacing the office, staring in front of her. There were too many thoughts crowding her head to think clearly.

Brody put his hand on her arm.

'Bec. We'll get him. We will. But we need to focus and keep a clear head. He's not going to hurt Chloe. He wants her for something else. You know that. We just have to work out where she is. We all need to be present for that.' He spoke softly, but there was a firmness that insisted.

Pope knew he was right, and not for the first time recently. She worked to bring herself back from the crippling power of her own emotions. This was not the time to lose control.

Pope was not used to this. She'd had cases that had touched her life in the past, things had gone wrong. Tina Waterson. Others. But this was different. Brody was right, she had to do what she had been trained to do: compartmentalize and prioritize. There would be time for soul-searching and recriminations when they had found Chloe. She had to believe that they would find her.

'What's our next step?' asked Fletcher.

Brody spoke. 'We really need something from his place in Greenwich. There has to be something there we can use.'

'Or I can go on TV and appeal to him,' said Pope suddenly. 'It's me he wants to target, one way or another. I'll go on TV and talk directly to him. Offer to trade myself with Chloe. He has to go for that.'

'Wait a minute, Bec,' began Fletcher. 'We need to think about this. I'm not sure it will do any good to—'

'That's what we'll do. It'll flush him out and we'll be ready for him,' said Pope, the idea gaining momentum in her mind.

'It might do more harm than good, Bec,' said Brody. 'There's no point putting yourself in danger.'

Pope was about to counter his argument, when the door burst open and Adam Miller flew into the room.

'I've got something, I think,' he said, breathless from running up several flights of stairs. He rushed to his desk and punched the password into his computer.

Pope, Brody and Fletcher stopped and looked at Miller, crossing to his desk.

'What is it?' asked Pope.

Miller opened his documents folder and navigated to the page he had evidently been working on downstairs. He found what he was looking for and opened it on the screen.

'We were looking at the material we had gathered from the house, when I suddenly had an idea.' Miller looked up at the three senior officers, who were waiting for him to continue.

'Nothing came back from the nationwide request for any unsolved cases with similar MOs. Nothing. We were fairly sure that these were not his first victims, so that surprised me. I was sure that there had to be something, somewhere. The next step was to widen the search, to look abroad. At Europe at least.'

The others nodded.

'So I put out an Interpol request for information. It didn't take long until I began to get some hits,' continued Miller.

'What do you mean?' asked Pope. 'What have you got?'

'Well, it turns out that there are quite a bunch of unsolved homicides across the continent with a very similar MO to Susan Harper and Linda Wilson. I'm still collating the information and putting together a timeline, and more cases are coming in as we speak. But so far, we have very similar crimes in Paris, Frankfurt, Milan, Madrid, Barcelona and Berlin.' He paused.

'What's the timescale?' asked Pope. 'How recent are these cases?'

'That's the weird thing,' replied Miller. 'They date back over the past twenty years.'

'Christ,' exclaimed Pope.

'Twenty years! Why didn't we know about this sooner? Why isn't all this on our database?' asked Fletcher.

'You know what European inter-force communication is like. There's just too much information,' said Miller. 'But this looks promising.'

Pope's head was throbbing. It was too much. She sat at her desk and massaged her temples. Somewhere in the back of her mind an idea flickered. She couldn't quite formulate it into a coherent whole, but something was there.

* * *

As he opened the door the bottom scraped along the floor, making a low, harsh scratch. There she was. He'd tied her well, tight. She was exactly where he had left her. He carefully closed the door behind him. He looked around the space, took it in. Then he walked slowly towards her. There was no rush. Nobody knew they were here, and nobody would disturb them.

He'd planned this carefully and it had happened exactly as he had wanted it to. Taking her from the house had been easy. Far too easy for the house of a police officer. The timing had been perfect. He had been prepared to kill Alex Regis if he got in his way, but he was undisturbed. Regis had been lucky. But it suited him. He knew how he would be feeling at this moment, his daughter abducted by a killer. In a way that was better. The girl had gone down easily. They always did. Only Karen Tarling had proved a problem, but it was a problem he had easily fixed. Now Chloe Regis was sitting in front of him, looking terrified and alone.

He walked along the length of the warehouse, never taking his eyes off her. He saw that she didn't take her eyes off him, either. As he approached, he saw her tense. She tried to move backwards on her chair, to get further away from him. It was futile, but an understandable subconscious action. He smiled. He stopped a few yards in front of her, put a bottle of water and a sandwich on the floor by his feet.

'How are you feeling, Chloe?' he asked gently.

She said nothing, just looked at him. Terrified. Her vulnerability was irresistible. And he was unable to control the desire to exploit it. He took a step towards her, deliberately aggressive. She flinched, and he smiled. Sixteen years old. It was too easy. He would be able to control the whole thing.

'How is your head feeling?' he asked. In another context it could almost be taken for genuine concern.

She looked at him. Said nothing.

'Sorry about that. But I had to keep you quiet back there. You wouldn't have wanted me to wake your dad or sister, would you? I might have had to do something rather unpleasant to keep them quiet. I'm sure you'll agree this was better for everyone?'

She looked at him, and he saw tears fall from her eyes, the enormity of the situation hitting her. Up until now anything was possible.

223

A knight in shining armour might crash through the door at any point and rescue her. But now she had seen him, she knew. She knew there would be no dashing rescuer. No last-minute escape.

'Why am I here?' she said suddenly, through the tears. 'What are you going to do with me?'

So many answers he could give to that question. He could even tell her the truth. Not yet.

'I thought it would be good for us to spend a little quality time. Get to know each other. We might even become friends.' As he spoke, he lifted his hand and moved to touch her hair, a strand that was in front of her eyes. She snapped away.

'Fuck off! Leave me alone,' she screamed, finding an impressive volume.

'Chloe!' he said unperturbed. 'What would your mother and father think if they heard you talking like that, and only sixteen.'

She stared at him.

'Oh, sorry,' he said. 'I forgot that your mother is dead. Apologies. How about Bec, then? What would she say if she heard you telling me to "fuck off"?' The last words were said with more force than those preceding.

He could see that she didn't know how to respond. Couldn't understand what was happening here.

'How do you get along with Bec? Is she a good stepmother? Not around that often, I would imagine. Spends all her time trying to catch people like me,' he laughed. 'You've worked it out by now, of course. I'm the one your stepmother is hunting. I'm the one.'

Chloe's face changed as she realized. He knew that until now she had not understood. But now. . . This was the killer her stepmother had been looking for. She had been taken by the Cameraman. She couldn't say anything, it was too overwhelming, too terrifying.

'You're not much of a talker, are you?' he said, very close to her now. 'How about some water?'

He reached down and picked up the bottle of water from the floor and removed the lid. He held it up.

'Open wide,' he said, ready to pour some into her mouth.

She stared at him, mouth firmly closed.

'Come on, Chloe. You need to have a drink. It will make you feel so much better.'

'You're insane. Let me go, you arsehole!' she suddenly screamed. 'Let me go!'

Without warning he brought his fist down on the side of her face, punching her in the same place as he had before. Chloe bit off a scream as her head flew backwards, then ricocheted forwards. Then her head dropped to her chest and she passed out.

'Stupid kid.' He spat on the floor.

He dropped the bottle of water on to the floor, allowing the contents to slowly drain from the bottle. He turned and walked the length of the dim warehouse. When he reached the other end, he left through the door, locking it behind him.

* * *

Pope was wrestling with something, but she couldn't pin it down. She knew something was sparking somewhere in her brain, but she couldn't make it come to the surface where she could identify what it was. She had a feeling that she was on the verge of something important in the case. She just needed to work it out. The frustration didn't help her think but the adrenaline was just about winning at the moment.

The phone rang and Brody picked it up. He passed it to Miller. 'It's for you, Adam. Stephen Thompson.'

Miller took the phone, had a brief conversation and hung up. 'I've got to go down to Thompson's office. He says he needs to show me something. He wants you too.' He said, looking at Brody.

'Why does he need both of us?' asked Brody.

'I don't know. But he said it was important.'

Brody sighed, looked at Pope. 'Bec, we'll be back in a moment.' He put his hand on her arm, then left with Miller.

Pope got up from her desk, walked over to the wall of pictures, maps, notes and diagrams that Brody had put up. It reminded her of the wall they had found at the house in Greenwich. Some of the photographs were even of the same people: Susan Harper, Linda Wilson, Karen Tarling.

Now they would have to add a photograph of Chloe, another match to the other wall.

She felt impotent. This case had been just a series of setbacks. Every time they got anywhere, they ran into yet another dead end. The difference now was the stakes had been raised. Chloe was somewhere with him, and clearly Pope was key, the connection to all this. She had to find out how. But the pressure of Chloe's abduction only made it more difficult to think. She had to channel her fear into something more constructive, into finding this man.

'What are you thinking?' asked Fletcher, coming up to stand next to her, looking at the images. Pope had forgotten that he was still there.

'I don't know. There's something, but I can't quite get it. Something that connects these things to me.' She looked at Fletcher. 'How can he have acted in so many countries with impunity? How can he have escaped capture for so long? And we still don't know who he is.'

'There has to be something in your old cases, Bec. There has to be a clue there. I think we need to go back through those again, especially now we have new information that he may have acted abroad and for such a long period of time. We need to look again with fresh eyes and go back even further. Since the very start of your career with the Met. This started a long time ago. We need to reassess Mick Waterson and Edward Boyd.' Fletcher looked at Pope, waiting for a response.

Before she could reply, the door opened and Brody walked through into the office, followed by Miller and Thompson. The expressions on their faces told Pope it was something bad.

'Chloe. . .?' she said, the worst possible thoughts crowding into her mind.

'No,' said Brody quickly. 'It's not Chloe. We haven't heard anything about her.'

Pope sagged with relief. Pope looked at him expectantly, then at the other two. Miller was looking at Fletcher, who looked implacable. Stephen Thompson was staring awkwardly down at his feet.

Brody hesitated, moved a step closer to Pope. She straightened, knew the signs of delivering bad news from having spent years doing the same thing herself. She looked in his eyes, saw the empathy.

'Stephen has been following up from the house in Greenwich, trying to establish who owns it. Stephen, can you explain the process?'

Thompson looked at Brody, then at Pope, obviously alarmed. He cleared his throat. 'I managed to track the owner of the house, but it led back to a shell corporation, which is essentially anonymous.' Thompson drew on all his reserves of courage to continue. 'But the shell corporation is connected to a company registered in the British Virgin Islands. This is well known as a tax haven and so it's nothing unusual on its own that the parent company should be registered there. But if you have the right access, you can sometimes get to the registered owner.' He stopped, looked at Brody. He was leaving him to pick up from there. Deliver the bad news.

Pope turned her attention back to Brody. He hesitated again.

'The company is registered in the Virgin Islands, as Stephen said, and the shell corporation is owned by that company. So the owner of the company is the owner of the house in Greenwich.' She understood that, but he was ensuring that it was clear.

'Bec. The company is owned by John Pope. Your father.' They looked at each other. 'Your father owns the house in Greenwich.'

The air seemed to have been sucked out of the room. The walls came closer, the ceiling drew lower, she couldn't breathe, unable to speak. Her body had frozen. The only noise she could hear was the thundering of the blood in her ears.

She saw it all now. Her father had travelled all his life with his work. Pope had received postcards from the exotic locations her father had visited, ever since she was a young girl. Paris, Frankfurt, Milan, Madrid, Barcelona and Berlin. Her father had gone to all those places.

She was aware that Brody was speaking to her. 'Bec. It means he owns the house, but it doesn't mean anything else at this stage. He's connected, but. . .' He didn't know what else to say, how to make it better.

'It's him,' said Pope emphatically. 'My father is the Cameraman.'

CHAPTER 28

Immediately after he had walked out of the foster home in North London, John Pope went straight to the nearest British Army recruitment centre and signed up. He had a canvas bag with all his belongings, which didn't amount to very much, and a small sum of cash.

He began his training in Harrogate, then moved to Pirbright, about thirty miles southwest of London. He undertook general training, then moved into Army Medical Services.

His decision to join the army had been motivated by a number of factors. Firstly, he wanted to escape the foster care that he had been a part of for nine years. It was difficult for a seventeen-year-old to find employment and accommodation independently, and the army seemed to offer both of those things. It was, as is so often the case at that age, an escape. He also wanted to develop the skills that came with training in the armed forces: discipline, strength, stamina. He knew he needed all of these.

But he also found a number of unexpected benefits came with this new life. His work with the Medical Services taught him about basic anatomy, how the body works and how to save lives. Paradoxically, it also taught him how to take lives. Very effectively.

He became ruthless, and this was in many ways the most important thing he learned. He spent three years in the army, serving several tours overseas. He became an accomplished armed services medic, patching up injured soldiers and assisting the trained doctors who could operate on the more serious cases. But he went about his business quietly, no fanfare. He was known to those who worked closely with him, but went unnoticed by others. This was the way he wanted it. He honed the skills he needed, taking what he wanted.

It was also here that he first killed a man.

There had been an accident during a combat operation, a young recruit fresh from training in the UK. The soldier had been brought to him to triage and then Pope was to refer to the senior medical personnel for further treatment. The patient was about his age and in a bad way. But when he looked at him, he suddenly saw his father. The resemblance was tenuous, but it was definitely there. He stood, paralyzed. Thoughts of his mother's death came to him, the hurt he had buried so successfully for so long rolled over him like a wave. It was overwhelming. He reached out to the steel tubes along the side of the bed, held tightly to steady himself. Head bowed, sweating, he felt that for the first time in many years he was not in complete control of his emotions. He had to fix this.

Then, all of a sudden, he knew exactly how to regain control. He looked at the young man, knocked out by painkillers and sedatives. He saw his father. Then he looked around to check he was alone. He was. He placed his hands around the soldier's throat and felt tentatively for his hyoid bone. His anatomy training enabled him to find it quickly. The visions of his mother's death, and his father's suicide, leaving him all alone, swam before him. The feeling was overwhelming. Without knowing exactly what he was doing, he began to apply pressure. The patient didn't wake up and John Pope steadily increased the pressure until he heard the bone snap, and continued until the soldier was dead. The confusion and disorientation he had felt disappeared. He had taken back control, ruthlessly and effectively. He felt euphoric.

It was easy to explain away the death. In his report he said that the wounds to the young man, and in particular the trauma to his neck and throat, caused him to have trouble breathing, especially when sedated, and by the time John Pope had got to him, he was dead. With the number of dead and injured, frankly no one paid too much attention to checking cause of death once it had been reported. There was far too much else to occupy medical personnel.

John Pope had committed his first murder.

* * *

When he was twenty years old, after serving three years in the British Army, John Pope resigned and started applying for jobs in the civilian sector. It didn't take him long to find something suitable. He applied for a job with a company that sold medical equipment to small private companies and hospitals in the United Kingdom and abroad, primarily Europe. The market was large and expanding, because advances in technology, married with continual medical advances driven by relentless research, meant there were always new products to sell. In the interview, he talked about his medical work with the armed forces. The company had recently expanded into supplying military facilities abroad and they knew that a salesperson with military experience and connections would prove invaluable in securing sales. So John Pope was hired and became a medical supplies salesman.

He was fully trained in the use of everything he was selling, including some complex, and very expensive, machinery and electronic equipment. This took up much of his time initially. But there was also travel and plenty of it. He visited cities in Europe and, after some time, travelled further afield. He was good at the job, knew how to talk to people and make them trust him. Consequently, he sold well and the job was very lucrative.

He had only been there a few months when he met Bec's mother. She worked at the same company, as the PA to the sales manager. They came into contact often and eventually John Pope asked her out on a date. Then they were a couple, and then she fell pregnant. Within seven months of meeting, they were married, and three months after that Rebecca Pope was born. Her parents didn't warm to John. Her father thought there was 'something about him' and her mother felt that he was overbearing and intimidating. But the marriage went ahead and all seemed well.

However, it wasn't long before John Pope began thinking about his mother and father again. It was on a trip to Paris. He had been sent by the company to meet representatives from a small, but very successful, private medical facility in the seventeenth arrondissement. They were looking to update their equipment, and their suppliers. The meetings went well and John Pope managed to secure contracts for a great deal of equipment, including some high-end, very expensive imaging machinery. His manager was delighted and insisted he stay on in Paris for an extra couple of nights, at the company's expense, as a reward. He took full advantage of the opportunity.

On the first night he met a young woman in a club and, after a copious amount of red wine, she invited him back to her apartment. After making love several times, she fell asleep. But John Pope was awake, wide awake. He began to think again about his mother, and, much like with the young soldier, he was overwhelmed with feelings he was unable to control. He strangled her. It was easier than the first time, and even though she woke up, terror in her eyes as he squeezed her throat, he did not stop and she was unconscious swiftly, and dead soon after that.

He got up from the bed and looked at her. Something was wrong. His feelings of loss of control were better, but there was still a residual sense of incompleteness within him. He saw the disarray, the result of two people struggling on the bed, and knew what he had to do. He lifted her body and placed her head on the pillow, smoothed the sheets, and pulled them over her body, tucking them neatly over her chest. He stood back and admired the scene. It was better, and so was he. The feelings were gone. He wiped down each of the few surfaces he had touched in the apartment and quietly let himself out. When he walked out on to the street, just as the sun was rising over the roofs of the apartments opposite, he felt wonderful. He had found the cure.

When he returned home, all was well again. He was the dutiful husband and father and no one knew anything about what had happened in Paris. There was no way to connect the murder to him. The feelings came over him only occasionally and when they did, a business trip soon offered the chance to deal with the problem. He travelled throughout Western Europe, usually big cities, which afforded the opportunity and the anonymity he needed. Again, he was visible only to those he wanted to see him, and invisible to everybody else.

Although the killings remained expertly hidden, the affairs eventually caught up with him.

John Pope returned one day from a business trip to Barcelona. He had been away for three nights, one of which he had spent with a Spanish woman he had met at a sales conference. She worked for a competitor, and after a long evening in the hotel bar discussing the intricacies of modern medical electronic machinery, they went up to her room. He left the next morning and flew back to London.

When Bec's mother was sorting her husband's laundry, she noticed a strong smell on his shirt of a perfume she didn't recognize. Powerful and intense, and certainly not worn by her. She confronted him, and an argument ensued, an argument that ended in him slapping her on the side of her head. She had fallen. Things were never the same after that.

He had felt remorseful, but not as much as he knew he should. She became distant, and he buried himself in work, volunteered more frequently for sales trips and conferences, and their relationship continued to deteriorate.

The other casualty of his infidelities and the arguments was his relationship with his daughter. Bec was too young to really understand everything that was going on and her mother went to great lengths to make sure that she didn't know the exact nature of their problems. But she certainly picked up the tension between them and the lack of intimacy. This manifested in a suspicion towards her father and she withdrew from him. For his part, John Pope let it happen. He wanted to be close to his daughter, but more important was the lifestyle he had carved out for himself away from the family. He could live without his family, but he couldn't live without the opportunities he found while travelling. He reasoned that he had survived without family, so Bec would be fine with a limited relationship with her father.

The uneasy existence continued for a couple of years, much too long, until Bec's mother had had enough. She knew her husband was having affairs and finally she snapped. She told him to leave, to be gone by the end of the day. He agreed.

Bec was twelve years old. Despite her weakening relationship with her father, he could see that she was devastated. She pleaded with her parents to reconsider. But her mother explained that it was over and that they would be fine, and that she could see her father whenever she wanted. He tried to help her understand the structural and emotional change to her family, but she blamed her father for abandoning them and had seen her father hit her mother on one occasion, and consequently her relationship with her father deteriorated irreparably. He knew she felt she had to take a side, and the side she took was her mother's.

After that, she saw her father infrequently. John Pope was busy with work and Bec was becoming increasingly reluctant to spend time with him. The separation was gradual but definite.

After leaving the house, John Pope stayed with a colleague for a couple of days while he found somewhere to live. He moved into a two-bedroom flat on the second floor of a Victorian building in Kilburn in North London. It was private and he rarely saw his neighbours. His daughter stayed with him occasionally, but apart from that he could do as he pleased. This was the lifestyle he needed, and he embraced it.

The manager of his company started to offer him more trips abroad and within the UK, in an effort, he supposed, to distract him from the ruination of his private life. In reality, it gave him more opportunity to do what he wanted to do, but also gave him the chance to sell more, to make more money and to make an impression with the company. What they saw as dedication to his job, was merely a context for him to further explore the darker corners of his psyche.

Eventually his boss offered to make him the senior salesperson, training and managing the entire sales force and overseeing the expansion of the rapidly growing company. It meant less travel, and more work based in London and the UK. But it also meant more money, substantially more, and he formed an idea. He realized that he needed to separate his work from his killing, find a base from where he could operate his extracurricular activities. By now this was taking over much of his time and he knew he had to strengthen his anonymity.

Through the lawyer at the company he set up a number of tax-evasion measures, which included the forming of several shell corporations and offshore companies. Many of the senior people in the company already took advantage of these types of financial loopholes, and so it was a natural step for him to get involved. He insisted that his anonymity be preserved in these dealings to protect his financial assets, he explained, from his wife in future divorce proceedings. The lawyer understood, of course — this was common practice among many of his, largely male, clients. Once this was all set up and finalized, John Pope then approached another solicitor, completely unconnected with the company, and arranged to purchase a small Victorian two-storey house in Greenwich. He felt that this was a suitable distance from his own apartment. The whole process would be through his anonymous and untraceable shell corporation. The purchase was completed quickly, and he took possession of the keys.

He told nobody about the house in Greenwich. He visited frequently, usually after dark, and saw very few people around the area.

He fitted it out with everything he needed and installed state-of-the-art security and surveillance equipment. He purchased all of this abroad and had it shipped to London, paid for through his anonymous company. He had everything he needed and for a long time he operated with impunity.

Then, one day, he was preparing to go to work. He was at the flat in Kilburn, shaving in front of the mirror, when he was overtaken by a wracking cough, coming from deep within his lungs. He was shocked to see blood splattered across the mirror and in the sink. Standing, looking at his reflection, he knew.

He visited a private clinic in Berlin that he had sold equipment to many years previously. The specialist told him gently that it was inoperable. The cancer had spread to the rest of his body. He asked how long, and was told six months.

John Pope wasn't afraid of dying. He had taken so many lives and watched so many final breaths, that he was at peace with the process. He knew what it involved, and he was ready.

But there were two problems.

The first was that John Pope was anonymous. This had been vital, of course, in order for him to be able to kill without consequences, and he had orchestrated that anonymity with skill and an enormous amount of patience and planning. But now. Well, now, he wanted to be known, to come out from the shadows, so that he would be remembered. He wanted to be in the company of others who had trodden the same path. Nobody knew his name. This he would need to rectify.

The second problem was his relationship with his daughter. This was difficult and it took him some time to decide how to deal with it. But after a while he realized what he had to do. He knew that it was no use simply telling her. He had to show her. Show her something that she would not be able to ignore and would not forget. Ensure that she realized the brilliance of what he had achieved.

So John Pope set about planning his personal denouement in intricate detail. He spent a great deal of time organizing and arranging what he needed, at the same time dealing with his deteriorating health.

Eventually he was ready. He had what he needed at the house in Greenwich and he was ready to put his plan in motion.

Susan Harper would be the first piece in his final performance. And this time, unlike all the many others, it would indeed be a performance for all to see.

CHAPTER 29

'This has to be a mistake. There has to be another explanation. Bec?' Richard Fletcher was looking at Brody, then at Pope.

They all stood still, frozen by the suggestion.

'We'll have a look at it again, Bec,' said Brody. He wanted to do something to make this better.

He looked at Thompson, who nodded, eager to offer some grain of hope. 'There has to be another connection we're not seeing. Your father may well have no idea. . . We need to look again at Mick Waterson, Edward Boyd, look for a connection.'

'It's him,' Pope interrupted Brody. 'Thanks for what you're trying to do. But it's him. I should have seen it before. It was all there if I'd looked harder. Too much time wasted on Waterson and Boyd when they were nothing to do with it. The timings are all off.'

The others in the room looked confused.

'How can you be so sure?' asked Brody.

Pope paused, took a breath. She knew that once she'd said it, there was no going back. This would be final.

'When I was a kid, my father left. Walked out on us. I was twelve years old. But both when he was living with us, and once he'd left, he travelled a lot for his work. Sometimes in the Middle East, in the Far East. But mostly Europe.'

They all watched her intently.

'When Miller told us that there were unsolved cases that fit the description of our killer's MO all across Europe, something started ringing bells. I knew there was something, but I couldn't quite put my finger on it. Now I know. All the places you mentioned, my father had visited. He used to send me postcards from some of his trips. I remember all those places.' She slumped into a chair, deflated by the effort of having to recount this.

'That's still pretty circumstantial, though,' said Miller. 'They're all just major cities.'

'I still have a couple of postcards. I think the dates will match up to some of these unsolved cases.' Pope looked at him and attempted to smile. It didn't work. 'He was in the hospital when Karen Tarling was murdered,' said Pope. 'That explains why we couldn't see him enter or exit the hospital. My father is ill, has lung cancer. He was in a ward on the floor below all the time. He ended up at the same hospital as his intended victim. Although I doubt that was a coincidence.'

No one said anything.

'That's also probably why Chloe opened the door so late at night. She doesn't know him well, but they've met on a couple of occasions. Chloe would have recognized him.' She stopped, suddenly remembering that the killer, her father, had abducted her stepdaughter.

'But the precision with which he attacked them. . .' said Miller.

'He was part of the Army Medical Service for some years when he was younger. He never talked that much about it, but I know he had medical training.' Suddenly the gravity of talking about her father in this context hit Pope, and she stopped talking, looked down at her hands clenched together on top of the desk. Dropped her shoulders.

The room was all silent.

Pope thought about her father, the tenuous relationship the two of them had had for the last thirty years. The irony of Pope joining the police force was not lost on her and she imagined how her father must have reacted to the news. Perhaps that was one reason for the lack of contact, her father wanting distance between himself and the police officer in the family. Certainly, he had been seemingly uninterested in his daughter's career achievements as she rose through the ranks.

But despite this distance, despite the lack of a close relationship, how could her father have operated in this way, for so long, without Pope having any idea whatsoever about it? It was unfathomable to her that she could have been oblivious to his activities.

It was her father who had left her the cards, the photograph. Her own father had played this like it was a game. What kind of father did something like that?

Brody sat down opposite Pope. 'Why do you think he's taken Chloe, Bec? What's he doing?'

'I don't know, honestly,' she replied.

'He must have an endgame,' he said. 'He risked a great deal to come to your house and take her.' He didn't need to say the rest. Pope knew full well that if Alex or Hannah had woken up, had seen her father, then it was highly likely that he would have killed them. He wouldn't risk being identified at that stage or, worse still, being caught.

'He's been very careful so far,' said Brody. 'He clearly has a plan now, and I'm guessing it involves you.'

Pope thought. 'The others were to get our attention. To get my attention. This is now the main event.' She shuddered even as she said the words. 'He wants me involved.' Then added, 'We have to find them now. Before anything happens to Chloe.'

She stood up, purposeful. She looked at the other four in the room. It was time to take control again, both of herself and the operation.

Pope took out her mobile and called her father's number. Predictably it went straight to answerphone.

'Thompson, Miller. We need to know where he went after he took Chloe. Find out where he is. See if they've found anything on the traffic cameras near the house yet, follow the leads from the shell corporation. Find something. Put a tap on my phone. And his. He's not answering his mobile but he might call me at any point.'

They both nodded, glad to have an opportunity to leave, and quickly exited the room. Pope heard them hurry down the stairs, saying nothing.

Fletcher walked towards the door. 'I'm going to mobilize all available units to look for them and send out an APB on your father and Chloe.'

'Send a couple of cars to my father's flat in Finsbury Park. I'll give you the address. He won't be there, I'm certain. But you might find something. I'll join them, if Thompson and Miller don't have any luck.'

Fletcher nodded tightly. He left the room.

Only Pope and Brody were left alone in the office now. He walked over to her and put his arms around her shoulders. He hugged her, and she felt the warmth of his body, the comfort of closeness.

'Whatever you need, Bec,' he said, and held her gaze. 'We'll find him, and we'll find Chloe. And she'll be fine.' They let go, separated.

Pope sat on the edge of the desk. 'Why the hell has he taken Chloe? As you said, it was a risky move. He's careful, but he still needed a lot of luck. There could have been units outside, or passing. Why did he risk that? Why does he want her so badly?'

'You said it earlier,' replied Brody. 'He wants to get your attention. And presumably now he has it, he's going to want to do something with it. Do you think he'll contact you?'

'I don't know. Either way, we have to do something fast. For Chloe.'

'Yes, we do,' he replied. 'But he didn't. . .' He paused. 'He didn't do what he has with the other victims. Kill her and stage the body. He took her, which suggests that he has other plans for her. That's a good thing, isn't it?'

'I guess so,' replied Pope.

'Have you considered that he might have taken Chloe as bait? For you?'

'Yes,' she replied. 'I have considered that.'

* * *

The daylight in the long room was becoming more pervasive as dawn began to break. The few rays of light crept up the walls, mixing with the mildew and dirt produced by years of neglect. The warehouse had not been used for its intended purpose for many years and natural decay had begun to take over.

Chloe Regis had woken up, the pain in the side of her head sharper than ever. This time she remembered exactly what had happened, remembered the pain of the blow to her head. The memory made her flinch.

She suddenly became aware of a small movement in the far corner of the large room. It was dark there, neither the two hanging lights nor the sliver of weak light from outside reached into the corners. But something was there. She craned her neck, squinted her eyes, trying to make it out. And then she saw definite movement, saw a shape rise up and begin to move towards her. And then she saw who it was.

* * *

As she began to come round, he watched her body start moving. Slowly, groggily at first, then she became more alert and responsive to her surroundings. Then she was looking straight at him, trying to see into the shadows. He smiled at the apt metaphor. Chloe Regis was indeed about to see into some of the dark shadows that life had to offer.

He stood up, smoothed down his jacket, and was aware that she sensed movement. He walked slowly towards her, and knew by her expression the exact moment that she finally saw who had been sitting in the corner. Not that there could really be any doubt, but he supposed she had to hope.

He approached her. A smile as he saw how utterly hopeless she was. He hadn't really intended to hurt her, as long as she behaved herself. But he did want to talk to her. And he would make sure that she listened.

He stopped a few feet away from her chair. They looked at each other, said nothing for a few moments. Then he spoke.

'Chloe. How are you feeling? How's your head? I'm sorry about that, but one thing I can't abide is rudeness in the young. It's so disrespectful.'

Chloe stared at him warily, didn't speak.

'Your reticence is only natural. We don't know each other very well, and you must be very scared, imagining all kinds of horrific things that I could do to you here if I chose.' She did indeed look terrified.

'Don't worry. I'm not here to kill you. If I wanted to do that, I would have done it already. I'm hoping it won't come to that.' He smiled, but Chloe just looked more afraid.

'Don't get me wrong, though. If you talk to me like you did earlier, then you will get hurt again. So, I'd watch your mouth if I were you. Make sure you remember who you're talking to. I suppose I am your step-grandfather, after all.' He laughed at the incongruity, took a step forward. She continued to keep her eyes locked on him.

'You're probably wondering what you're doing here. Wondering what's going to become of you. Well, you don't have to worry too much. It's not you I'm after. You're simply a device to bring your stepmother here. She's the one I want to talk to. You may even make it out of here relatively unscathed. We'll see how it goes.'

* * *

'Have you got anything yet?' Pope asked Miller, the phone balanced on her shoulder as she attempted to type on her computer at the same time.

She listened for a few moments, then told him to keep digging, and hung up the receiver.

'Anything?' asked Brody.

'No, nothing. There are various holdings and companies linked to the shell corporation, but it's all well hidden, of course. They're still looking. Miller's trying to get hold of traffic camera feeds in the area,' said Pope.

Almost immediately the phone rang again. Pope answered, it was Fletcher. The units had raided her father's flat in North London. Nobody was there, and there was nothing obvious that suggested where they might find her father or Chloe. Forensics were on their way and would let them know the moment they found anything. Pope replaced the receiver again.

'Nothing at my father's flat,' said Pope. 'You know what this means?'

'What?'

'He has a third site. Where he's holding Chloe.'

Brody thought for a minute, looked down at his computer then back at Pope. 'You know you're going to have to talk to Alex soon. You can't put that off much longer.'

Pope nodded. That would be one hell of a call.

* * *

'You know, Chloe, we should get to know each other a little better.' John Pope was walking slowly around her in circles. Each time he disappeared behind her, she twisted her neck around to try to follow him, to make sure that he wasn't out of her sight, then snapped it back as he came around again.

'Do you know anything about my childhood? Has Bec told you anything about me?' he asked.

She just stared at him. Terrified to say anything.

'No, I suppose not. Let's just say there were reasons why I killed people, and I won't bore you with those, but eventually the desire for control takes over. There is simply nothing in this world that offers us as much control as taking another human being's life. It's a truly wonderful experience. I urge you to try it one day.'

She watched him in horror.

'But recently my health has deteriorated and there are some things I need to sort out. Most noticeably with my daughter. And that brings us right up to the present. The reason you're here.'

'So why am I here?' asked Chloe.

'She speaks! How nice to hear your voice, I was getting a little tired of just hearing myself.'

She glowered at him.

'You'll know soon, Chloe. Have a little patience and all will become clear.'

Chloe suddenly snapped. 'She'll find me! Bec will find me and when she does you'll go to prison for the rest of your life. Your pathetic, sad life. She'll come here and she'll get me, I know she will. Help! Help! Somebody! Help!'

'No one can hear you, Chloe. I wouldn't waste your breath if I were you.'

'She'll find me,' she said, but this time her words lacked conviction.

'That's exactly what I'm counting on,' he said. 'You see, Chloe, I'm dying. I have very little time left to live. So I need to talk to your stepmother.'

CHAPTER 30

Pope needed to clear her head and think. She'd been up all night and her head was thick. Everyone at the station was working on finding her father and Chloe, but she had the distinct impression that her father would be found only when he wanted to be found. He had been one step ahead of them the whole time. She was certain her father would contact her. Otherwise, they were in trouble.

She stepped outside the open-plan office. She had to call Alex and attempt to explain. How the hell could she explain this situation? She took a deep breath. Putting it off would serve no purpose. She dialled the number and he picked up on the second ring. Pope realized she hadn't thought through what she was going to say.

'Have you found her?'

'Hi, Alex. No, not yet.'

Silence at the other end of the line.

'But we think we know who she's with.' She wanted to offer some hope to Alex as soon as she could.

'Who? Who's taken Chloe?' His voice was rising.

Another deep breath.

'Who is it?' Alex repeated.

Pope steeled herself. 'We think it's my father.'

There was a long silence. Was Alex processing the news, or did he not trust himself to speak?

'What do you mean, your father?' he said at last. 'What are you talking about?'

'I think my father has taken Chloe because he wants to talk to me.' She was making an unholy mess of this.

'What are you talking about?' Alex repeated. 'What do you mean? Why would your father need to take Chloe to talk to you?' Pope could hear the confusion.

'The case I'm working on.' She couldn't bring herself to say the name. Or use the word "killer".

'What about it?'

'We think my father might be involved somehow.'

'So let me get this straight. Your father has abducted Chloe. From our house. And he is somehow involved in the murders of three women? How?' Alex was raising his voice now.

'I can't go into the details. But it means that Chloe is OK. My father won't hurt Chloe. He won't.' She was reassuring herself as much as Alex.

'Involved how?' he demanded.

'Alex. I can't get into this now. I'm going to find him and I'm going to bring Chloe back.'

'You need to come home, Bec. This is crazy. We need to sort this out.' His tone had changed.

She heard the fear.

'I can't, Alex. The best chance of me bringing Chloe back is if I'm here.' She immediately regretted her choice of words.

'"Best chance"? You said he wouldn't hurt her!'

'I will bring her back. I'll find her. But I need to be here, working on it, to be able to do that. You're going to have to trust me.'

There was a pause.

'I'll call you when I know anything. I promise.' Silence. 'Alex?'

'Fine.' He hung up.

He had no choice but to accept what she had said, but Pope knew that he was keeping a lid on things until this was over. He knew that she needed to be in the best psychological state if she was to find Chloe, so he held off telling her what he actually thought. But she knew that when all this was over, it was coming.

She'd had to make difficult calls to family members in the past, but this was entirely different. She really hoped the next call would be good news. Ever since Pope had entered their lives, she'd only caused trouble. She and Alex loved each other, but would that ever be enough? Her life, her attitude to her work, made this relationship, any relationship, almost impossible. The parallels with her own father were clear.

Pope had to put her personal issues aside if she was going to do her job. But the pressure she was feeling was so intense, she didn't know if it was possible. She needed to focus.

She looked around the office. They were all keeping busy, chasing leads that were likely to go nowhere. But really they were waiting for the call. Her father's call. Thompson and Miller now had access to the traffic camera networks in the city and were searching to find the vehicle Pope's father might be driving. Fletcher was in his office, trying to organize city-wide APBs for John Pope and Chloe Regis, circulating photographs and descriptions of both, and authorizing overtime for all available officers. Brody was still at his computer, trying to sift through the reports that were still arriving as a result of Miller's requests to multiple European police agencies.

But her father was in complete control. Pope felt powerless. She didn't know what to do. There was nothing she could do.

Her thoughts were interrupted by a knock at the door and Tobias Darke strode into the office. Pope stood up as Darke walked over to her and gave her a big hug.

'So, how can I be of help?'

Pope was glad to see another friendly face, a face she had known for many years. She was also glad of Darke's no-nonsense attitude.

Darke knew the basics. Brody had explained what had happened and had arranged for Darke to be brought to the station. Pope filled in the details. As he listened intently, Darke's expression grew more and more serious. When Pope had finished explaining what they had discovered in the last few hours, Darke sat back, exhausted by the emotional energy it had taken to process what he had heard.

'And you had no idea?' Pope raised her eyebrows. 'No, of course you didn't. Stupid question. So where do we go from here?' asked Darke.

'Well, what do you think his next move could be?' asked Pope. 'You know about these kinds of killers? What's he likely to do next?' It hurt placing her father in the company of serial killers familiar to Darke, but she needed to get straight to the point, ask the difficult questions.

'That's a good question,' said Darke. 'It's difficult to tell. I mean, there's a level of volatility and unpredictability here.'

'I know,' said Pope.

He considered what he was going to say carefully. 'I think this feels like the endgame, or at least the precursor to the endgame, if that makes any sense.'

Pope nodded.

'The other women, the last three, were to get our attention. To get your attention. He was sending you a message: "I'm here, look at me". It's classic narcissistic behaviour. Now he has your attention. The next stage is the finale, for him. It's like he's putting on an elaborate show, with him and you as the key participants.'

'How do we handle him?' asked Pope.

'He has to believe that he's in charge. Play along as far as is possible. What you don't want is him feeling that he is cornered and has nowhere to go. Not while he has Chloe. He has to feel that he has options.'

'So, what's the endgame?' asked Brody.

Tobias Darke looked at him, thought for a minute. Then turned back to Pope.

'Bec, you mentioned that your father had been admitted to the same hospital as the third victim. What for? What's wrong with him?'

Pope hesitated. Despite everything, it was still difficult to say the words. 'He has lung cancer. They diagnosed it for certain in the hospital, but I suspect he knew exactly what was wrong with him before he set foot in the hospital. It was all a set-up to get to Karen Tarling. I must have mentioned the hospital.'

Darke's brow furrowed.

'What is it?' asked Brody. 'What are you thinking?'

Darke took a deep breath. 'If he has a terminal condition, if indeed it is what he says it is, then we may have an additional problem.'

'What do you mean?' asked Pope.

'Well,' continued Darke. 'If he's dying, and he's aware that he's dying, then whatever he's planning is likely to be dramatic. Because, if he hasn't got long to live, he has nothing to lose.'

* * *

Now there was a weak, watery light from outside, making the warehouse space lighter, though the shadows retained their depth. It looked like a film noir movie set from the 1940s. John Pope stood in front of Chloe Regis, watched her feel uncomfortable under his gaze.

Again he offered her a bottle of water. Again she turned away, refused the drink.

'Chloe,' he said. 'If you don't drink, your head isn't going to feel better.' She said nothing. 'OK, if that's the way you want it,' he said, replacing the bottle on the floor in front of her.

He looked at his watch. 'Are you surprised Bec hasn't arrived to rescue you yet, as you predicted?' He smiled. Chloe looked uncomfortable. 'Are you wondering where she's got to? Wondering what she's doing to try to find you? Your father will be frantic by now, I imagine. I didn't really want to cause him so much distress, but these things are soon forgotten in families, aren't they?' He laughed at his own joke. He paced back and forth in front of her now, her eyes following his every move.

'Shall I let you in on a little secret, Chloe?' he asked, relishing the question, the theatrics. 'I'm afraid Bec has absolutely no idea where you are, and absolutely no hope of finding you. I mean, they try hard, but this place is completely untraceable. It's hidden behind so many layers of ownership, they'll never get through the maze I've created. They'll never find you,' he repeated.

'She'll find me,' she said quietly.

He smiled. 'Your loyalty is admirable, if misguided.'

He let her consider that for a minute, while he continued pacing. 'However, it's your lucky day, Chloe. You see, while Bec and her henchmen have no clue where we are, I do actually need her to find us, otherwise it's not going to work. She needs to come and join our little family party so we can catch up and have a chat.'

She stared at him, unsure whether to believe the madman standing in front of her. But as she watched him, he reached into the inside pocket of his jacket and brought out a phone. He looked at her and smiled, then looked down and dialled a number. He placed the phone up to his ear and waited.

Then: 'Bec. How nice to hear your voice.'

* * *

Pope heard her phone ringing in her pocket. Brody froze, Darke and Fletcher looked at Pope.

She took out her phone and saw *No caller ID* flash across the screen. She looked at the others.

'Unknown number,' she said, then pressed answer.

They watched her, knew immediately who it was from her expression.

'Dad,' she said, and Fletcher visibly flinched. 'Where are you?'

Her father was speaking.

'Is Chloe with you? Is she OK?' asked Pope. She let out a breath. 'You need to let her go. Now.' She listened some more.

'Why do we have to do this? Just come to the station. Let Chloe go and come into the station. We can talk then.'

Pope looked frustrated, then picked up a pad of paper and a pen from her desk and started to write.

'One hour.' Pope looked at her watch. 'Right. One hour.' A sharp tone could suddenly be heard. The phone had obviously gone dead, and she put it down on her desk.

'What did he say?' asked Brody.

Pope didn't speak for a few moments.

'He has Chloe, says she's OK. He won't let her go, says I have to go to him. Alone.'

'No, that's not going to happen,' said Fletcher decisively.

'He gave me an address. Told me to be outside there in exactly one hour, then he would call again and give me directions. To where he and Chloe are,' she clarified.

'How did he sound?' asked Tobias Darke.

'He sounded normal. Like my father,' said Pope. 'Calm, relaxed. It's ridiculous.'

Fletcher said, 'There's no way you can go alone.'

'I know that,' said Pope. 'But he has to think I'm alone, or we'll have problems. He'll expect me to bring backup, so we need to think carefully about how we handle it.'

'I'm going to alert Armed Response,' said Fletcher. 'And I'll get a couple more units on standby. We'll need to meet first and work out how we're going to do this. It's not going to be easy to send in the cavalry without him noticing, especially as we don't have a final address yet.'

'That's exactly why he hasn't given us an address,' said Pope. 'He wants to be completely in control.'

Miller arrived at the same time as the commander of one of the Armed Response teams. They gathered round the table under the gaze of the wall to discuss their options. There weren't many. Time was tight. Without knowing the location, they couldn't send teams in advance to get in position and wait, with the element of surprise on their side. They were working blind until the very last minute.

The decision was the only one they could make. The armed teams and extra units would follow Pope at a discreet distance, wearing a wire and maintaining radio contact at all times. As soon as she knew where she was going, they would know and they would pass her and set up as quickly and inconspicuously as was possible. It wasn't perfect, and it certainly wasn't foolproof. But there was no alternative.

'Brody, Miller—' Fletcher's voice was strained but firm — 'I want you in a car right behind Bec. Do not let her out of your direct line of sight at any time. Where she goes, you go. Understand?'

They both answered in the affirmative.

'I don't want any mistakes today No heroics, no fatalities. Are we clear?' Fletcher left the room.

Tobias Darke was standing by the window. 'One thing you might consider. I don't think he wants to hurt you, Bec.' The others were all looking at him, their concentration evident. 'He's set this all up for you, essentially. He clearly has an agenda, but I don't see him killing his own daughter. That's not how these people tend to work in my experience.'

'I hope you're right,' said Pope. 'But he has Chloe. It's not really me I'm worried about.'

'You do have a point there,' conceded Darke.

Pope looked at her watch. She had just under an hour. She needed to get her Kevlar vest, her taser, and then she needed to go.

To meet a version of her father she hadn't even known existed.

CHAPTER 31

The car pulled up to the address that her father had given her. Pope parked in a space on the left-hand side of the road, in a residents' parking zone. She recognized the area, of course. Her father's flat was on a parallel road. Her father had directed her right to where he lived in Finsbury Park. His idea of irony, no doubt.

She was ten minutes early, so she switched off the engine and listened to the silence. She looked in the rearview mirror and saw Brody and Miller in an unmarked car, several spaces behind and on the other side of the road. She also saw the Armed Response team, this time travelling in unmarked cars, some way behind. She wondered if her father was watching, surveilling her every move. He had to know that Pope wouldn't arrive alone. Withholding the final address was designed to offer an extra degree of control.

Pope had spent the journey running through as many possible scenarios as she could imagine, what her father might do and how she might respond. But in truth, she had absolutely no idea of her father's plans. He had Chloe, so whatever happened, he had the advantage.

All she could do was wait, and as each minute ticked by Pope became more and more on edge. She now knew what her father was capable of, knew that she didn't really know him at all. Never had. She drummed her fingers on the steering wheel, trying to control the adrenaline that was coursing through her. Waiting was intolerable. She was sweating underneath her jacket, although the morning was cool and fresh outside the car. She looked at her watch: three minutes to go. She wondered if her father would be on time. The sun was slowly rising above the trees to the east and Pope wondered if her father had timed this carefully to coincide with the early morning. And if so, why?

She jumped as her phone rang. It sounded deafening in the car and she answered it quickly.

'Pope,' she said.

'Me too,' said her father. 'I'm glad you made it on time, Bec. Do you have a pen handy?'

'Is Chloe there? Can I talk to her?'

'Yes, she's here. No, you can't talk to her. You'll see her soon enough.'

He gave Pope an address and the instructions how to get there.

'And, Bec. Come in alone. Tell your acolytes to wait outside. Otherwise I can't be responsible for what happens to Chloe.'

He ended the call.

Pope considered what her father had said. Her father had killed many people, and he was certainly capable of hurting Chloe, or worse. She called Brody and gave him the address.

'But I need you and the Armed Response team to wait outside until you have my signal.' She repeated her father's threat.

'OK. I'll let them know the details. We'll wait to hear from you, but we'll be just outside. And, Bec?'

'What?'

'Be careful.'

'I will,' she replied.

She put the phone away and punched the address into the GPS. It was about a twenty-minute drive north. She started the car and pulled out.

Pope tried to clear her head as she drove, to empty it of all the thoughts that might impede her judgement. But it was impossible. She played through the episodes she could remember from her childhood, tried to get a handle on who her father really was. Certainly not who she thought he was. She thought about the distance, the business trips abroad, the postcards, and it sort of made sense. But it was difficult to confront a reality that was so different to the version of his life that she had believed. It still shocked Pope that she had had absolutely no idea about her father. She had missed the signs, failed to see what was right under her nose.

This train of thought was counterproductive and she needed to be sharp and clearheaded when she arrived. She tried to focus on the road, switched on the radio, realized how ridiculous that idea was and promptly switched it off again.

As she drove through Wood Green and headed northeast, the GPS told her that she was only a couple of minutes away from her destination. Her heart began to beat faster and she could feel it in her chest. She took a right off the main road and then she was arriving at what looked like a disused industrial estate. She stopped at the entrance and surveyed her surroundings. Beyond the iron gates was wide road, leading to a gravelled area. No silent approach. She texted a warning to Brody to park outside. In a horseshoe around the gravel entrance there were four units, the type used to house small businesses. But these all looked abandoned many years ago, rundown and uncared for.

She was still convinced that her father wouldn't kill her.

Parking outside Unit Four, as her father had instructed, she got out of the car and closed the door quietly. Then she walked towards the building, trying to locate the entrance. At last she saw a door at the far end. A sliver of light spilled between the cracks in one of the pieces of wood nailed up behind the window. Pope peered through, but couldn't see anything through the grime. She felt suddenly vulnerable. She had a taser, but nothing else. She was at a distinct disadvantage.

She arrived at the door, she hesitated, drew breath, and then opened it.

The space was clearly a warehouse, or at least had been in its better days. Pope estimated it to be about fifty metres long and twenty wide. Now it was empty, a large, dingy rectangle of space with no obvious purpose. She squinted into the gloom.

Then Pope saw her.

Chloe was sitting at the far end of the room, on a metal-framed chair. She seemed to be staring straight ahead. Her hands appeared to be tied to the arms of the chair. Her hair was in disarray, her face bruised and swollen. Was she alive? Hurt? Pope fought against the urge to run to her. She had to be careful.

Then she saw Chloe's eyes focus, the terror clear, but also relief at seeing Pope.

Pope looked around, saw nothing, no one else. She began to walk carefully towards her. She was aware that she was out in the open, in the middle of the space. But she needed to get to Chloe.

'Are you all right? Are you hurt?'

Chloe shook her head but didn't speak. She guessed she had been warned not to.

'Where is he?' asked Pope, as she continued to get closer.

'Right here, Bec. Good to see you.' Pope froze at the voice as her father emerged from the shadows in the corner of the room, just behind where Chloe was sitting. 'I see you've found my second hideaway.'

He stepped out towards Pope, and stopped just by Chloe's shoulder. He was dressed, as usual, in a suit and tie. In his right hand he held a pistol. Pope again felt vulnerable, too far away to get to Chloe, too close for him to miss if he took a shot.

Pope looked at the gun. 'Do you need that?' she asked casually, but inside her heart was hammering. She should have let the Armed Response team come in first.

'I don't know, Bec. You tell me. Where are the boys with guns?'

Pope hesitated. Was it worth trying to pretend that she was all alone? Probably not. 'They're outside, but they're not coming in unless I tell them to.'

'Good,' said her father. 'I think it's much better if it's just you and me for a while, don't you?'

Pope didn't agree, but she didn't say this.

'What are we doing here, John?'

'Oh, it's "John" now, is it? How disappointingly modern.'

'Well, I think we've got past the father-and-daughter routine by now, don't you?'

'I suppose we have. A shame, but these things happen.'

But these things didn't just happen. Pope wanted to scream.

'Why did you have to involve Chloe? Couldn't you just have come to see me?'

'Ah, well. I had to ensure that you would come alone. Give you something worth coming for.' Her father was standing right next to Chloe now, his gun beside her head.

'Why don't you put the gun down, John. Then we can talk.'

'We're talking now,' said her father.

Pope was straining to read between the lines, anything that would help her get a handle on her father's mental state. But he was just as aloof as he always was. She needed to occupy her father and control the situation. She changed tack.

'Why the envelopes, John?'

'Ah, yes. Did the invitations amuse you? Give your forensic team something to occupy their busy little minds? It certainly got you involved. I had to make sure of that.'

Pope stared at her father. 'And the church? Why did you leave Susan Harper in the church?'

'St Paul's. Beautiful, isn't it?' He looked past her for a moment, seemingly lost in a memory. 'You probably don't know this, Bec, but you were baptized in St Paul's.'

Pope started.

'Yes. Your mother used to live right next door in Deptford and felt quite attached to St Paul's. It just seemed appropriate. Beginnings and endings. You know.'

'I don't really know, John.'

'There's little point in us discussing that now, Bec. I'm sure you'll be able to talk about that to your heart's content when all this is over.'

'How is this all going to be over?' Pope asked.

'It won't be long, one way or another. I'm sure your team will get bored of waiting soon, so let's use the time wisely, shall we? Let's focus on the present, and the future.'

'What did you have in mind?' Pope was slowly moving forward, towards her father and Chloe, taking a furtive step whenever she thought he was looking at the ground or at Chloe. She wasn't sure what she could do, if anything, but she knew she had to keep moving.

'Don't come any closer, Bec. Stay where you are.'

Pope was frustrated at being caught out. Her father's tone was different, harder. He stood still.

'I think it's time I came out of the shadows, Bec. I've been quite prolific over the years, extremely successful. But also, as you'll no doubt discover, extremely successful at hiding what I've done. I think now is the time to come clean, to confess my sins, if you will.'

'And what exactly are those sins?'

'I mean that in the broadest sense of the term. I don't regret what I've done, quite the contrary, in fact. But I think it may have affected you somewhat. And in turn our relationship as adults. I want to try to make that right. I want you to understand me.'

Understand him. Pope felt nauseous. She focused on Chloe, who was silently begging her to get them out of here. She needed to find a way out, to find a way to seize control away from him. She couldn't allow him to end things in the way he wanted to. Whatever that may be.

'You and I, we could have been. . .' He seemed unsure, searching for what he wanted to say. 'I'm not sure you ever really knew me, Bec. I very much want you to see the real me. I want you to know what I've done, what I've accomplished. I think you'll be impressed.'

Pope wasn't so sure she wanted to know the real John Pope.

Her father continued. 'The press has got hold of this ridiculous epithet "the Cameraman". Such lazy journalism, always looking for the shorthand, the sensationalist sound-bite. Anyway, it seems to have some traction and it won't be long before at least some of what I've done becomes public, if not the full extent of my history. I think you should be the person to end my activities now, don't you? A step up the ladder in your career. A feather in your cap.'

Pope wasn't sure what her father was talking about, but she had the feeling that she wouldn't like it. 'What do you mean?' she asked.

'I'm dying, Bec. I don't have long. I've had a good life, and I'm going to be remembered for a very long time. I might as well use my demise to show you who I am. To finally reveal your father to you.'

'Are you suggesting that I arrest you?' Pope almost laughed. 'Take you in and bask in the glory of a successful resolution to the case?'

'Not exactly,' said her father. 'But you're on the right lines. Why don't you call in the cavalry, and we can get Chloe out of here?'

Pope looked at Chloe. She had been silent all this time, terror on her face. Pope tried to send her a message: *It will all be fine. It will all be over soon.*

'You want me to bring the others in?' clarified Pope.

'Yes. Do that now,' said her father, still very much in control.

Pope was uneasy, but couldn't think of an alternative. Pope spoke for the wire. 'He has a gun. He wants you to come in now.' She didn't take her eyes off her father. 'Why don't you just give me the gun and we can take you to the station, talk about this in a bit more detail. We have lots to talk about,' said Pope.

'No. It's better this way,' said her father.

'What do you mean by "this way"—?'

Then it all happened very quickly. The door to the warehouse cracked loudly as a boot smashed it open. Pope swung round, as four armed officers exploded through the door, Brody and Miller and several other uniformed PCs behind them. Repeated shouts of 'Put down the gun'. The room echoed with boots, shouts and running.

Chloe screamed, looked terrified, instinctively ducked. Then John Pope raised his pistol and held it to Chloe's head.

The officers continued moving forward. 'Put down your weapon. Put down your weapon now or we'll fire.' Shouted. No doubt allowed.

Her father held the gun against Chloe's temple. Chloe whimpered. Pope felt powerless to help her. Stood rooted to the spot. The armed officers stared at John Pope, each one holding an automatic rifle trained on his heart.

Then her father looked at Pope. Smiled. 'Goodbye, Bec. Remember me.' He pointed his gun at his daughter. Pope barely had time to register what was happening, before four rifles let loose a salvo of bullets. Her father's body lashed back, then twisted, bent over and finally collapsed on the ground.

Pope moved a step towards her father, but stopped, paralyzed by her emotions. She knew her father was dead.

Brody and Miller ran to Chloe and untied her, checked she was all right. Then Pope was there, taking over, Brody stepping back to allow them space. Chloe threw her arms around Pope sobbing, her chest heaving with the effort. Pope held her, rocking her back and forth, murmuring softly. She glanced over her shoulder at her father, at the blood pooling on the ground under him.

She looked away, back to her stepdaughter.

'Let's go home,' she said.

EPILOGUE

Highgate Cemetery lies north of the River Thames, and east of Hampstead Heath. More than 170,000 people are buried in its overgrown, slightly ramshackle grounds. If you enter from the east, you walk past the tomb of Karl Marx, its most famous resident, unironically bloated and ostentatious in the context of the more modest gravestones that surround it. Like a number of cemeteries around the world that are the last resting place of famous people, Highgate Cemetery is often visited by tourists, but also by Londoners who enjoy the relative solitude and space. It is a beautiful place, and one in which many people in the city wish to be buried.

Today the cemetery is closed to visitors, as there is a burial underway. Standing beside the grave, into which the coffin has been lowered, are five people: Bec Pope, Alex Regis, James Brody, Adam Miller and the minister conducting the funeral, Michael Conlon. The cemetery is about three miles from where Pope's father had lived and it seemed like the natural place for his burial.

It had been just two weeks since her father had been shot by the Armed Response unit that had accompanied her to the warehouse in North London. But it seemed a great deal longer. Busying herself with funeral arrangements had been one way of dealing with her father's death. But there had also been a great deal of work to do in trying to unravel the details of the case involving John Pope.

It rapidly became clear that her father had been a prolific serial killer stretching back forty years. Now that the links had been made, the scope of his activities was becoming clear. Miller and Brody had been collating the suspected cases and to date they had identified eighteen victims that they thought could reliably be attributed to John Pope. It seemed likely that there would be more to come.

The press had got hold of it all, of course, and "the Cameraman" case was splashed all over TV screens and newspaper front pages worldwide, particularly in those countries where John Pope was thought to have committed murders. The fact that his daughter had been leading the investigation had sent the media into a frenzy.

The records they had managed to obtain from her father's employer, although patchy, showed that John Pope had visited a number of European cities at the same times as a great many unsolved murders had been discovered, each with a similar MO to the recent killings. It was clear that his business trips had been anything but for that purpose. Cross-referencing all this information would take a long time, but Pope knew they would uncover more. Some, she was sure, would never come to light. Her father's use of cameras to record what happened after he killed the victims seemed to be a recent development. At least it hadn't been noted in any of the historic cases that they were now examining. Tobias Darke's theory was that John Pope's narcissism finally drove him to need to watch his handiwork after the fact and observe the people discovering the bodies, particularly his daughter.

Fletcher was still searching for the source of the leaks of information to the press. He made it clear to the entire station that he was hunting for the person responsible, but Pope dismissed it. Early on in her career she had been told that when it came to information, police stations were like sieves. She didn't think that had changed in the intervening years.

Mick and Trish Waterson had been found. They were on holiday in Spain and had missed the whole thing. Pope imagined that they were relishing the chaos that had been surrounding her. She had the feeling that she had not heard the last of Edward Boyd.

* * *

The funeral service had been quick, with the same five attendees, and the burial was similarly brief. Pope chose not to say anything, so the minister spoke briefly and generically, aware of the sensitive nature of the situation. A few camera crews were hovering outside the cemetery gates, but had been prevented from coming in, a fact for which Pope was extremely grateful.

The burial took place on one of the arteries that extended out from the main paths running through the cemetery. Sinewy and shadowed, the light dappled by the mature overhanging trees, dipping down as if in mourning or quiet contemplation. Pope was struck by the silence of the place. Even the birds seemed quieter than usual, respectful of the circumstance, and she appreciated the overwhelming peace after the raging storm of the previous weeks.

It was a clear afternoon, cool but sunny. A good day to be buried, she thought. Alex stood beside her, held her hand. Pope looked over the grave and considered the hundreds of other gravestones she could see from where she was standing. Each one a life at the centre of a web of family, friends, colleagues and acquaintances. She wondered who would attend her own funeral.

When it was all over, the minister shook everybody's hand. Pope thanked him as he left to attend another funeral for which he was already late.

Alex was staying at his parents' house outside London, taking the girls with him. He needed some space to think and make some decisions. He had returned to support her during the funeral, she decided that was a good sign. Chloe had, naturally, refused to come to the funeral, and Hannah had stayed with her. Now Alex was leaving to go back to his parents straight afterwards. She needed him, but he needed to be away from her. She didn't resist, knew it was pointless.

'I'm going to go now, Bec,' said Alex. He kissed her, lingered for a moment, but then pulled away, looking down at the ground.

'How long do you think you'll need?' she asked.

'I don't know, Bec. I need to work out what's best for the girls. And for me. It's not good for us to be around you at the moment.'

Pope felt the words like a kick in the gut, but she tried not to show it.

'Are you coming back?' she asked. She regretted the question as soon as he had said it.

He looked at her. 'Give me some time, OK?'

'OK,' she said.

Pope watched him walk away, felt that she needed to go after him, say something. But she had no idea what and thought it probably wouldn't work anyway. Head down, he threaded between the graves and monuments to other, past lives, and then he was gone. Pope stared after him for a while.

She was aware of others, and looked round to see Brody and Miller standing beside her.

'He just needs time,' said Brody. 'Think about all he's been through, and Chloe. He'll come round when he's had time to think.'

Pope wasn't so sure.

Brody changed the subject. 'Mike Hawley's woken up. We just got a message from the hospital. Jade Leigh says he's doing well.'

Pope was relieved. It was good to find something positive. 'That's great news,' she said.

'We're thinking of going to see him,' he said, indicating Miller. 'Do you want to join us? We can go for a drink afterwards?'

'No, thanks. I'm going to hang around here for a while.'

'Why don't we wait for you?' asked Brody.

'No, it's fine. You two go. Give Hawley my regards. Tell him I'll be in to see him soon.'

'OK. I'll let you know where we end up in case you want to join us for a drink later on,' said Brody.

'Yeah. I really want to sit in a pub with you today and discuss the thermodynamics of the Twin Towers.'

He grinned and gave her a hug, held her tight, rubbed her back with his hand. Then he stepped away and Miller shook Pope's hand, formally, offered his apologies for the fourth time today, and then they left. Pope was alone in the cemetery.

She stood looking at her father's freshly dug grave. She had no idea what to think, what to feel or what to say. She felt a hollow space inside. She had lost her remaining parent and it hurt like hell. But it was far more complicated than that. Her father had been a serial killer, had brutally murdered women in cities across the world. And Pope was a cop, who had known nothing about it. How could she not have seen something? How could she continue to be a detective with her father's shadow hanging over her? She knew the answers wouldn't come now. She knew this would be a long process.

She looked around her at the empty space, filled with the dead but devoid of the living. There was one more thing she had to do.

She picked her way through the overgrown bushes and overhanging trees. The ground was littered with weeds. She guessed the inhabitants of Highgate Cemetery didn't object too much about the state of the place, even if their visitors might. Eventually she found what she was looking for. She moved a couple of low-hanging branches away from the gravestone, snapped them off and threw them to one side. The stone read *Mary Anne Pope. Beloved wife and mother. Rest in Peace.* Pope was aware that she hadn't visited her mother's grave in a long time. When she had arranged the burial, they had suggested that her father could be buried in a plot adjacent to her mother. Pope had decided that this was the last thing her mother would have wanted, and opted instead for a site some way away. She stood looking at the grave for some time. The sun was lowering in the sky now, disappearing behind the trees, and it was becoming cooler.

'I'm sorry,' she said, looking at her mother's tombstone. She wasn't sure what she was apologizing for, but it seemed the right thing to do.

Pope had parked on the west side of the cemetery, guessing, correctly, that the TV and press hounds would be waiting by the east entrance. She climbed over the fence and escaped quietly to her car, undetected. She started the engine and chose John Coltrane's *A Love Supreme* to accompany her. As the music started, she looked in the rearview mirror. The sun was dipping low on the horizon, but that was not what caught her attention. She could see Alex, walking towards her. Had he changed his mind? She got out and started walking towards him, towards the figure in the sunset.

THE END

Thank you for reading this book.

If you enjoyed it please leave feedback on Amazon or Goodreads, and if there is anything we missed or you have a question about, then please get in touch. We appreciate you choosing our book.

Founded in 2014 in Shoreditch, London, we at Joffe Books pride ourselves on our history of innovative publishing. We were thrilled to be shortlisted for Independent Publisher of the Year at the British Book Awards.

www.joffebooks.com

We're very grateful to eagle-eyed readers who take the time to contact us. Please send any errors you find to corrections@joffebooks.com. We'll get them fixed ASAP.

CPSIA information can be obtained
at www.ICGtesting.com
Printed in the USA
BVHW051330161222
654327BV00002B/475

9 781804 056479